Conan was about to sit down and enjoy the show when his gaze sharpened upon one of the attackers. He recognized the raven-crested helm of the man who had dared to consider him as slave material. That decided him.

Conan leaped to his feet, screeched a wild Cimmerian battle cry so blood-freezing that the fighting stopped below, and charged. Some of the attackers turned to face him, and one walked toward him with shield high. Without breaking stride, Conan cast his spear. The man raised his shield, but too late. The iron point smashed through the shield, struck him below the chin, and had enough force left to drive through to stand out a hand's breadth from the back of his neck.

As the man toppled, the rest spotted Conan. "The foreigner!" one shouted. "I warned you not to stray from the merchant's steading, fool! Now come to your death."

"Deliver it yourself, *nithing*!" shouted Conan, smiling. "I am Conan of Cimmeria, and I will take any or all of you on!"

CONAN
THE CHAMPION

Look for all these Conan books from Tor

CONAN THE CHAMPION

JOHN MADDOX ROBERTS

A TOM DOHERTY ASSOCIATES BOOK

CONAN THE CHAMPION

Copyright © 1984, 1987 by Conan Properties, Inc.

First printing: April 1987

A TOR Book

Published by Tom Doherty Associates, Inc.
49 West 24 Street
New York, N.Y. 10010

Cover art by Ken Kelly

ISBN: 0-812-54260-6
CAN. ED.: 0-812-54261-4

Printed in the United States of America

0 9 8 7 6 5 4 3 2 1

For Harriet McDougal
and James Rigney
Editors and friends

WESTERN SEA

VANAHEIM

ASGARD

CIMMERIA

PICTISH WILDERNESS

BORDER KINGDOM

Velitrium

BOSSONIAN MARCHES

GUNDERLAND

TAURAN

Galparan

NEMEDIA

Black R.

Shirki R.

Tanasul

Numalia

AQUILONIA

Belverus

Tarantia

Thunder R.

Shamar

Tybor R.

Ianthe

OPHIR

Kordava

Khorshemish

KO

ZINGARA

ALIMANE R.

Khosalas R.

ARGOS

Eruk

ZORILIAN MTS.

SHEM

BARACHA ISLES

Mezomitra

Asgalun

River Styx

Khemi

Luxur

STYGIA

SIPTAH'S ISLE

Sukhmet

KUSH

DARFAR

Xuthal

BLACK

Zarkheba R.

Xuchotl

CHAZAUD

Tundras

HYPERBOREA
• Haloga

Deserts

Steppes

BRYTHUNIA

ZAMORA
KEZANKIAN M.

TURAN

HYRKANIA

CORINTHIA

KARPASH MTS.
Shadizar •
• Arenjun

KHAURAN

Sultanapur

VILAYET
SEA

→ KHITAI

T H

IKHORAJA

Isle of
Iron Statues

Akit •
• Aghrapur

Deserts

Samara •

Zaporoska R.

• Zamboula

Khawarizm

Kapur

• Kuthchemes

Ilbars R.

Preion •

KESHAN
• Kassali

PUNT

Keshia •

KINGDOMS

ZEMBABWEI

VENDHYA

IRANISTAN

One

The Sea of Storms

For two days and three nights the terrible storm had carved the sea into a clashing army of shifting mountains, battling one another like the giants and the gods in the days when the world was young. Not for nothing was the Vilayet named the Sea of Storms, the Mother of the Tempest, and other titles that expressed the awe of men at the way the usually-placid inland sea could turn without notice into a savage, primeval chaos, the Grave of Sailors.

The man who tossed helplessly upon the waves, lashed to the stump of a mast and a bit of decking, thought none of these things. Since the midst of the second day of the storm, when his ship had broken up under the relentless pounding of the sea, he had been afloat. By now he was nearly senseless from the tossing of the waves and the numbing cold of the water. He was able to keep only a single thought in his mind: The storm was taking him north, and the Vilayet narrowed to the north. Soon he must be tossed ashore, and that

1

was his only chance for life. When he neared the land, he must cut himself free of the mast or risk being crushed as the heavy timber was dashed against beach or rock. Still in his belt was his long, curved Kothian dagger in its hide sheath. Frequently the man flexed his fingers so that he would be able to grasp its hilt when the time came. This and nothing more occupied his thoughts as the wind howled like demons in agony and the sea writhed beneath the flogging of the wind.

Dawaz rose early on the morning after the storm to find what the sea had left. Many interesting things were yielded by the sea on such occasions, and sometimes they were things that could be turned to profit. Profit was never to be taken lightly. Thus, he wrapped himself warmly in woolen cloaks of local weaving and left his little trading post, the northernmost of many maintained by Kyros Brothers of Aghrapur.

The post was situated in a tiny cove on the western shore of the Vilayet, where the sea was no more than a league in breadth. The water was calm this morning. The Vilayet was a shallow sea, thus a wind that would cause no more than a heavy swell on the Western Ocean could stir titanic waves on the surface of the Vilayet. For the same reason, the cessation of the winds left the tideless sea calm within hours.

Dawaz found a great deal of storm-wrack in the form of tree trunks, seaweed, and shredded vegetation, much of this blown up from the south. There were dead fish and an occasional marine mammal, but he saw no amber, which was among the sea's finest gifts. Finest of all would be a complete shipwreck, with a salvageable cargo. Dawaz determined to send his servants north and south along the coast to search for such. It must be done discreetly, of course, for the kings thereabout claimed all such sea bounty as their personal property. He was about to go back to the post for his breakfast when he saw the corpse.

Corpses were among the more common of the sea's yieldings, and had no value whatever. Sailors rarely had more jewelry than an earring, and this loinclothed figure plainly had not been a wealthy passenger. It had been a big man, and Dawaz would need his servants' aid to push the body back into the sea. He did not want this fellow's spirit haunting his post. The ghosts of drowned seamen properly belonged at sea, which was their element.

He was about to turn his steps to the post when the corpse moved and groaned. Dawaz stared, fascinated. This human hulk was battered, savaged by the elements, and blue with cold, yet it lived. The man on the beach began to vomit copious amounts of seawater, and Dawaz went to fetch his servants.

Conan awoke in the dim interior of a low, boothlike building, its walls constructed of flat stones piled without mortar and chinked with moss. The upper half of one long wall was a swinging, top-hinged shutter, designed to be propped outward in better weather so that the whole building might be used as a shop of sorts. Just now the shutter was tied down and draped with rough cloth against drafts. Bales and bundles filled most of the building, kegs and stacks of goods, some of them with Turanian writing upon them. A driftwood fire burned on a low hearth, the salt in the wood making crackling, multicolored sparks.

He lay on a pallet of skins, and over him were rough woolen blankets. The room was heaving as if in a slow earthquake, but Conan knew that this was caused by his long sojourn among the tossing waves. It seemed that he had survived. He did not find that as surprising as many might have. He had survived more mortal threats than he could readily remember.

There were at least two other men in the room. They could not be too unfriendly, since they had not cut his throat when they had the chance. As the lettering he could see was Turanian, he decided to try that tongue first.

"What is this place?" His voice sounded more like the croak of a crow than the speech of a man, but it brought a heavily-bundled man to his side. The man's features were Turanian, as was his speech.

"Welcome back to the land of the living, friend. I am happy to tell you that it is a dry land, albeit cold."

"Any solid ground is better than the Vilayet in a storm," said Conan. "You are a coastal trader?"

"For Kyros Brothers." The trader placed his fingertips against his breast and bowed very slightly. "I am Dawaz."

"I am Conan of—" He was about to say "of the Red Brotherhood," but thought better of it. "—of Cimmeria. I was serving on a ship somewhere to the south of here when we were caught by the storm." His stomach grumbled loudly, and his host signaled a servant. The servant, a Turanian of low caste, brought a carved wooden cup of steaming spiced wine.

"This should settle your stomach a bit," said Dawaz. "Then we may try some solid food. Doubtless you've not eaten in days, and your belly was quite full of salt water, which I witnessed myself."

"The only thing that's ever kept me from eating," Conan said with a little more life, "is already having a belly full of food.'' He took a long drink of the spiced wine, which was wonderfully bracing to a half-drowned man. ''What land is this? Our ship had just paid a visit to a settlement near the northern border of Turan when we were struck by the storm.'' He thought it best not to mention that they had just finished looting the settlement.

''You are far north of there,'' Dawaz told him. ''We are no more than fifty leagues from the northern tip of the Vilayet, and beyond that is the land of snow-giants and dragons. Here there are no true kingdoms, just the petty domains of the local kinglets. Each of them claims wide lands, but none truly rules beyond the reach of his sword.''

Conan nodded. This was true of most of the North, which was still primitive and tribal in nature.

The servant brought a bowl of thick, fragrant stew and a stack of flat loaves, tough and leathery.

''You are here late in the year,'' Conan observed as he ate. ''Do you plan to winter here?''

''We may have to,'' Dawaz admitted. He filled a cup for himself and poured more wine into Conan's. ''The last ship of the season was supposed to come for us many days ago, to take us and the year's trade goods back to Aghrapur. Something must have befallen it. Perhaps the storm.''

Conan wondered whether that ship might have been one that he and the Brethren had looted. ''Much can happen to a ship on the Vilayet. Will one of the local kings protect you through the winter?''

''Perhaps,'' Dawaz said moodily. ''After all, they depend upon the southern trade for many goods they cannot produce. However, they are also greedy, and there are many bands of outlaws as well. It shall be a hard winter, and we shall be fortunate to get through it with our lives and goods intact.''

"Who rules here?'' Conan asked.

"The king who claims this stretch of coast is called Odoac. His nation, or more properly his tribe, are the Thungians. They are a crude people, who lust after gold and the silks and other luxuries of the South. For these they trade the furs they trap and the slaves they capture from other peoples.''

"Do you trade slaves?'' Conan asked suspiciously. It was always possible that the merchant had saved him for other than generous reasons.

"No. We have an agreement with the House of Yafdal that we trade only for nonliving goods and they have the slave trade. You really must have special ships to transport slaves, so it is not practical to deal in both. The slave compound is now empty, as the factor for Yafdal left a moon ago.''

Conan was relieved. There were many other questions he wanted to ask, but sleep overcame him before he could finish one of them.

For the next two days the Cimmerian recovered from his ordeal. By the third day he was as strong as ever and fretting to be away. Dawaz wondered at the man's swift recovery. He had thought that Conan would have to be nursed along for at least a month, but except for a little shakiness in the first two days Conan had showed little effect from his experiences. Dawaz studied the strange barbarian. The man prowled catlike about the compound, eyeing the surrounding, tree-clad hills. Had Dawaz been a slaver, he might have entered Conan on his ledger as: "male, age about thirty, very powerful, black hair, blue eyes, skin fair but darkened by sun and weather, tall and sturdy, all teeth present and sound, northern in origin, prime stock.''

In the rare sunlight of early winter, Dawaz sat bundled in his woolens, writing with a brush upon a scroll set on a low table before him. Conan strode up to him in the midst of his writing. The Cimmerian wore a wolfskin tunic, which Dawaz had given him, and leggings of wolfskin above his heavy sandals. This left his arms and thighs bare, and that seemed to suit his northern blood. ''What do you write?'' he asked.

''I flatter myself that I am a bit of a scholar. Since I seem to be stuck here for a while, I am adding to my writings about my travels, although Mitra knows there is little to write about these northern lands.''

''Are there any wars going on?'' Conan asked.

''Why do you ask?''

''Because I must have something to do. There shall be no ships this way until spring. When I am not on the sea, I serve as a soldier. As long as there is a war brewing, I can earn my bread.''

''Stay here with me,'' Dawaz said. ''I enjoy your company. You have traveled far, and I should like to hear more of the places you have visited. We have plenty of provisions for the winter, and the local fishermen and hunters come often to barter their catch. We'll not go hungry.''

''It is good of you to ask,'' Conan said, ''and I thank you. But it is not my way to while the months away in idleness. If you can lend me arms, I can pay you for them from my earnings.''

''Very well,'' sighed Dawaz. On the table before him he began to draw a crude map. ''Here we are north of the steppe. The land is hilly and covered with dense forest, most of it pine. There are no great rivers, but there are many streams, most of them soon to freeze.

Besides King Odoac's people there are the Tormanna to the north. Their king is Totila. To the east of them both lie the lands of Queen Alcuina of the Cambres. She is said to be beautiful, but I have never seen her. Both kings would like to strengthen themselves by marriage to her. Both pay court to her, but she will not choose between them. The two kings fight one another incessantly. There are other peoples and kinglets, but these are the only considerable ones in this area."

"Not much to choose between them," Conan mused. "I think I'll offer my services to one, then see if the other will better his offer."

"I do not understand why warriors affect to despise merchants," Dawaz mused, "when they barter themselves as eagerly as we do our wares."

Conan grinned. "We have more of a stake in the quality of what we sell. After all, if this sword arm fails"—he flexed the massive limb—"the matter cannot be settled by exchanging it for a better." He threw his head back and laughed uproariously, as if the prospect was vastly amusing. "Now, what arms have you? I never yet saw a merchant who had not a sword or two in stock."

Dawaz had his servants bring out a small hoard of weapons and armor, all of which Conan examined closely. "These are all I have," Dawaz said. "There is no market for them in the South, but I do a little trading for them because the local warriors or would-be warriors often want them. When I bring up swords from the South I bring only the blades because the local folk will just put their own style of handle on them anyway."

Conan picked up a sword. It was heavy and old-fashioned, with a wasp-waisted blade of decent steel. Its leaf-shaped blade broadened above the waist and then tapered to a long, sharp point. Its handle was of bronze wrapped with leather.

The cuirasses were of bronze plate embossed with studs and extending only to the middle of the waist. Conan tried them until he found one that would cover his big chest. The helms were of bronze as well, decorated with studs like the cuirasses and sporting a variety of nose, cheek, and neck guards. Some had small animal figures for crests. Conan settled on one with cheekplates and a small, silver-worked bronze boar for a crest.

For his right forearm he found a bracer of thick leather studded with bronze. Since he would be bearing a shield, he sought no armor for his left arm. The shield he chose was all but identical to the others: round and made of oaken planks of two thicknesses laid with the grain crossed. It was bound and bossed with iron for strength. He selected an ash spear tipped with steel, and was ready for whatever might befall.

"The warriors here favor bronze," Conan noted.

"And they work it well," said Dawaz. "They cannot work iron into the designs they like, so they use it mainly for weapons and plain purposes such as the strapping on your shield. What you have is the gear of a free warrior, although many cannot afford the breastplate and wear instead a cuirass of many layers of elkskin, which is at least warm if not as protective as metal. The chieftains and kings have richly-worked arms, decorated with gold, silver, and amber."

"What is their style of combat?" Conan asked professionally.

"I know little of war," Dawaz said, "but to me they seem to be little more than armed mobs. I have seen the armies of Turan drilling outside the walls of Aghrapur, each man in his own place, the lines neatly arranged and the cavalry riding by in rows as if all were on but a single horse. The people here get together on a field and swing their weapons until only the men of one side are left on their feet. I understand that it is not rare for nobody at all to be standing after one of these battles."

"Then they fight like all the other northern people of my acquaintance," Conan said with satisfaction. "That is well, since I am a northerner and I like to fight that way too."

One of Dawaz's servants called to him. "Master! Men come riding!" Dawaz looked inland, toward the tree line. A little knot of mounted men were barely visible, black against the dark trees.

"Four men on horseback," reported Conan, his keen eyes glittering. "All armed. Do you think they mean mischief?"

"We shall know when they get here," said Dawaz uneasily. "If they are Odoac's men they will probably not rob me. They could be bandits, though."

"Bandits or king's men," Conan said, "you may rest easy. There are only four."

Dawaz stared at him. "You are nothing if not confident." Conan just smiled.

The bronze-girt warriors rode stocky ponies with uncut manes and tails. The riders were similarly shaggy, with brown or yellowish hair and beards spilling from their helmets over their shoulders and breasts. All wore armor similar to that which Conan now wore. They rode into the little compound, and one with a stylized raven cresting his helmet rode a little forward. He addressed Dawaz, but his eyes were on Conan.

"Greeting, trader. We are Odoac's men, and our

king wishes to know if aught of value was washed ashore during the great storm a few days agone.''

"Naught but the driftwood and trash of the sea," said Dawaz smoothly. "Has there been better picking along the coast?"

The man gestured to the bags tied over the back of one of the horses. "Some fine amber and some coral." He pointed at Conan, who gazed at him unflinchingly. "But who is this? He is no man of our nation, by his look."

Before Conan could speak, Dawaz said: "Just an unfortunate seaman, cast ashore by the storm. Of his ship, nothing came ashore but the stump of a mast, too tar-soaked even to make good firewood."

"Did you not hear me ask if aught of value came ashore? If he washed up then he is part of the sea's bounty and belongs to the king. A fine, strapping rogue like that will fetch a good price from the slave traders."

There had been a time when Conan would have instantly split the man's skull for these words, but age and experience had taught him to be prudent, especially in a strange land. He said simply: "I have no desire to dispute with you here in the home of my friend. But if you really want to sell me to the slavers, let us go over to yonder field, and I'll carve your guts out and strangle your friends with them." Dawaz paled, but the spokesman smiled.

"You speak loudly for a man outnumbered four to one."

"I'll kill you first," Conan said, "then it will be three to one. I've often fought three to one, and it has seldom taken me more than three blows to settle matters." He smiled calmly.

"Boasting fool!" blustered the rider. "It is your

good fortune that this trader enjoys the king's protection. Best for you that we never encounter you away from here.'' Without giving Conan a chance to answer, he wheeled his mount and rode out of the compound, followed by the others.

''That was a close matter,'' Dawaz said when he could draw breath again. ''They might have slain you out of hand for your words.''

''What would you have me do? Surrender myself to them as goods for the slavers? Besides, there was never aught to fear. That one with the raven on his helm was nothing but wind, albeit encased in bronze. And a little wind never hurt anybody.'' He clapped Dawaz on the shoulder, causing the slight man to stagger a few steps. ''Come, friend, let's to dinner. In the morning I'll be off to seek my fortune!''

Two

The Queen of the Snows

Conan trudged in a vaguely northerly direction. Just now King Odoac's court did not seem to be the best place to sell his sword, but that did not bother him. He would give King Totila a try. One employer was much like another. He was three days' march from Dawaz's trading post, wending his way through the silent forest and using his spear as a walking stick. Snow had been falling heavily since the night before, and he was happy that his friend had pressed upon him a good cloak, a long-sleeved undertunic, and a pair of trews. His recent sojourn in the balmy lands to the south had somewhat softened his innate resistance to cold weather. His Cimmerian kin would have shaken their heads pityingly to see him so overdressed in this mild weather.

The pines grew thick on every hand in these low hills, and the quiet of the forest was broken only occasionally by the eerie howling of wolves. This caused him no anxiety. It was too early in the winter for the wolves to be desperately hungry enough to attack a man; and an armed warrior, unwounded and possessing his full strength, had little to fear from wolves in any case.

Thus Conan proceeded, perfectly contented and even happy. The Northlands were his home, and although the seductive South had its attractions, he found these cold lands very much to his taste. He knew that by spring he would be half-mad with boredom and yearning for the soft, southern lands, but for now he was ready for a winter of fighting among the little northern kings. It took him several minutes to realize that the sounds of battle he had been hearing were not solely in his head but were real.

Conan grinned and ran toward the sounds. The song of clashing weapons was the peculiar music of his life. Even at a distance he could discern the sound of iron sword crunching into bronze armor, the singing screech of iron spear point glancing from helm, the singular clatter of steel weapons against wooden shield. The shouting was loud and continuous. He knew that it was a small group fighting, or else a large group was letting a few fight. If he knew his northerners, though, there would be few laggards.

Conan crested a rise and saw a road winding through the shallow vale below. In the midst of the road, bronze-girt warriors battled savagely. Conan studied them to see whether it would be worth his while to join one side or the other.

As he descended the hillside he began to see details. One group of fighting men were clustered around two figures, one a graybeard, the other a woman. The surrounding warriors were more numerous, but identical in look to the defenders. Here was where a civilized army's use of standards and uniforms and livery would be of use, Conan thought.

He was about to sit down and enjoy the show when his gaze sharpened upon one of the attackers. He recognized the raven-crested helm of the man who had dared to consider him as slave material. That decided him.

Conan leaped to his feet, screeched a wild Cimmerian battle cry so blood-freezing that the fighting stopped below, and charged. Some of the attackers turned to face him, and one walked toward him with shield high. Without breaking stride Conan cast his spear. The man raised his shield to block it, but the iron point smashed through the wood and pierced him below the chin, dividing his beard and going through to stand out a handsbreadth past the back of his neck.

As the man toppled, raven-crest spotted Conan. "The foreigner!" he shouted. "I warned you not to stray from the merchant's steading, fool! Now come to your death."

"Deliver it yourself, *nithing*!" shouted Conan, smiling. "I am Conan of Cimmeria, and I will take any or all of you on!"

The man in the raven helm had to meet this challenge or suffer loss of status in the eyes of his peers, so he strode forward, shaking his sword. "I am Agilulf of the Thungians, and I fear to meet no man!"

Attackers and defenders seemed to find this a good occasion to take a rest from the fighting, so they lowered their arms to watch this rare entertainment.

Conan caught the cool, gray eyes of the woman upon him, and made a sketchy salute with his sword. Then he was fully occupied with the man before him. Agilulf advanced in the fashion of a practiced sword-and-shield fighter: legs bent, spine erect, shield held well before the body, ready to drop to protect the legs or raise to cover the head. His sword arm was raised high and bent so that the blade slanted across his back. With only a slight shifting of that arm, he could strike with full strength at head, at side, or at the leg below his enemy's shield.

Conan favored his own highly individualistic style. He fairly ran in, crouched low, shield before him and held almost horizontally. His sword was held low and well to the rear. His opponent could see little except the shield and Conan's eyes above its rim.

Agilulf struck first, for Conan's helm, but the Cimmerian raised his shield slightly and at the same time swept his sword at his opponent's leading leg. The raven-crested warrior dipped his shield to catch the blade and both swords clattered against the shields. Agilulf leaned far over and tried to strike past Conan's shield at the briefly exposed shoulder, but Conan sidestepped and threw a powerful, looping blow at his enemy's flank. Agilulf interposed his shield in time and neither blow found its mark. Both men jumped back at the same time and the watching warriors shouted acclaim for the excellent exchange.

The two circled warily, now having a bit of each other's measure. Sweat dipped from beneath the rim of Agilulf's helmet, but he was as windy as ever. "Not so easy to defeat the champion of the Thungians, eh, Cimmerian?"

Conan's grin was hard between his cheekplates. Then he struck. The watchers saw only a whirlwind of metal as the Cimmerian's first blow sheared through the tough shield as if it were parchment, breaking the arm beneath with a loud snap.

The second blow divided the raven between the wings, cleaving downward through the helm, splitting skull and teeth and finally stopping at the top of the cuirass. Conan needed a powerful wrench to free his sword from the ghastly wreckage that had been Agilulf, champion of the Thungians.

Conan shook the clotted blood and brains from his blade and glared at the attackers. "Who else would play at swordstrokes? I stand here, dogs, come to me!"

The Thungians were shaken by the sudden demise of their hero, but they were brave. Besides, there were many of them. With a mass howl, they converged on him. In their preoccupation with him, as he had anticipated, many made the mistake of turning their backs on their erstwhile victims. The encircled men attacked them from behind and before the more numerous foe could reorganize, the tide had turned and they were at a disadvantage.

This turnabout did not mean an easy fight, though, especially for Conan. He was quickly surrounded by enemies, and only his armor and his amazing quickness saved him. As each man attacked, Conan ducked and dodged, springing over blows or dipping beneath them, striking return blows when he could. Working in his favor was his enemies' lack of coordination and the determination of each to be the sole killer of this alarming foreigner.

Then the attacks on Conan abated as most of his opponents were engaged and slain by the defending force. At length he found himself opposed by only one man: a yellow-bearded swordsman in an elkhide jerkin. A few blows sufficed to splinter his shield, and Conan finished him with a quick jab to the throat, the most merciful of battle-deaths.

The clangor around him had ceased, and Conan looked to see many bodies lying about in the grotesquely stiff poses of death. There was more red on the ground than white, and survivors went from fallen man to fallen man, tending to their own wounded with bandages and to enemy wounded with daggers.

Conan stuck his sword into the earth, dropped his shield, and untied the chin strap of his helm. As he pulled the helm off, his thick black hair tumbled almost to his shoulders. From the upturned helmet a mist of steam arose. Fighting in armor was always a warm business.

The woman approached him, with the graybeard in tow. She stopped before him and looked him up and down for a few moments.

"I am Queen Alcuina of the Cambres." Her gray eyes were cool to the point of iciness. "How came you here?"

She was as haughty a woman as Conan had come across in a long time, but he sensed that now was no time to take an arrogant pose.

"I was looking for employment for my sword, lady," he said, bowing slightly. "I heard the sounds of battle, and I came to investigate. I met that man Agilulf a few days agone, and he spoke ill to me. I was minded to improve his manners."

"So you did. He is not nearly so talkative now."

"Why did these rogues fall upon you, lady?" Conan pulled his sword from the earth and began to clean it carefully.

"Are you my peer that I must satisfy your curiosity? I will hire your sword, stranger. Your counsel I do not need. Find a mount and ride with my escort.'' With that she walked away. The graybeard seemed on the verge of speech, then he thought better of it and followed the woman.

Much nonplussed, Conan finished seeing to his weapons and went to look for an undamaged spear. The men were now in the woods, trying to catch their scattered mounts. Apparently, these people did not have the art of mounted combat, and dismounted to fight. With so many dead, there were plenty of spare horses. Conan climbed aboard one and joined the escort. Perhaps, he thought, he would go look for King Totila after all.

As they rode through the lengthening shadows of afternoon Conan made the acquaintance of the other members of the little guard. As an experienced soldier, Conan was careful to learn all their names.

Like all the folk he had met hereabout, they spoke a variant of the tongue common to much of the Northland, not much different from that spoken in Asgard and Vanaheim and by the Gundermen of Aquilonia. They were fair for the most part, with blue eyes more common than brown, their hair ranging from yellow to dark brown. None had truly black hair like his own. All the men who were old enough had flowing beards, although some partially shaved their faces the better to show off especially fine scars. They did not seem to favor paint or tattooing. Scalps hung from the bridles of some.

A yellow-haired man with a boar crest like Conan's rode up beside him. ''That was a fine fight, Cimmerian. I for one am glad to have you among our number. I am Siggeir.'' The man held out a gurgling skin. ''Here, have some ale. It has gone stale, but it will have to do until we return to our hall.''

Conan took a long pull at the ale. It was flat, but of good quality. He tossed the skin back. "Thanks, friend. Tell me, is your queen always so short with those who would take service with her?"

Siggeir smiled ruefully. "That is just her way. She was the only child of the old king and has always been haughty. She is a good queen, though, and she will not let her people become subject to some inferior king." By *inferior* Conan knew that the man meant a chieftain of another tribe. "But do not worry. Serve her well and fight as you did today, and she shall treat you well and reward you as you deserve. She is open-handed and generous."

"Well, that's something," Conan grumbled. "Why were you attacked by Odoac's men? If I'm going to fight them, I might as well know why."

"They wanted to capture Alcuina," said Siggeir. Like most northerners he used titles sparingly. "Odoac wants her to wife. They say he has already murdered his last one to make way for her. Many think this is commendable optimism, but I call it presumption."

"Can a king have only one wife among you?" Conan asked.

"That is the law. Concubines and such, he can have as many as he flatters himself he can tend to. Many kings have come to grief in this fashion."

"What of this King Totila of whom I have heard?" Conan pressed. "Does he not court Alcuina as well?"

"Yes, Totila and his pet wizard would have her, but she rightfully disdains the Torman swine."

Conan did not like the mention of a wizard. He had had little joy of that breed in his life and travels. Still, the man did not speak as if the wizard's wiles bothered him overmuch.

"Who is the graybeard?" Conan asked, jerking his chin toward the old man who rode ahead next to Alcuina.

"That is *our* wizard, Rerin. He is a wise old man, and he can protect us from the spells of Iilma, who brews spells for Totila."

"And has Odoac no wizard?" Conan asked, fearing the worst.

"Not that I ever heard. Wizards are rare, and Totila is richer than Odoac."

"Which wizard is the stronger?" Conan knew that it is always wise to know the relative strengths of friends and enemies.

"I cannot say," Siggeir said, pondering deeply. "It seems to me that every time one of them tries a spell, the other uses a counterspell, and thus they cancel each other. This suits me well."

"Aye," Conan said with the sincerity of experience. "When these wizards and necromancers and suchlike meddle in the affairs of honest warriors, there is always trouble that cannot be set aright with steel." Conan had a great dislike of problems unsettleable by steel.

Night was falling when they rode into the compound of Alcuina's hall. The compound sat atop an oddly regular mound, which stood higher than the surrounding fields. A wall of gigantic stones encircled the top of the hill, and upon the stones was set a palisade of sharpened logs. The massive gate was raised for them to enter and immediately dropped once all were inside.

Within was a wide yard dotted with small buildings: smithies, stables, sheds of various sorts. There was much livestock in evidence. In the center was the queen's hall: a long, low building with a steep-pitched roof covered with turf. Goats grazed on the roof, and smoke drifted from its gable ends. A southern king would have smiled to hear such a structure called a royal palace, but to the northerners it was all a palace should be; it was a place where warriors sat and feasted with their lord. They could have no respect for a king they saw but rarely if at all.

The smell of freshly-cut wood filled the place, and Conan could see that these people had not been living in this place for long. He followed Siggeir to a stable built against the stone wall and there left his borrowed mount for the boys to groom and care for. As they left the stable he examined the wall. Even in the dim light he could see that it was ancient, built of huge stones, and heavily grown with lichens.

"Who built this?" he asked.

Siggeir looked uncomfortable and made a sign with one hand. "Giants' work from ancient times. I like it not. Come, let us go eat and find some decent ale."

As they walked back to the hall Conan saw the bodies being taken from the horses. There was some muffled sobbing, but northern women did not mourn their dead with the extravagant, screeching lamentations favored in the South. It was well, he reflected, that it was still early enough in the winter for gravedigging. Soon the ground would freeze solid, and corpses would have to be kept in a shed until spring.

Inside, the hall was far more ornate than its exterior suggested. New though the hall was, artisans had already carved much of the visible wood with fanciful designs; patterns of interlace, deeds of heroes, strange beasts were everywhere abundant, most of them stained with crude but bright vegetable dyes. Horns of stag and elk and other creatures adorned the beams overhead, and hangings covered the walls, brightening the interior while they kept drafts at bay. The floor was paved with flat stones and strewn with rushes. In its center massive logs blazed and crackled upon a huge hearth. Near the flames meats turned on spits.

Conan's mouth watered from the smell of roasting meats as his eyes watered from the smoke. Long benches had been set up, and tables were laid across trestles as the warriors divested themselves of armor and weapons. Siggeir showed Conan where he would sleep on the straw next to the wall. Above his sleeping-place were pegs whereon he could hang helm and swordbelt, shield, and corselet, always to be kept ready against attack. He set his spear in a rack near his sleeping-place. With his belongings settled, Conan took his place at the bench. Every man sat opposite his sleeping-place so there was never any arguing over seating. Also, should they be attacked in the midst of their feasting, each man had his weapons close at hand. These people gave much thought to the possibilities of hostile action.

No sooner than he was seated, a girl brought Conan a massive, pitch-coated wooden tankard of ale. This he drained in one long pull and slammed down upon the board, to be refilled almost instantly. Platters of smoking joints were laid down, and for some time there was little speech as the famished trenchermen made up for their time spent on marching rations.

When appetites were somewhat sated, the men fell to boasting of their prowess in that day's battle. Each recounted his own feats and praised what he had witnessed of his companions' fighting. Every man was generous in praising Conan's contribution to the battle, although none went so far as to suggest that they might have been annihilated except for Conan's timely arrival.

In his turn Conan arose and praised his hosts, now

his comrades-in-arms. He explained some fine points concerning his defeat of the late Agilulf, which his listeners followed closely with the interest of professionals hearing the words of a master. Never overburdened with modesty, Conan did not underappraise his effectiveness in the subsequent fighting. He ended with compliments for his new employer and companions, proclaiming his eagerness to fight their enemies. There was loud applause and much thunking of tankards when he resumed his seat.

Finally Alcuina rose and, after the northern custom, lavishly praised her men and distributed gifts among them. Her words of praise for Conan were, he thought, rather sparing when one considered his signal contributions to her defense. He could not fault her generosity in material things, however. His own gift was a massy arm-ring studded with coral and garnets. Its weight in gold alone would have been considered a year's wages for a skilled swordsman in southern lands. Conan slipped the ring above the thick muscle of his right arm and thanked Alcuina courteously. She seemed to take no notice.

As the torches were being taken down, Alcuina announced that the rites for the dead were to be held upon the next eve, as the sun set. All then prepared for sleep. Alcuina disappeared behind the arras that screened off the end of the hall, and her wizard went to seek out the little building where he performed his sorcerous duties. Everyone else slept in the straw, wrapped in their cloaks.

Conan did not feel ready for sleep yet. Taking a fresh tankard of hot, spiced ale, he went outside, not knowing the source of his unease. The yard was quiet, with all the folk abed and the fowl roosting in their sheds.

Only a dog roamed about, doubtless hoping for a late handout from the feast.

The Cimmerian caught sight of a glow coming from the wall above the gate. He crossed the yard and found a stair made of split logs ascending to the top of the stone wall, thence to the wooden platform that ran around the palisade built atop the wall. Over the gate he found a single sentry standing next to a glowing brazier. In the fire's glow he recognized the man as one of his companions from the fighting earlier in the day.

"Greeting, Hagbard," Conan called. "This is a cold night for such duty."

Hagbard drew his cloak more closely about him. "Colder than it should be, Conan."

Indeed, the temperature had dropped considerably since Conan had entered the hall. He handed the tankard to Hagbard, and the man drank the warm ale gratefully. "The frost giants march south early this year," the Cimmerian said.

Hagbard handed back the tankard. "Thanks, friend. Yes, this is the sign of a bad winter. If the cold increases much more, we'll not be able to bury our dead tomorrow."

"Do you never burn them?"

"Never. A warrior is buried with his weapons, a craftsman with his instruments, a wife with her distaff and spindle. That is the custom. Even the children are buried with their toys, and the thralls with their field tools. If we cannot bury them tomorrow, we shall have to build a lich-house without the walls to hold them until the ground thaws."

Conan surveyed the bleak and rather uncanny ground surrounding the enclosure. Here they were in a broad, open field, almost a small plain, in strange contrast to the wooded hills that characterized most of this district. In the bright light of the full moon, Conan could see that the plain was dotted with several of the steep-sided mounds, of which the one upon which he stood was the highest. Several of those had similar stone walls atop them. Out in the flat ground, many standing stones were arranged in straight lines or circles. Some stood in configurations like doorways, with a great stone laid horizontally across two standing ones.

"How long have you folk lived here?" Conan asked. He touched one of the palisade logs, and his hand came away sticky with sap.

"Only since midsummer. We had been living in the old place for ten years, and the fields were worn out. The game was getting scarce as well, and the fish were few in the streams. It was decided that we should move."

Most northern peoples were seminomadic at best. There had been times when entire nations had simply picked up their belongings and migrated for no better purpose than a change of scenery. Great wars often resulted. The most common reason, however, was the simple wearing out of land settled too long by people whose agricultural practices were primitive in the extreme.

Hagbard shook his head. "I wish Alcuina had not picked this place, though. Better we had stayed to the hills and forests."

"I can see why you do not like it," Conan said, sipping at the rapidly-cooling ale. "It is uncanny, with all those mounds and stone circles. Why did she pick this place?"

"She deems we can better defend ourselves here, behind these giant-wrought walls. I speak no disloy-alty," the man said hastily, "but Alcuina is not the leader her father, Hildric, used to be. He knew the way to deal with enemies was to kill them, not hide behind walls of stone.''

"What kind of place is this?" Conan asked, sweeping an arm to take in the uncanny plain.

"Long ago," Hagbard said, "even before my grandfather was born, giants lived in this place. It was their stronghold. They fought a war with the gods for many generations, with neither side having the victory. Then the giants hired dwarfs to build them a great wall engirdling this whole plain. The fee claimed by the dwarf master mason was the daughter of the king of the giants. The wall was built, and the wedding was held. But"—by now Hagbard's breath was steaming heavily with the cold—"on her wedding night, the bride murdered the groom, as what princess would not, given so inadequate a husband? In a single night, the dwarfs tore down the wall and the gods stormed in and slew all the giants, who were still besotted from their feasting. These ruins are all that is left of that ancient slaughter, but I think the spirits of the slain giants linger here still.''

Conan pulled his cloak closer around him. The mulled ale was gone, and he was beginning to feel the effects of all the food and drink he had taken on that night. "Well, restless or not, they are dead now," Conan commented. "Good night, friend. I think it is time to seek my bed in the straw."

"Good night, Conan. Would you wake my relief? It is Oswin, who sleeps nearest the door tonight."

Conan assured Hagbard that he would not sleep until Oswin was awake and headed out into the cold. He descended the stair to the courtyard. As he crossed to the hall he noticed a light burning and wondered who stirred so late. Then he saw that the light came from the

little stone hut where the wizard lived. With a muttered
malediction on all dabblers in magic, Conan went into
the hall and rousted the snoring Oswin.

Picking his way among the sleeping forms, Conan
found his way to the still-glowing hearth, where he was
cheered to find a half-full pitcher of ale still warming
by the coals. He poured some into his tankard and
drank deep. He wondered whether he had made the
right choice in joining Alcuina's band. An air of doom
overhung these stark stone ruins. However, he had
accepted her gold and her food and her roof, so he
would accept whatever might befall. It was not his
custom to worry about the future. He found his sleeping-
place, rolled himself into his cloak on the straw, and
soon was as deep in sleep as any there.

Three

The Hall of Totila

King Totila sat brooding on his high seat. He took no joy in the jeweled cup before him, nor in the singing of the harper who sat upon the hearth. His elbow was propped on a great carven arm of the chair, and his chin rested on a knotty fist on which every finger blazed with the gleam of gold and jewels. He was the wealthiest of the northern kings, but Totila of the Tormanna brooded upon that which he could not have. Queen Alcuina of the Cambres.

He wanted her fair body in his bed almost as much as he wanted her lands annexed to his. With his eastern flank thus secured, he would be able to swallow up Odoac and his Thungians to the south. Thus would Totila become the greatest king of the North. With such a beginning, he would forge a northern empire such as men had not seen since the last great migration of the northern peoples, many generations before.

In dreams such as this did Totila pass his days, but he was not one to confine himself to dreams. He had

begun as little more than a robber-chieftain, with only
the most tenuous claim to royal blood. By dint of iron
will and unrelenting savagery he had forged a small but
solid kingdom. Fighting men he had in plenty, and
what swords could not do would be handled by the man
who sat at Totila's right hand: the wizard Iilma.

Years ago the man had come to Totila, claiming to
be from Hyperborea and claiming as well that the des-
tinies of king and wizard were intertwined. Totila would
furnish him with protection, and Iilma would strike at
those enemies Totila's swords could not reach. The
wizard had been as good as his word, and the two had
grown fat together, waxing in power and wealth. Totila
never stayed content for long, though, and each victory,
each kinglet swallowed up, caused his appetite to grow
along with his power.

"I would know how it fares with Alcuina, wizard,"
said the king. Below him, on benches at the long
tables, his warriors ate and drank, their mood subdued
in recognition of their lord's brooding spirits.

"As my lord wishes," Iilma said. "I shall go and
prepare the pool. My messengers have told me"—he
waved toward a pair of large magpies that perched on
the back of his chair—"that she returns to her hall this
day, after touring her lands."

The white-bearded man arose. The skins of reindeer
draped him, and the antlers of that beast crowned his
headdress. Bones and skulls of small animals rattled on
strings about him, and the feathers, claws, and beaks of
many birds adorned his crude garments. He took his
curiously-wrought staff from its place by the chair and
walked rattling from the room. The magpies hopped
after him, and conversations stilled as he passed. All

men feared the wizard almost as much as they feared the king.

Totila sat for a while in desultory conversation with his counselors, but his mind was elsewhere. In time, he took his helmet from atop the cornerpost of his chair. It was the most famous helmet in the realm, and he wore it even when no battle portended, in lieu of a crown. It was of bronze plated with gold and silver, and its hook-beaked nasal was flanked by a pair of lowering silver eyebrows. Long cheek pieces framed his face, and strips of silvered bronze wrought in the semblance of feathers dangled behind to protect his neck. Embossed upon plates of silver, a file of warriors encircled the crown, and above all brooded the fierce eagle-crest, its eyes glaring feral hate, beak agape for prey.

With the helmet settled upon his head, Totila donned his cloak. It hung from his huge shoulders to drag on the ground, its colors curiously piebald. This cloak was entirely made of the scalps of men Totila had slain with his own hand, and not one of them lower in rank than chief or champion. He picked up his great sword and carried it by the sheath as he strode from the hall. Crown and scepter meant nothing in the North. Helmet, cloak, and sword spelled kingship in runes the savage northerners could read.

King Totila's hall was encircled by no wall or palisade. It was his boast that he feared no king enough to bother with such defenses. His warriors were wall enough for him, he claimed. He strode past the tilled fields where his thralls toiled away their lives to raise the grain for the free men's bread and ale. Grain was practically the only crop grown in the North. For the rest of their food, they depended upon their livestock, the beasts of the forest, and the fish in their streams. A race of meat eaters, the northerners despised free men who would work upon the land as men did in the South, and taste meat only once or twice in a year.

Taking a little-used forest path, Totila soon reached a small grove, which was warm despite the surrounding cold. The wizard Iilma wielded great power over the forces of nature. In the midst of the grove was a small pool, fed by no visible stream, and from which no stream flowed. It never froze, no matter how bitter the weather beyond the grove. Iilma stood by the pond with a magpie perched upon each shoulder. Totila placed himself by the wizard.

"This is what took place earlier in this day," intoned the mage. He touched the surface of the stream with his staff, and a bright picture appeared with the widening ripples.

Totila watched with absorption. He was now used to these magical displays, although he had been frightened when first he saw one. Gazing down into the pool he saw a file of men marching through a snowy forest, seen from above as if by a flying bird. Ahead of the marching men were other men, more numerous, lying in ambush. His eyes narrowed as the viewpoint lowered, as if the watching bird were descending to a convenient tree the better to see the coming entertainment.

"Those are Alcuina's men," Totila muttered, "and she among them. Odoac's warriors lie in wait. Had I known she would be traveling away from home, it would have been my own men there to take her." He looked at Iilma. "Why did you not inform me that she would be thus vulnerable?" He did not speak angrily, although he felt much anger. He did not dare offend the wizard, even though he lose a queen. Totila possessed a capacity to hide his feelings far in excess of the control owned by most northern kings.

"This journey was hidden from me until this day, my lord. I suspect that the wizard Rerin, whom you see riding beside the queen, erected a screen to foil my farseeing eyes on wings."

Totila snorted noncommittally, unsure how seriously to take the wizard's protestations. "Now they spring the trap!" he said. He watched excitedly as Alcuina's men were surrounded, forming a shield-wall around their queen and preparing to sell their lives at bitter cost. "They cannot protect her long," Totila observed as the snow reddened. "That means I must take her from Odoac." He gnawed at a nail in annoyance. "But what if he gets her with child before I kill him? This is an ill business, wizard."

"Watch what happens now," the wizard said. As suddenly as it had started, the fighting ceased. Now the viewpoint changed, as if the bird were swiveling its head. A single man stood on a hillside, and he looked to be shouting, although they could hear nothing.

"What is this?" Totila wondered. "A youth? Nay, that is a grown warrior, though beardless. What breed is he?"

"From his look," Iilma said, "a Cimmerian. They are a race my nation knows to its cost. They come from a mountain country to the west of Hyperborea. Their god is called Crom, and they have no skill of magic, although they are matchless fighters."

"My own men are matchless fighters," Totila grumbled, "and I the most matchless among them. What does such a one here?"

"Observe this. It is most interesting." They watched one of Odoac's men come to meet the stranger.

"A challenge fight!" Totila said happily. "That is Agilulf, Odoac's champion. He's a fine swordsman but a loudmouth withal." They saw the first exchange played out. "Good fighting on both parts," Totila said judiciously. "Now they have each other's measure. The next clash must tell the tale." They watched the bewildering flurry of blows, and Totila slapped his thigh in delight. "You spoke true words, wizard! That one is a warrior of rare skill."

The rest of the combat was played out for their enjoyment; then they saw the bodies loaded and watched as the stranger mounted and rode off with Alcuina's escort. Then there was nothing but the stiff forms of Odoac's men, the reddened ground, and the gently falling snow. The picture in the water faded.

"So, Alcuina has a new champion," Totila said, tugging at his beard. "I may just have to try that one myself. It has been many years since I have found a man worthy of my steel. Besides," he mused, looking down at his cloak, "black is the only color missing from my cloak of chiefs' hair. Such a mane as that rogue sports will make a collar better than a wolf's winter coat."

"With that brute among her guard," Iilma said, "Alcuina will be more difficult than ever to possess. Why do you not forget her for the moment and move against Odoac? He lost many men this day and is weaker than ever."

Totila thought for a moment. "No, it is as I have told you before, wizard. When I move south, it shall be in a great push that shall take me to the borders of Zamora and Turan. I shall swallow up Odoac and his tribe like a fish snapping up an insect upon the water."

Iilma knew that these dreams far exceeded even the

abilities of a man like Totila. The North simply did not contain enough men to hold so much territory for more than a few years. Still, he wanted to make Totila the greatest king of the North. That much he could assure. "If my lord wishes, I have command of certain spells. They are spells that will make use of allies I can cause to do my bidding. My servants are the frost giants of the North, and the dead who lie stiff beneath the snows."

"I care not how you go about it," Totila said, not wanting to hear more. "Just see to it. If you pave the way for me to take that woman and make her my queen, I'll reward you well, as always."

"So my lord shall," Iilma said. "Now, return to the hall and feast with your warriors. I shall be busy here the rest of the night and tomorrow and tomorrow night. Then, we shall see."

Totila left to make his way back to the hall. Behind him Iilma stirred the waters with his staff and began a high, eerie chant. Outside the grove, the weather grew colder.

Four

Battle with the Dead

When morning came, Conan woke as the hall door opened, admitting a cold wind and a near-frozen sentry. The man shut the door and ran to the hearth, where he held blued arms over the warm ashes of last night's fire. Conan rose, wide awake as always when not sodden with drink. The others in the hall roused from sleep in a more leisurely fashion, groaning and scratching. Indeed, on so cold a morning it was a hard task to rise at all.

Conan went to the hearth, wondering that a hardened northerner could be so affected by a few hours' sentry-go in the night. "Good morning, Regin," Conan said. "Is it so cold out there?"

Through chattering teeth, the man managed to say, "Go look for yourself!"

Conan went to the door and threw it open. "Crom's teeth!" He slammed it shut again. Snow was blowing on the wind, and the wind was as cold as any Conan had ever felt in all his years in the Northlands. The loud crack of trees splitting echoed in the distance. A fur-swathed form came to stand by him.

"Open the door," Alcuina ordered peremptorily. Conan obeyed.

The woman stepped through, and Conan was forced to marvel at the way she stood in the stern wind without making the slightest sign of discomfort.

She turned back to the hall and called in a commanding voice, "Get up, you lazy sluggards! We must see to the livestock or they shall all freeze. Build up the fires, and get all the spare hangings on the walls!" She beckoned to her steward and the man came running, pulling up his trews. "Aslauf, get all the stock you can into the stables with plenty of fodder. We cannot afford to lose a single horse or cow. Get all the fowl into the stables or the sheds as well. If need be we'll move any beasts that have no place else into the hall with us until this weather breaks. Better to put up with the smell and the mess than a winter of hunger."

"Yes, Alcuina," the steward said, and he hurried off, calling the names of the boys and the thralls who had charge of the stock.

The queen turned to Conan and beckoned. "Come, stranger, we must see whether the old man is well."

For a moment Conan did not understand who she meant; then he remembered the old wizard, Rerin. "A moment," he said, and rushed back into the hall. He reemerged, buckling on his sword.

"Why do you need that?" she demanded.

"You hired me for my sword, lady," he said with an insolent grin. "I am of precious little use to you without it."

She led the way to the little hut near the stone wall. Conan admired the way her hair, now braided into a single plait thick as a maiden's arm, swayed with her purposeful stride. The shape of her body was a complete mystery beneath the swathing gown and fur robe, but her carriage was light and graceful.

"The old man was awake late last night," Conan told her.

"How do you know that?"

"I came out after everyone else was abed and spoke awhile with the gate sentry. As I returned I saw a light in his window."

"He works in my behalf most of his waking hours," she said. "Unlike warriors, who fight once in a great while and spend the rest of their time gorging my food, and swilling my ale, and bragging of their feats."

Conan smiled mirthlessly. This one did not yield an inch. He rapped on the door of the hut, and it was opened almost immediately. The old wizard looked as though he had had no sleep, but he seemed to be strong and alert.

He nodded to Conan and turned to Alcuina. "Come inside. I have unwelcome news."

Alcuina entered and so, unbidden, did Conan. She turned on him.

"Wait without. Who bade you come in?"

"I'm accursed if I'll freeze my backside out there while you warm yours at the wizard's fire, lady. You have hired a warrior, not a lackey." He folded his arms and leaned against the doorjamb. She grew red in the face and seemed on the point of loosing a scathing tongue-assault when the wizard touched her shoulder.

"Let him stay, Alcuina. I think this outlander may be of great use to us in the trials we face." The queen instantly quieted.

"Very well," she said. She paid no further attention

to Conan. "What means this sudden onslaught by the frost giants? It is unnatural."

"Unnatural, indeed, my lady. I am sure that it has been cast upon us by our enemy, Iilma."

"Who is Iilma?" Conan asked. The name sounded vaguely Hyperborean to him. He had never had pleasant dealings with that race.

The queen turned on him with stormy brow, but once again Rerin quieted her with a gesture. "He is a wizard, young man. He works evil magic for King Totila of the Tormanna. Last night, as I left the hall after the feasting, I could smell his magic in the air. I searched the sky, but I saw no sign of his magpie-familiars. I knew then that his work was in the very air all around. I returned to my house, and all night I have sought the nature of his working."

"What have you discovered?" asked Alcuina.

Conan leaned against the jamb, deeply troubled. He did not like it when sorcerers were at work. This old man's cottage was filled with things that disturbed the Cimmerian. Bundles of dried herbs dangled from the roof-posts. Small, stuffed animals that were not native to the North, instruments of bronze and glass that were of some manufacture he did not recognize lay scattered about.

"He has been rousing the frost giants, as you can well tell for yourself. Beyond that, he is up to some foulness that I cannot fathom yet."

"Does he hope to weaken us by freezing our stock and crippling our people?"

"I do not see how that can be," said the old man. "This bitter cold must be afflicting Totila's folk fully as severely as our own. I fear that there is something far worse than cold in store for us."

Alcuina rose and turned to go. "I must go see to the garth, Rerin. We must be ready before another such night comes upon us. I want you in the hall with the rest tonight. So long as there are evil things abroad at night, I want none of my people sleeping without the walls."

"But, Alcuina, if I am to serve you properly I must—"

"Inside tonight," she said in a voice brooking no dispute. The old man bowed assent.

With Conan following, the queen strode outdoors into the teeth of the wind and began giving orders. The Cimmerian grudgingly admitted to himself that she commanded as well as any professional soldier he had ever seen. While the stock were being seen to, and fuel and fodder gathered, Conan was ordered to mount and was sent out with three others, one of several bands whose task it was to seek out and report on the outlying garths and steadings, and the tiny villages in the forest clearings, who owned Alcuina as their queen. They were to ride as far as they could, while leaving themselves time to return before nightfall.

It was a long and cold ride, over snowy hills and through dark forests. Here and there they saw the stiff forms of small woodland animals, caught in the open during the night.

"I like it not," said Siggeir as they sat at midday, letting their horses rest. "The creatures of the wood should know when a great freeze comes, even when our dull senses do not tell us. I have seen unseasonable freezes in plenty, but never one that caught the beasts by surprise." Conan nodded but held his own counsel.

The sun was just dipping below the western hills as they rode back into the garth. Alcuina came to hear their report as they stiffly dismounted.

"Most of the farmers and villagers weathered the freeze well enough, my lady," said Siggeir. "In the outlying garths we heard of three men out tending flocks and herds who froze. Perhaps one beast in ten perished in the cold."

The queen heard these words with a grim countenance. "It might have been far worse. Between the fight with Odoac's men and the weather, I have lost more than one hundred of my people. We are weakened, but at least tonight people will be prepared."

At mention of the fight of the day before, Conan glanced at the space beneath the eave that ran around the great hall. A row of blanketed forms lay there, lightly covered by snowdrift. "Were they not buried today?" he asked.

Alcuina followed his gaze. "The men tried to dig, but the ground is frozen solid. Barring a late thaw, we'll not see them properly interred this winter. Tomorrow we shall have a lich-house built for them outside the wall. Doubtless there shall be other winter dead for it to house." She was gloomy but stoical. Death and the pitiless elements were commonplace in the North, and one who would be a ruler there must learn to cope with both. She turned to Conan. "You are the last party to return. Close the gate and see to your mounts, then join the rest of us in the hall."

That night there was a meal, but no feast. Until it was certain that this was a freak storm rather than the harbinger of a terrible winter, they would be kept on short rations. No joints smoked on the fire this night, and they made do with bread and cheese and hot porridge, and each man was restricted to no more than three tankards of the ale.

The hall was far more crowded than it had been the

night before. At the benches, where before only free
warriors and their wives had been permitted, there now
sat thralls and children and all the other inhabitants of
the garth. At the end of the hall where the thralls would
be quartered for the emergency, several horses and
cattle assured that the atmosphere was noisy and fragrant. Nobody complained of the noise or smell, since
the beasts generated more heat than a good-sized fire.

There would be no sentry posted on so bitter a night.
Instead, youths took it in turn to perch in the gables and
peer out into the yard through the smoke holes at either
end of the hall. It seemed unnecessary to post a watch
in any case, since an enemy would hardly choose such
a night for an attack, but Alcuina insisted that vigilance
never be relaxed, whatever the weather.

Finding that two tankards of ale scarcely took the
edge off his thirst, Conan wagered his last tankard with
a warrior, the ownership to be settled by an arm wres-
tle. He won easily and drank his winnings. He was
soon challenged again, and in this way won six more
tankards before his arm had tired sufficiently for him to
be beaten by a burly, red-bearded thrall whose arms
were like tree trunks. He took part in some impromptu
wrestling matches, which set the men rolling in the
straw, scattering piglets and chickens who were sharing
the amenities of the hall with their future diners.

Nursing his last tankard of ale, Conan watched with
admiration as an old warrior carved a supporting post.
First the man drew his design on the wood with a piece
of charred stick from the fire. It was a complicated
interlace of serpents and vines. He then roughed out the
design with a corner of his belt-ax, wielding the crude
weapon with the delicacy of a surgeon. His finishing
work he performed with the same knife that he used for

eating, fighting, and all the other chores a knife is called to do. When the work was finished, Conan ran his fingers over it, feeling no splinters or gouges. In the course of a long winter evening, the old man had performed a task that would have taken a Zamoran wood-carver a week to finish with a shopful of specialized tools.

To Conan's compliments the man only nodded curtly, saying, "I'll paint it tomorrow, if I can find the pigments."

Throughout the evening Alcuina looked grim but determined. She had done all there was to be done. Conan tried to cheer her, but she was in no mood for it.

"Just keep your sword arm limber, Cimmerian. You may have need of it ere long."

"My sword arm is always ready," Conan said. "And it's at your service. What enemy do you fear?"

"Pray you never have a king's worries, Cimmerian. By this day's work I may have preserved my people through a long, hard winter. It may be that others have not been so foresighted. If the season continues as hard as this, they will grow hungry, and they'll begin looking about for those who have food and fodder to raid."

Conan nodded. "Aye, you've the right of it there. Kinging is not just fighting battles and lolling about on a throne drinking wine from a jeweled goblet."

Soon Alcuina gave instructions for a watch to be posted and the torches extinguished. The fire was banked for the night, and the people and livestock bedded down. Alcuina retired to her bower behind the arras, and soon the hall shook to the snores of its packed inhabitants.

Conan jerked awake to the shout of the boy perched

in the gable. "Someone stands without!" There was fear in the young voice.

Conan rolled from his bed of straw and snatched his sheathed sword from its peg. A great pounding began upon the door. "Keep the door barred!" he shouted. People stirred and groaned, calling out questions in the darkness.

"Build up the fire!" Conan called. He made his way toward the gable nearest the door, kicking a pig out of his way. He climbed the crude ladder and joined the youth in his perch. "Where did they come from?" he asked, leaning out for a look.

"They must have got in over the wall," the boy said. "I have kept a watch on the gate, but none have come that way."

Below Conan a dozen men cradled a log of wood in their arms, gradually pounding in the door. Oddly, their heads and shoulders were covered with snow. "So few?" Conan wondered.

"The gate!" the boy shouted. Conan looked that way. Two of the invaders were struggling with the gate-bar.

Conan turned back to the hall. "I'm going down there. You warriors follow me as soon as you are armed, but come through the gable. Keep the door barred. Thralls, block the door with benches and whatever else you can find." He turned back and looked down at the men trying to pound the door in.

"You are not going down there?" said the boy, appalled.

"Sooner or later," Conan said philosophically, "a man must do something to earn his bread." He leaned out, balanced briefly on the sill, and jumped. He held his sword well out to his side lest he stumble and fall on it, but he landed lightly, taking the shock on bent knees. Bearing no shield, he took the hilt of his sword in both hands as he called out to the would-be raiders. "You're a hardy pack of rogues to be out on such a night! Who sent you?"

One of the raiders turned to face him, and Conan's blood turned as cold as the night. The man's eyes were turned up so that only the whites showed. His movements were stiff, and he creaked with every motion. His garments were rent to show gaping wounds and they were crusted with frozen blood.

"Crom!" Conan swore. "They are dead men!"

The lich came toward Conan, its movements swift and sure despite a certain stiffness. The others continued their monotonous pounding.

Live men or dead, Conan had only one way of dealing with enemies. As the lich attacked with clawlike fingers outstretched, Conan hewed with all his might at the thing's side. It was like hitting a log. The sword chunked into the flank, biting into frozen flesh and bone and organs, showering Conan with frozen crystals of blood. The thing seemed not to notice. Its claws closed around Conan's neck and commenced to squeeze.

Conan released his hilt and grasped at the thing's wrists with desperate strength. The cold fingers pressed inexorably inward, cutting off his air. Conan was forced to his knees, growing dizzy as the undead creature's frozen countenance registered nothing and the log continued to thud-thud-thud against the door. With a final, desperate wrench, Conan broke both hands off at the wrists. Using all the strength left in his own hands, he grasped the thumbs and broke them off, then tore the hands away from his throat. The lich continued to club at his head with the stumps of its forearms. The door was giving way.

Conan grasped his hilt and hauled his sword free of the frozen corpse. Desperately, he hewed at the icy flesh until the head flew into the snow. His next blows took away one arm at the shoulder. The blade was growing dull with all this unaccustomed ice-chopping.

"They're walking dead men!" he bellowed. "Bring axes and mauls! Swords are no good!"

He became aware of a warrior standing beside him, gaping at one of the things. "Hrulf!" he said. "That is my friend, Hrulf! But he was slain in the ambush two days ago!"

"Some wizard's raised the dead we could not bury," Conan shouted. "Kill them again, or they'll slay us all!"

He hewed at one of the log-bearers just as the door gave way. Now there were more warriors about, and torches were thrown down to give the men light to fight by. Conan saw a young warrior borne to the ground with cold fingers buried in his throat while the corpse gnawed at his face.

A pandemonium had erupted inside the hall as the doors broke in, with the screaming of women and children, and the frantic cries of the beasts that knew something unnatural was happening. Now several warriors chopped at each frozen corpse with axes and clubs of firewood, slowly battering and hacking the things to crystalline fragments.

"The gate!" someone shouted. Conan turned to see the gate swinging open.

"Go get the gate shut!" Conan looked down to see Alcuina standing beside him, wild-eyed, her hair streaming in the cold wind.

"Get back inside," he growled. "We'll deal with these things."

Not waiting to see how she responded, Conan sprinted for the gate. Dead they might be, but it seemed that they could be killed again. He came to a halt as a ghastly horde stormed through the gate. In hideous silence came a pack of creatures, some missing arms or other members, all bearing wounds, their eye sockets packed with ice, more ice and snow lacing their beards and showing inside their gaping mouths.

"Odoac's men!" Conan said. "The dead we left in the snow after the fight!"

He dropped his sword and picked up a massive stone, fallen from the ancient wall. With muscles straining, he cast it upon the nearest of the walking dead. The lich fell back with a crunch and lay twitching beneath the weight. Conan looked about for another stone and saw the thrall he had arm wrestled smashing a corpse down with a great wooden mallet.

All about men battled the things with improvised weapons, and Conan breathed silent thanks that they had stripped the dead of arms before abandoning them upon the field where they fell. From behind him Conan heard a scream and spun to see Alcuina writhing in terror, grasped by one of the ghastly liches. Trying to bear her off, the thing lifted her, now apparently unconscious, to a shoulder.

With inhuman strength and speed, the creature ran for the gate while its fellows continued their now losing battle against the living. In the yard, a fear-maddened bull had broken from its pen and crunched a horn through a corpse, tossing its head and casting the thing onto the hall roof. As Conan raced in pursuit, he saw that a boy had doused a corpse with a pan of grease; another set it alight with a torch.

"Good thinking," he shouted to them as he passed.

Outside the gate Conan saw the lich running with its burden across the field of standing stones, headed for the forest to the west. Conan loped after it, amazed that a thing with ice for blood could move so swiftly. His breath lay behind him in a streamer of steam as he chased them, his black mane streaming in a wind of his own making. An ordinary man might have slipped in the snow and stumbled in the pale light from the moon, but Conan had been raised in mountains so treacherous that this was as a field at high noon to him.

When they came to a circle of stones gleaming in the moonlight the thing seemed to sense that Conan was near. It stopped and turned, and at that second Conan grasped Alcuina. Half of the queen's robes were left in the lich's hands as Conan wrenched her from the thing's grasp. He hurriedly set her upon the ground, half-conscious, and whirled to face the creature he had pursued. It made the others look normal, for its head was divided into two parts, with clotted, frozen brains hanging from the division. Its eyeballs lay frozen upon its cheeks, started from their sockets by the blow that had slain it.

"Agilulf!" Conan breathed.

The thing attacked. Conan had no weapon, and he saw no stone within reach small enough for him to lift but large enough to do any damage. A claw-fingered hand reached for him and he grasped the wrist, seeking to bend the arm back. The fiend's other arm wrapped around his back, and his own sought a grip near his other hand. The hard, frozen flesh made a firm grip all but impossible. It was a good thing, he thought, that the ruined jaws could not get a teeth-lock upon him.

They swayed and tottered, each trying to get a deadly hold, the lich wrestling as cleverly as any living man. Its strength was abnormal, and it rushed Conan back to slam him against a standing stone. The Cimmerian shook stars from before his eyes, but it had given him an idea. If he could not cast a great stone at this thing, perhaps the opposite could be arranged.

Grappling and staggering, the two forms tottered toward a huge slab of stone, one of the rock sentinels that had toppled in ages past. Conan forced an arm away from him and stepped back, giving himself an instant to get his other hand free and grasp the thing's leg. With a sinew-cracking effort, he raised it above his head and brought it smashing down upon the stone. There was a sound of many small fractures, and the thing lay still for a moment. Then it began to move.

Once again he raised it and brought it down, with an incoherent scream. This time the internal crunching was much louder. Still, the thing moved. A third time, Conan, with a superhuman straining of muscles, heaved it above his head. It was like lifting a sack of stones, only its relatively intact skin holding its sundered fragments together.

"Die for good, Crom curse you!" he shouted as he smashed the ruins once again upon the unyielding stone.

This time it lay still. Even a physician would have difficulty in recognizing that this had once been a man.

"Well, Agilulf," Conan said when he once again had breath, "you could not slay me when you were alive. Did you think you would have a better chance dead?"

"You have slain him twice," Alcuina said. "Must you insult him as well?"

Conan turned to see her standing shakily by one of the standing stones. "Of all the masters I have served," he said, "you are the hardest to please. Are you hurt?"

"I am sore all over, but I think I bear no serious hurts." Her hands clutched together gaps in her tattered robes, which exposed far more of full breast and rounded thigh than was her wont. Even so, she stood pridefully, seeming to ignore the cold. "I came to my senses just as you caught up with that thing. I saw the whole fight. I think I did well in taking you into my service."

"I never thought I would live long enough to hear that," he answered.

"Your work is not over, swordsman. I fear that this is merely the opening affray of this war."

"Come, lady," Conan urged, "let us go back to the garth and see what damage is done and who is dead. Even with these things out of the way, it is still possible to freeze."

"You are right," she said. She tottered slightly, ripped garments gaping to expose pale, trembling flesh, and he put a strong arm about her shoulders. She did not object.

As they crossed the moonlit plain they could see the light of small fires coming from the garth, but there were no major blazes to be seen. At least they would have a roof that night.

A cheer went up as they came in under the gate-lintel. "We had thought you lost," Rerin said. "So busy was everyone, nobody noticed you had been borne away until all these creatures were finished." The old man chattered in nervousness and relief. "Then we sought you but could not find you. A boy said he saw a monster run through the gate with someone over his shoulder and the Cimmerian chasing both. We were about to send a party in search."

"Are all done for?" Alcuina asked.

"Yes, it took some time and the efforts of several men for each lich, but they are all dead. Again."

"There is one more out in the great circle of stones. The outlander killed it with his bare hands." Murmurs of admiration arose. "Go send a party to fetch it," Alcuina continued. "Build a great pyre without the wall. We must burn all the dead. How many did we lose this night?"

"Two warriors, lady," said Siggeir. "And three thralls. Had the Cimmerian not taken a hand when he did, the toll would have been far higher."

"Yes," she said distractedly, "he did well. Get plenty of fuel together. I want all the dead reduced to ashes, and the ashes scattered."

"It grows warmer," Conan noted. A wind had sprung up that would have been cold at any other time, but that seemed warm after the last two days.

"So it does," Alcuina said. She turned to her wizard. "What make you of this?"

"It is plain now what Iilma has been up to. He brought the great cold upon us to freeze the ground so we could not bury our dead. He used them against us, both to attack us and to let in Odoac's men, or, rather, the liches who were once men."

"Let's go pay King Totila a visit," Conan suggested. "I would very much like to kill this Iilma."

"First we must put this place aright," Alcuina said. "With the door repaired and the dead safely disposed of, then we can discuss action. To work."

All the rest of the night they toiled to set the house in

order. While the women saw to the hall, the warriors and thrall-men went to the woods and cut trees to build a pyre. They could not spare seasoned firewood, but the winter pine would burn fiercely, even though it was still green. With teams of oxen and horses, they dragged logs back to the garth. Just outside the wall they stacked them into a great heap, upon which was poured all the grease from the kitchen-midden.

The bodies of the freshly slain were cast upon the pyre, along with those of friend and enemy. Even a few beasts that had perished were tossed on. The sun was high in the east when the pyre was set alight. The arms of the slain warriors were thrown into the blaze, since they could not be buried together.

"Look," said Rerin as the flames ascended into the clear sky. He pointed a gnarled finger straight upward. Far overhead a pair of magpies circled.

Five

Wizard-Craft

"Iilma," said Totila ominously, "you have failed."

The wizard shrugged beneath his reindeer skins. "It was not I who failed you, Totila, but the dead."

"I ask little of the dead, wizard," said the king, barely able to restrain his temper. "From my wizard I expect results, not excuses. First you bring an unnatural cold upon us, costing me dear in livestock and thralls, then your army of dead men fails of its mission." The two men sat in the hall arguing while the men all around made merry, celebrating the passing of the unnatural spell of cold weather.

Iilma rose to his feet haughtily. "If my lord has no further use for my services, perhaps another king may see fit to engage me."

The king turned conciliatory. "Oh, sit down, Iilma. I spoke overhastily. We must devise a better plan, it is clear. It must be nothing that can devastate the whole countryside, though. Like it or not, a king lives by plows as well as by swords. I would not have thought it when I was merely a chieftain over a dozen men, but the loss of oxen can hurt a ruler as severely as the loss of fighting men. Even thralls have value." He ran beringed fingers through his luxuriant, red-gold beard. "How may we set this matter aright?"

"Master," Iilma said, "let me meditate upon this. There are mysteries I am privy to that might provide the answer for us. Certain powers commune with me. Let me summon them and take counsel with them. Have I your leave to go to my spirit-hut?"

"You have my leave," said Totila graciously.

The men quieted as the wizard rattled from the hall, then fell once more to dicing and wrestling. King Totila himself sat brooding, from time to time running his fingers through the scalps of dead chieftains and champions.

At that same time Alcuina was taking counsel with her warriors and her wizard. "What may we do to counter this threat from Totila? It is plain that he will destroy us all if we do not do something."

"How many warriors has King Odoac?" Conan asked.

"Several hundred, if he calls them all up," she answered. "More than I have. Why do you ask?"

"Why not ally yourself with him? With your combined armies, you could destroy Totila. It would be of profit to you both." He drained his tankard and held it out for more. Since the passing of the freakish cold Alcuina had lifted the rationing.

"I know well what the price for his alliance would be!" she said hotly. "I'll not lie in that pig's bed for a score of kingdoms!"

"So much for that, then," Conan muttered.

"I fear," Rerin said, "that his next attack will be

magical as well. After all, why should he risk his men when he has the evil Iilma to do his work for him?"

"Is there no way we can kill this wizard?" said Siggeir.

"Aye, I'm for that," Conan said. "Just tell me where to find this spell-caster, and I'll take care of him. He must sleep sometime. Ordinarily I'll not kill a man who has no chance to fight, but one who raises dead men to fight the living has no claim on any man's mercy or justice."

Alcuina turned to her own wizard. "What of it, Rerin? Could Conan steal upon Iilma and kill him? That is an order for murder I'd not hesitate to give."

The old man shook his head. "No wizard has wrought as Iilma has without seeing to his defenses. He will be surrounded with traps and warnings. Most especially, there are his magpie-familiars. They could be perched in the eaves, watching us even now." Many heads jerked around, eyes wide with fear and searching the surrounding shadows. "No, they or some other agency would warn him of an approaching killer, be the man ever so stealthy and crafty."

"Crom take it!" Conan said, slamming down his tankard. "These are mortal men. There must be some way to deal with them." But none there had an answer for him.

Iilma the wizard strode through the forests and across the hills. Above him flew his magpies, spying out his path, their eyes bright and keen for the sight of enemies. Iilma gave no notice to the cold or the snow, once again those of a normal winter. The pouch at his side contained a little food, which was all he needed.

To a magician, the needs of the flesh were the pettiest of concerns.

Ten years before, he had come to these strange lands, driven from his native Hyperborea by jealous rivals. He might have gone south, to the rich kingdoms he knew were there. He had communed with southern mages in his spirit-trances. But his magic, of which he was a matchless practitioner, was the magic of the snows and the forests. His was the magic of the North, the land of frost giants and fog giants, of the spirits that lived in stone and wood and water. To the south was the magic of other gods, equally ancient, and dominated by the serpent cult of Set. In those lands his power might not be great, and he was too old to learn a new art.

Thus, he had come to this land of squabbling kinglets and chose one such to bend to his will. Totila was strong and fierce, but he was also crafty and saw no reason to use men and treasure when magic would do his work. He was the perfect instrument for Iilma's plans. The wizard would make Totila the greatest king of the North, and Iilma would in turn become the greatest of wizards. Lesser mages such as Rerin would be no stop to him, since they feared to traffic with the truly great powers.

On his third day of travel Iilma came to a dead heath. Such vegetation as it supported was stunted and withered, and it took strange shapes not pleasant to look upon. Iilma journeyed there two or three times each year to find plants that grew nowhere else in the North. Almost everything that grew there had powers and properties that were valuable to him. This time, however, he was not in search of magical plants.

As he progressed into the heath the plants grew fewer, until there were none at all. Here the ground was frozen and cracked, like a dried lake-bottom in the midst of a drought. In the center of the wasteland towered a mound, curiously regular in shape and crowned with an encircling wall, much like those that dotted the plain where Alcuina had built her hall. Leaning upon his staff, Iilma trudged to the top of the mound.

From its crest he surveyed his surroundings. He could see the cracked plain he had crossed, but neither hills nor forests were visible in the distance. Only a wavering haze was to be seen. The laws of the ordinary world did not always apply to this demon-haunted place.

The wall was breached by a narrow doorway, and within the top of the mound was empty save for a beehive-shaped hut made of stones piled crudely, without mortar. Ordering his familiars to keep watch outside, Iilma ducked through the low doorway into the hut. The inside was dark and smelled of damp, and the wizard quickly kindled a fire from the bundle of sticks he had gathered on the way. As it blazed high the fire revealed a conical chamber with walls of rough stone and a floor of packed earth, nothing more.

Onto the fire Iilma cast small objects from his pouch: bones, feathers, clots of dried blood, and certain plants plucked from the withered heath. A thick smoke of many colors arose and gathered thickly in the chamber, for there was no smoke hole at its peak. For reasons peculiar to this place, no smoke found its way out through the door. Iilma breathed deep of the murky fumes. Rocking back and forth, he began to chant, occasionally stirring the embers of the fire with his staff. In time with his chant, Iilma shook a gourd rattle in a monotonous rhythm. Gradually he lost all sense of where he was. The hut and the smoke disappeared from his senses, and he entered the spirit world.

He was never sure at what point he would enter that strange realm. The spirit world and the world of men were not like nations, whose borders remain in the same juxtaposition. He had many times entered the spirit realm through this gate, and never had he twice entered the same place. This time he found himself sitting in the midst of a limitless plain, twilit, its sky beginning to display stars that were not those to be seen from the world of men. In the far distance he could just descry the hulking shapes of mountains, which seemed to move subtly, in a disturbing fashion. Sitting in the middle of this plain, Iilma continued to rattle and chant. The flames of his fire were still before him, but of the fuel and the smoke there was no sign.

From time to time strange creatures drew nigh him, their forms gaunt and hideous. Great, glowing eyes and long teeth shone in the dim light, and many-jointed fingers were tipped with claws. Bloodlust burned in their eyes, but none ventured within the circle of light cast by the little fire. In time they departed, at the approach of something far larger.

The thing that came to the wizard Iilma upon the darkling plain of the spirit world was evil to behold, bloated of body and with a face like that of a toad, if a toad's face were capable of expression and malice. Wartlike growths covered its leprous skin, which hung in loose folds about its repulsive body. It squatted before the wizard and waited with an air of intelligent expectation.

"What would you?" it asked in a hissing voice. The tongue it spoke was one known only to wizards and demons.

"I have an enemy," Iilma said, "and I desire that my king should have a certain woman. It is my desire that you attend to my enemy and procure this woman that I may present her to the king.''

"The woman is a queen?" the thing hissed.

"Yes, but you may not have her! You must deliver her to me at this place, alive and unharmed. I invoke the pact we made many years ago."

The thing glared at him with hideous amusement, then said, "I abide by the pact. Now, show me."

Iilma's flames flattened and spread into a broad whorl, like his forest pool. Pictures began to take form. First they were looking down through a bird's eye upon Alcuina's garth, the hall looking tiny within its surrounding wall in the midst of the plain dotted with its cairns and stone circles.

"This is where they live," Iilma said. "Since midsummer has the queen dwelt among the stones of the dead."

"She wrought foolishly in her choice of a dwelling place," said the demon with obscene glee. "For many turns of the gyre we have felt strange vibrations emanating from our point of contact with that place."

The flames swirled again, and then the form of Alcuina was revealed. The queen of the Cambres sat in her chamber, her robe pooled around her hips, baring the voluptuous perfection of her upper body, a handmaiden brushing her luxuriant hair. The red-gold tresses fanned gloriously over her shapely, white shoulders. The queen looked pensive, but what thoughts lay behind her level brows remained a mystery. She spoke, but they heard no sound.

"The queen is fair, as men judge such things," Iilma said. Now the flames brought forth the image of Rerin the sorcerer. The old man stood upon the walk that ran around the palisade. "This is my enemy. He is a wizard, but his skill is small compared to mine, and he has no pact with you."

"A trivial business," the demon said in boredom. Then another man joined the wizard, a tall, powerfully-built man, with flowing black hair. "Who is this?"

"That is Alcuina's new champion," Iilma said. "A mere adventurer, and of no consequence."

The demon looked upon Iilma with a smile so terrible that even the hardened wizard was frightened for a moment. It pointed toward the Cimmerian with a tal-oned finger. "This one has the aura of destiny about him."

Iilma looked, but could see nothing. He shrugged. "Many are born to destiny, yet die before they have any chance to fulfill it."

In the image that floated before them, the wizard looked up, seeming to stare straight at them. He pointed a finger toward them, and the black-haired man fol-lowed the gesture. The warrior snatched a spear from its place against the palisade and cast it upward. The weapon seemed to soar straight at Iilma, then the vantage-point shifted and they lost sight of the two.

Iilma smiled frostily. "The foolish Rerin has learned to keep watch for my familiars."

"We shall take them," the demon said. "The queen, the wizard, and the warrior."

"The wizard you must kill," Iilma said. "The warrior"—he made a dismissive gesture with his hand—"you may do with as you like. But the queen you must deliver to me unharmed. Her mind, of course, may be slightly damaged by the experiences she shall undergo, but my king is interested primarily in her body, her pedigree, and her ability to produce strong heirs."

"None of those things shall be damaged," the demon promised. "This shall take time to arrange. I shall contact you in the spirit-trance when I have her for you. At that time you must come to the place whence you came here and perform as you have this day. Then shall I deliver her to you, in accordance with the pact between us."

"Be it so," said Iilma.

At his gesture the flames were extinguished, and he found himself once more within the beehive-shaped hut of stone. Before him lay the cold ashes of his fire, and outside he could hear the cawing of two magpies.

Conan stood at his guard-post, brooding over the stony plain. He did not like this place. He liked his companions well enough, and he could not fault Alcuina as an employer, but the ancient stone lines and circles depressed his spirits. The massive posts with their stone lintels could never have been the work of men, he was sure. The stones were too great to lift by any means he could imagine. They squatted in brutish silence, and he was sure they were haunted by the spirits of the builders. The old man Rerin agreed with him in this, but Alcuina insisted that they needed the wall while they were in so weakened a condition, with so many enemies all about.

The snow fell gently, but Conan, perched above the gate, had had a small shelter built to protect the man on duty. It had no sides to restrict his vision, but a thatched roof kept off the worst of the snow or rain.

He whirled at the sound of someone ascending the ladder. He wondered which of his friends, sleepless this night, was coming up to while away an hour in tale-spinning. Great was his surprise to see Alcuina herself.

"Good evening, my lady," he said, sheathing his sword.

"You are a nervous man to draw your weapon even at one coming from within the garth," she said.

"I have not arrived at my present age by assuming a man was my friend merely from the direction of his approach. What's more, many an officer has given me extra duty for *not* challenging him while on guard, even though I knew him as my own commander. It was a lesson I was slow to learn, but it may be the only sensible one the southern armies use."

"It is rare that I even find one of my sentries awake when I come upon them this late. How do your southern officers deal with sleeping sentries?"

"It depends. Some hang them. Others are content with a mere flogging. I would not recommend that you employ such means. Northern warriors are not like southern soldiers."

"I could not sleep tonight," Alcuina said. She stood by Conan and leaned upon the palisade, looking out over the vista that so disturbed the Cimmerian. "I went to Rerin's hut, but he is abed. You are the only other one wakeful in the garth."

"What disturbs your sleep?" Conan asked, not without a gentle malice. "The feast was a good one, I saw that you put away your share of the ale, the snores within are no louder than usual, the livestock are back in their sheds, and no dead men have come calling—"

"Do not mock me!" She turned on him. "I feel uneasy tonight." She looked back out over the plain. "I feel that something out there is stirring. I know now that this is not a good place for us to live. I should have trusted to a timber wall such as we always used."

"Too late to be worrying about that," Conan said

uneasily. He did not like this talk of things stirring in the outer darkness. The fight with the dead had been bad enough. Now that it was past, he hoped there would be no more supernatural doings. An open sally by Totila was what he wanted. He had no unease about an honest fight with real men and real weapons, no matter how bad the odds. "We must make the best of it here until spring. Let me take some men into the hills, then I'll find you a good defensive position in the upland."

"Spring may be too late." Alcuina shivered, but not from the cold. "Perhaps I'll be forced into alliance with Odoac after all."

It occurred to Conan that her sleeplessness might be occasioned by lack of suitable male companionship. Surely she would not be out in the middle of a winter night talking with Siggeir or any of the other men who, Conan complacently realized, did not share in his abundance of the qualities women find attractive in a man. He was about to test this thought when he was interrupted by the arrival of Rerin. The old man came puffing up the ladder just as Conan had stepped closer to the queen.

"I had thought you abed," said Alcuina as she hastily stepped away from Conan.

"As did I," said Conan sourly.

"An evil dream woke me," Rerin said. "I doubt not but Iilma is up to some mischief. I came to find whether the sentry had seen aught. I did not expect to find you here, my lady."

"This has become a popular gathering place," Conan said. "But we've not seen those accursed magpies in many days, so why think you that Iilma is busy this night?"

"For one thing," Rerin said impatiently, "we've not seen his magpies in many days, young man. Does that not make you suspicious?"

Conan shook his head. "The less I see of wizards," he said pointedly, "the happier I am. The same goes for their familiars. I have seen worse creatures than magpies lurking about magic-mongers, but these birds are bad enough."

"I felt it too, Rerin," said Alcuina, ignoring Conan. "Strange shapes move through my sleeping hours."

"Speaking of which," Conan broke in, "I wonder where my relief is? I feel the need of a few sleeping hours, with or without strange shapes."

"Come, Rerin," Alcuina said disgustedly, "let us retire to my bower where we may confer without annoying this great warrior." The two descended the ladder and left Conan, arms folded, and sunk in gloom.

After all, he thought, brooding, there were plenty of other women hereabout. Because of the recent increase in mortality, there was a large supply of grieving widows, many who had let him know in no uncertain terms how desperately they were in need of consoling. He had yielded to some of their blandishments, but it was Alcuina who intrigued him.

Small though her kingdom was, she ruled it well, with the good of her people in mind. That was a rare thing in Conan's experience. Her warriors were intensely loyal to her, even though she was not a warchieftain, and that was even rarer. More to the point, he found her beautiful, and he was frustrated by her seeming indifference to him. Certainly a queen could have no intention of permanent attachment to a penniless adventurer, but surely she owed herself a little pleasurable dalliance. And who better to dally with than Conan? It was hard on a warrior's pride.

He saw a small point of light coming his way from the hall. Had she reconsidered? But then the light became a burning faggot borne by Ataulf, his relief. The man made his way up the ladder, yawning and scratching. Beneath the little roof, he tossed his brand into the smoking brazier. "Any sign of foes without?" he asked sleepily.

"You would know if there had been," Conan said shortly. "What took you so long to get here? I've been freezing my—"

"Peace, Conan. I am not late. It always feels that way on night sentry. Go find your bed."

Conan grumbled as he descended to the yard. He would show that stuck-up, queenly wench. He wondered which of the women who had been casting longing gazes his way to try first. No, they would all be asleep now, and in no mood for amusement. What he needed was a good fight. No, what he really needed was some sleep. He went into the hall and stumbled among the snoring heaps on the floor. He found his place and was beginning to unbuckle his cuirass when the screams began from behind the arras at the end of the hall.

"Crom's bones, what does a man have to do to get a night's sleep in this place?" He ripped out his sword and dashed for the arras. The glowing coals in the hearth illumined that end of the hall. With no patience for such niceties as formal entrance, he slashed the arras from top to bottom with his sword and leaped through.

Brilliant, unnatural light filled the chamber. Dazzled,

Conan could make out only shifting forms. Screaming came from the midst of animallike growls.

"Alcuina!" he shouted, sword held out before him and eyes squinted against the light. "Where are you?" A loud chanting rose among the other sounds. Behind Conan the hall stirred, but nobody joined him. "Alcuina!" Still no answer.

Gradually the light faded. The screams and the animal growls faded away, but the chanting continued. At last Conan could see. The queen's chamber was utterly wrecked, its furnishings splintered and claw-slashed. The logs that formed its rear wall appeared to have been burned through. Beyond the gaping hole footprints led away through the falling snow.

He looked to the source of the chanting and saw Rerin, his staff held stiffly before him in both hands, eyes tightly shut as he wailed out his chant. A nimbus of blue light surrounded the old man, pulsing and throbbing to his litany.

"Cease that bawling, old man!" Conan shouted. "Where is Alcuina?"

Rerin's eyes sprang open and his chant broke off. The nimbus faded as he stared wildly about. "The demons came! They came and tried to carry us both off! I cast a protective spell. It saved me, but I could not save Alcuina." His hands trembled as he clenched them in rage and humiliation.

"Then what good are you?" Conan demanded.

He crossed to the gaping hole in the logs, noting that the ends of the logs were blackened; but instead of being charred, they looked as if they had *melted*. He shook his head. "Wood should not melt." He kept his words steady and offhand, as befitted a warrior; but inwardly he was repelled at the unnatural sight.

"And demons should not bear off queens," Rerin said. "But it has happened. We must pursue."

Terrified, gaping faces peered in through the ruined arras.

"Arm yourselves!" Conan ordered. "We're going to get Alcuina back." Some moved with less alacrity than they might have had it been human enemies they faced. Conan pointed to a stableman. "You! Saddle some horses, quickly."

"Do not bother," said Rerin. "The beasts will never go near those creatures, nor even follow on their tracks. We must pursue on foot, and we have little time."

Conan pushed his way back into the hall and found his cloak and his helmet. Donning both, he returned to the queen's chamber and grabbed the old wizard by the arm. "Let's go, magician. The trail grows cold."

Out through the ragged hole Conan strode into the snowy night. The footprints in the snow were not quite human, but neither were they those of any beast he knew. He turned at a shout from the sentry. "Something crosses the plain! They go toward the great stone circle."

With the wizard in tow, Conan followed the prints to the base of the stone wall. Through the ancient stone another passage had been melted. His hair rose on the back of his neck, but his urge to rescue Alcuina was stronger. He turned to the mob of people behind him. "We must go get the queen!" he shouted. "Who goes with me?" Siggeir and a few of the hardier souls came forward. "Then curse the rest of you for *nithings!*" he said. "Come on!"

Out through the unnatural tunnel they went. Snow drifted into the tracks, but the men would remain visible for some time yet. They held torches aloft and shouted to encourage themselves and each other.

"I spend much time tracking this woman over the same ground," Conan muttered. "What did they look like?"

"Their shape was unclear," said the old man. "Such creatures are not intended to exist in this world, and they cannot hold any form here for long. I think they were man-sized, and almost man-shaped. More than that I could not tell."

"Why did they take her, and why did they want you?" The great stone circle loomed in the distance, and there was an unaccustomed glow about it.

"I can only guess," protested Rerin.

"Guess, then," Conan urged. "It was not for your beauty they wanted you."

"It must be some machination of Iilma. Totila wants Alcuina, and I am her only protection from Iilma's sorcery."

"Cursed poor protection, if you ask me," Conan growled. "I want to meet this Totila. A man who is already stronger than his enemies and has plenty of warriors and still would rather use wizardry has lived too long."

As they reached the circle of stone they could see a crowd of odd creatures huddled near a gatelike stone trilithon. Uncanny streaks of light arced between the standing stones and whirlpools of flamelike light filled the entire circle. Borne overhead by the pack of creatures was Alcuina.

"There she is," he said, pointing with his sword. "We must go take her back!" The men behind him stared with fear-widened eyes, and none came forward.

Rerin shook loose from Conan's grasp and gathered

his shaken dignity about him like a robe. "I shall lead," he said, chin high and only slightly quivering. "Follow me."

With his staff held rigidly before him, the old man stepped within the circle. The lights whirled about him, but none touched him. Conan followed close behind, heart pounding. The light formed into small, malevolent beings, fanged and clawed and flapping bat-wings of glittering light. They attacked him and he slashed at them with his sword, but it passed through them harmlessly. They circled around him, laughing maniacally.

"Do not waste your strength," the old man said. "They are phantoms of your own mind."

"Then give me something I can cut, damn you!" Conan bellowed.

"They pass through!" said Rerin in a quavering voice.

Conan squinted into the shifting light. Something like daylight gleamed through the gateway formed by the posts and lintel of the trilithon. The things and their burden were passing beneath the lintel.

At the gateway the old man halted. "We dare go no farther," he said. "Beyond is the spirit land."

"By Crom, I'll not return to the hall without her, and neither shall you!" With the wizard's robe knotted in one fist and his sword gripped in the other, Conan strode into another world.

Six

The Shifting Land

As Conan leaped through the gate he felt a shattering sense of disorientation. For moments that could not be measured in time, he felt suspended in a yawning gulf, with a sickening sensation of falling endlessly in some void between worlds. Such thought as he could muster he devoted to keeping his grip on his sword and upon Rerin.

Abruptly, the transition was over, and he was staggering upon solid ground. His grip on the old man's clothes broke and he whirled, sword outstretched, ready to be set upon by enemies. His dizziness passed, and still there was no attack.

"Alcuina!" he bellowed, but there was no answer.

Raging, he stormed about, seeking any sign of the demons that had borne her off. There were no tracks such as the demons should have made, either. He hoped that the wizard might have some answers for the things that perplexed him. Rerin sat dazed upon the ground, and the Cimmerian studied his surroundings as he went to the old man.

Instead of the black, snowy night they had left behind, it was an oddly dim day here. Conan helped the old man to his feet and said with unaccustomed hesitation, "I'm sorry I was so rough with you, old man. I thought that, with haste, we might save the queen."

"Quite understandable," said Rerin, brushing off his robe. "I do not suppose any more followed us?"

Conan scanned the gateway. The trilithon was identical, but instead of standing in the northern plain it stood in a little mountain glade. Nothing was visible through its doorway but more of the glade. "Not one," Conan reported. "I am not surprised. They were brave men to come as far as they did. It is easier to find a new ruler than to enter a demon land."

"And yet you come," said Rerin.

"I want her back," Conan said.

"And you are braver than most men."

"That may be," Conan agreed. "But I was as frightened as any."

"It takes a hero to ignore fear in the service of his liege. She did well when she hired you."

"Then it is time for me to earn my pay," Conan barked, weary of talk. "They were only paces before us when they passed through this gate. Why are they not here now?"

"The spirit land does not obey the same rules as our own world. They may not have emerged in the same place as we. It is fortunate that you and I came across in the same place."

"That remains to be seen," Conan said. He looked around at their surroundings. "What manner of land is this?"

If this was truly a spirit land it seemed to be common enough. They stood in a glade cupped in rolling hills. The light of the blue sky was slightly different than it should have been, its blue deeper and the bowl of the sky seeming somehow closer, and there was a haze around them, as if they were under water. Unclear things floated in the haze, but none seemed to be threatening so far.

"It's like the sea," Conan said, "as you see it through the crystal eye-shields worn by the black pearl divers of Kush."

"We have been fortunate, if I may use such a word," Rerin said. "I think we may be in the Shifting Land. The spirit world is really many lands, as is the world of men. I have been to some of these lands in spirit-trance, although never in body. Some of those lands would drive you mad instantly. This is one of the more bearable ones. We came through a gate in the northern part of the world of men, and this place somewhat corresponds to that part of the world. Had we entered through the land of Kush you mentioned, we might have come out into a hideous jungle, but there are far worse places even than that in the spirit land."

"Is there some way we may find Alcuina?" Conan asked, cleaving to the subject.

"There may be, but it will require time. And a number of magical substances, plants and minerals for the most part. Let us hope that they exist in this evil place."

"It seems that we have time. We'll find your substances, if they are to be found here. Can you get us back to the real world?"

"Yes, through gates such as this one. The time must be right, and—"

"Good," Conan said, dismissing inessentials. "Are there people here?" He gazed up at something that flew overhead on membranous wings. It took no notice of them.

"Of a sort. I have seen them in spirit-trance. They are not true men such as you and I, though. They—"

"How long until you know where we should look for Alcuina?" Conan asked abruptly.

The old man looked about. "I see some of the plants I need right here. Doubtless the others will be nearby. Then I must build a fire, perform certain ceremonies and chants—"

"Wake me when you know something." Conan dropped his helmet, stripped off his corselet, and flung himself on the ground. Soon he was deep in sleep.

Rerin shook his head in wonderment. Even in slumber the Cimmerian's hand still rested lightly upon his sword hilt.

Conan awoke when the old man touched his shoulder. Rerin jerked back as he exploded to his feet, sword in fist. "It is only me, Conan. I have found a direction where we may look for Alcuina. It is not a definite location, but at least we'll not be wandering about lost."

"Good," Conan said. He sheathed his blade and began to don his armor. "At least it is not too cold here."

Indeed, it was like a mild spring day in the North, just cool enough to know that winter had not wholly departed. Conan folded his cloak and tossed it over one shoulder. His life had taken him to many strange places. It was a consequence of being an adventurer. This was another strange place, and he could make his way anywhere.

"Let us go find her," he said.

For some time Alcuina thought she was mad. One moment she had been sitting in her bower, quietly talking with old Rerin. The next the log wall began to melt and flow, and a pack of nightmare demons entered in a burst of light, laying their loathsome hands upon her. She had thought that she called her men in her usual commanding voice, only later realizing that she had been screaming. As she was borne out she heard a bellowing voice that she was sure belonged to Conan. Then there had been a period of scattered impressions, of sounds and sights and concepts so confused that now she was utterly disoriented.

What was this place? For a moment she was afraid to breathe; the air appeared thick, as if it had turned to water. Giving in to the inevitable, she took a deep breath, then shuddered with relief. It was like any other air. Perhaps something had gone wrong with her vision. But then she realized that things nearby were perfectly clear. She could have wished otherwise, for now she saw clearly the nature of her captors.

Before, their outline had been unstable. Now she saw that they were gaunt creatures, vaguely man-shaped but formed as obscene parodies of humankind. No two were quite alike, but bird-beaked faces mocked her. Beaks fringed with stubby tentacles flapped and clacked with obscene laughter. Their eyes were huge, bulging, and lidless, each with two slit irises and pupils. The hands that gripped were many-fingered and their gray skins coarse and pebbly, chafing her fair skin. Their smell was, if anything, worse than their aspect. They had set her upon the ground and seemed to be conferring among themselves. Their attitude was watchful, but they did not seem threatening just now.

She sat up and examined her surroundings. The turf beneath her felt strange. The grass was blue-green, very short and springy. She had never seen such grass. Some of the trees nearby looked familiar, others had feathery fronds and ringed trunks. Colorful birds flew overhead in panicked flight, pursued by a reptilian thing on membranous wings. Whatever this place was, it was not her familiar Northland. The air was cool, but not bitterly cold like the land from which she had been abducted.

The creatures, deep in their deliberations, ignored her. Their voices croaked and clicked, and multijointed hands gestured excitedly. Something in their furtive aspect told her that this was alien territory to them as well, and that they sought not to draw attention. She wondered who or what they were afraid of. She knew better than to assume that the enemy of her enemy was her friend.

That this was some machination of Iilma on behalf of Totila she had no doubt. What it would lead to was another matter. She knew that she was on her own. None of her people could have followed them here. How could they? She fought off a wave of hopelessness. She was a queen, and she would not act like a terrified kitchen-girl. Her first priority was escape from these unthinkable creatures.

In the distance, over the trees, she could see hazy mountains. She thought she could descry a hulking shape on the side of one of the nearer mountains, like some unthinkably huge hall. If so, it must be inhabited by giants such as had erected the wall surrounding her own hall. That did not look like a good direction in which to flee.

♦

She was resolved upon flight, and the present seemed to be as good a time as any. Her captors were preoccupied with their own bickering, and their fearful attitude was such that they might be more solicitous of their own safety than zealous in their pursuit of her. Surreptitiously, she gathered her legs beneath her.

As the bickering ascended to a crescendo, she sprang to her feet and ran. Behind her rose loud hoots of consternation, but she did not look back. She had spotted the nearest patch of dense forest, and she headed straight for it. Sounds of pursuit grew closer, and something tugged at her fur robe. Shrugging out of her garment, she increased her pace and heard a disappointed screech from behind. Now she could run even faster. She took her fur-trimmed gown in both hands and pulled its hem above her knees as she ran, wishing there was some way for her to strip it off, too. Unfortunately it took the help of a maid just to lace her into the garment.

Then she was among the trees, winding her way among the densest of them in hopes that the demons chasing her would find the terrain bewildering. So far they had shown little sign of intelligence. She darted between the tree trunks as lightly as a barren doe, and the sounds behind her grew frantic as the demons crashed through the undergrowth.

The woods were dark and mysterious, but she limited herself to one fear at a time. The sounds of pursuit grew fainter, but she did not slack her pace, although her lungs burned with the effort. She leaped a small stream in which the water flowed with an odd slowness.

At last, panting raggedly, she collapsed in a heap beneath a busy plant with dense, fleshy leaves. She crawled under it as far as she could go, trying not to

breathe too loudly. She was almost certain that she was
far enough ahead of the pursuit that she had not been
seen taking cover. With every nerve stretched to the
snapping point, she listened for the demons. Once she
thought she heard shuffling sounds nearby, then nothing
but the noises that apparently were common in this
forest, not much different from the woodland sounds
she was used to.

Something lumbered by on big, soft feet, jarring her
from a half slumber. She wondered how long she had
been semiconscious. The light was dimming, and she
wondered at this since she had been wide awake when
she hid. Perhaps it was the shock catching up with her.
She still felt oddly drowsy and lethargic. A bunch of
the flowers of the plant she had taken refuge under
hung before her face, giving off a heavy perfume. Idly
she tried to brush the blossoms aside and found that she
could not move her hand. With growing horror she felt
her body pinioned by rootlike growths that trailed from
the branches of the plant above her. Eyes wide, she
realized that the ground beneath the bush was carpeted
with the bones of animals.

Trying to make little sound, she struggled for her
life. Gradually the roots yielded. They had sent out
fine, hairlike rootlets, which penetrated her clothing.
The rootlets stung as they pulled away from her flesh.
She thanked Ymir that the passing beast had awakened
her before the evil plant had had a chance to kill her.

One by one the roots tore away from her as she
dragged herself with her hands toward the open. With a
stinging wrench, the roots binding her legs ripped loose.
Quickly she scrambled out from under the bush and lay,
panting and exhausted, upon the ground.

The darkness increased rapidly even as the fumes

from the plant cleared from her head. A pearly, ambient light remained after the last of the sunlight was gone. What kind of place was this? She had been afraid of the demons. It had occurred to her to fear the beasts or people of this place. She had not expected that she would have to fear the plants as well. For the first time the extent of her isolation and danger was borne in upon her. Never had she been so lost and alone. She shivered upon the ground and not entirely from the cold. Where could she go from here? She was utterly exhausted, yet she dared not sleep, as much as she yearned for it.

Shakily she got to her feet and examined herself. Her fine, fur-trimmed gown was in rags where the roots had torn away, exposing far more flesh than a well-born northern lady was accustomed to display. Her fair skin was covered with welts where the rootlets had been pulled from her. It was a good thing, she reflected, that the weather here was so mild.

The light grew stronger as the moon rose over the trees. It looked much like the moon she was used to, but it appeared much larger, and its color was greenish. She had never traveled far from her home, but she was fairly certain that people saw the same moon in all lands.

She could neither smell nor hear the demons anywhere nearby, and direction seemed to be purely a matter of convenience, so she decided to go downhill. There were many clear pathways in the forest. She chose one that descended alongside one of the slow-flowing streams. There was little sound in the forest except for the occasional splash of a fish leaping in the stream.

She had been walking by it for some time before she realized that something was odd about the stream. She stepped closer to the water and squinted at it. Unsure of her sight in the dimness, she found a light-colored leaf and tossed it in. She had been correct. The stream flowed *uphill*. None of the widely-traveled people she had spoken with had ever mentioned this happening in the far places of the world.

In a half trance she staggered on for some time, until she wandered from the path and walked into a tree. The shock of hitting the unyielding trunk jolted her into wakefulness. It was plain that she must rest, but where could she do it safely? She came to an open glade that had no vegetation except the short, springy grass. She went to its center, as far as she could get from any large plants, and lay down. She was so numb from fatigue that she was unaware of the chill air or anything else. Gratefully she allowed sleep's black wings to enfold her.

She awoke stiff and sore. Her body was bruised and scratched, and she was chilled to the bone, but she was rested and clearheaded. A night such as she had spent would have killed or at least seriously weakened a highborn woman of the more civilized parts of the world, but in the frozen North even the queens were hard as steel.

She looked around her and gasped when she saw that a middling-sized tree stood near her. It had not been there when she had lain down to sleep, and now it was only a few paces from her. It stood upon a mass of tangled roots, and she now saw that the roots were moving with almost imperceptible slowness. Long, thorny, vinelike growths hung from its branches, and she had little doubt of their purpose.

She rose hastily and walked away from the menacing tree. Now, in daylight, she saw that she was at the foot of a mountain. Upon its slopes towered the great structure she had seen when she was still in the hands of the demons. That seemed impossible, for at that time it had appeared to be many leagues away, and she could have covered only a fraction of that distance in her flight. Could it be a similar hall on another mountain? And yet she had been sure that there were no mountains nearby when she made her escape. It was another mystery, but she put it from her mind. In any case she had no intention of going near that stronghold. It looked ominous, and she did not want to encounter the folk who might live in such a place.

The rising sun, which at least appeared to be normal, gradually warmed her. She was very hungry, but what did she dare eat? In a place where plants walked and ate living victims, how was she to know which things were poisonous? She had no weapons for hunting and no skill at trapping, no hooks, line, or net for fishing. She could endure much privation, but if she did not eat today, she would weaken, making it harder for her to find food, making her easier prey.

A lengthy, tiring trek brought her to level ground below the mountain when she heard a great commotion behind her. As she crossed a wide clearing she cursed her carelessness. She should have skirted it, keeping close to the tree line. The trees might be dangerous, but at least they seemed to be unable to catch moving prey. She broke into a run, striving to reach the tree line straight ahead, when she looked back to see a panicked beast break into the clearing. It was the size of a horse and had lyre-curved horns. Its hide was dappled white and brown. It ran straight for her but she could tell by its rolling eyes that it did not see her. She knew a hunted animal when she saw one.

She had not reached the far trees when the hunters entered the glade. Flight was now out of the question; she turned to face them. They appeared to be men, and the animals they rode seemed to be horses, but she could not be sure. The riders were clothed in fantastic costumes of leather and cloth and metal, in many colors. Masks of fanciful design hid their faces. The mounts were likewise caparisoned gaily in bards of silken cloth, and their heads were adorned with horns and antlers and other outlandish ornamentation, clearly artificial. Little of the beasts was visible but for their hooves, which looked like true horse hooves except for their bright colors.

One of the riders drew a short bow, and an arrow flew from it to plunge feather-deep into the fleeing beast's side. It staggered on a few more steps, then collapsed almost at Alcuina's feet. The riders rode up to her and reined in. Their speech sounded like the twittering of birds, and one of them seemed to address her.

She shook her head. "I do not understand you."

They seemed taken aback. The one who had addressed her wore a hawk-mask covered with feathers, and now he lifted it from his head, like a helmet. His features were elfin and his hair like spun silver. His eyes were featureless silver balls and his skin pale as milk.

"Are you from the world of men?" he asked. His smile revealed small, even teeth.

"What other world is there?" she asked.

They all seemed to find this highly amusing and laughed uproariously, the sound of their laughter high-pitched and warbling. Now the others removed their masks, and they were so much alike that they might have been siblings. Some appeared to be women, but in their heavy, fanciful costumes sex was difficult to judge.

A group of dwarfish figures emerged from the tree line, but the riders paid them no attention. The dwarfs ignored her as well and set about cutting up the dead beast with great efficiency.

"What kind of person are you?" asked the one who had spoken before.

"I am Alcuina, queen of the Cambres," she answered. They found this amusing as well.

"What are Cambres?" asked another.

"They are my people, my nation. I do not know what place this is, nor how I arrived here, but I must return home. I crave the boon of your hospitality until I may find a way to return." She had no idea who these people were, but their horses and rich clothing suggested that they were nobles. The tradition of hospitality between persons of high birth was observed everywhere that she had ever heard of, so she presumed that it would be so here as well.

The strange people twittered among themselves for a moment, then the one who seemed to be their spokesman said, "Very well, you shall be our guest. You shall ride with me."

"I thank you." She reached up to mount behind him.

His stature was not great, and he was slender, but he was inhumanly strong. He took her beneath her arms and lifted her easily to sit before him.

With incredible speed the dwarfs had dismembered the dead animal and were now packing off the joints. One bore the lyre-horned head and another the hide, and only the hooves and a pile of offal remained upon the ground.

The little group of hunters set off, taking a wide trail

that led uphill. Alcuina sat with her spine straight, seeking to maintain her dignity in the midst of these daunting changes in her life. She was ashamed of her ragged condition, now little more than near-nudity. But she made no futile attempt to restore her appearance, knowing that it would only make her look more helpless.

"Who are you?" she asked the man she rode with. "What manner of people are you?"

"I am Hasta, and we are Getae, the masters of this, the Shifting Land."

Alcuina thought this an odd name for a place. "How is it that you speak my tongue?"

"Many of us speak the tongues of men. Those of us who practice the great arts need such facility with speech." As if to confirm this, another rider drew even with them. The face was similar to Hasta's but the voice, although husky, was feminine.

"You appear to be in great distress, my dear. When we reach the castle I shall find you more suitable attire."

"Alcuina," Hasta said, "this is my sister, Sarissa. She is mistress of many arts."

The two smiled at her. She did not like the way they smiled, but she had never seen such faces, so how could she know how to read their expressions?

"And this," Hasta said, gesturing grandly, "is our home."

Alcuina looked up the mountain path and saw, to her dread, the great hall she had seen and had wanted to avoid. It was made of greenish-black stone, and she could see no joints between blocks. It was as if the whole structure had been carved from a single, massive block of stone. The doorway and the windows were strangely irregular, their outlines wavery and vague. It looked more like something that had grown there of itself than a thing built by human hands.

They rode beneath the lintel of a great gateway, its stone carved with peculiar and disturbing figures. Alcuina first stared at them, then looked quickly away. More of the dwarfs appeared to lead away the mounts.

She had expected a courtyard inside the gate, but instead they had ridden into a gigantic room illumined only by narrow windows high on the walls. Her entire garth would have fitted into the room.

Sarissa led her up a stairway and through a wide door. The door was flanked by crouching, sculpted figures that bore the lintel of the doorway upon their tortured backs. The whole massive, gloomy aspect of the building was oppressive and daunting.

Taking her hand, Sarissa led Alcuina through mosaic-decorated halls and sumptuously furnished chambers until they came to a door of richly-carved wood, which opened for them without human or even dwarfish aid.

Sarissa entered and began to strip off her colorful, leather garments. "Come, the bath is this way."

She led Alcuina into a room full of thin, fragrant steam with a pool in its center. The room, indeed the entire castle, felt warm despite the apparent absence of fires.

Sarissa had now removed her outer garments, and Alcuina saw that, in spite of her facial resemblance to her brother and the others, Sarissa was indeed a woman. Decidedly so. She now wore only a harnesslike arrangement of straps, buckles, and rings, to which her outer clothing had been attached. It covered nothing but instead framed and emphasized all her feminine attributes. Her body was so voluptuous that Alcuina felt like an adolescent girl beside her.

"Remove those rags, my dear," Sarissa said, beginning to peel the rags from Alcuina's trembling body. "You shall feel far better after a bath."

Hesitantly Alcuina complied. She was a little apprehensive of the pool. In her home, bathing had been accomplished in a sweat-room, with hot stones, buckets of water, and a stiff brush. Bathing with another woman did not bother her, since all the free women of the garth had bathed together, but actually submerging herself in the water was a decidedly outlandish idea.

Sarissa freed a few buckles and her harness dropped to the floor, to join the remains of Alcuina's clothing. For a moment she stood, pridefully naked, so challenging in her flaunted womanhood that Alcuina wanted to draw herself up in reply, yet a strange timidity filled her. To her surprise she found herself childishly stretching out a trembling hand. With a cruel smile Sarissa took the proffered hand possessively and drew Alcuina down a series of small steps into the water. As the warm water rose up her legs, it leached the sting from Alcuina's many small injuries. A languorous feeling of well-being replaced the alien sensations. She had never felt anything so pleasurable. Sarissa seated her on a stone ledge so that the water was just below the level of her chin.

Sarissa clapped her hands, and such was Alcuina's state of lazy contentment that she was not disturbed when several men and women, clad only in silken loincloths, entered bearing trays of gold and silver. As one of the men crouched by her to proffer a goblet of red wine she noticed that he wore a wide collar of plain iron, such as some northern peoples put upon their bondsmen.

"Are these thralls?" Alcuina asked dreamily.

"Slaves," Sarissa confirmed. "Toys, existing for
our convenience and pleasure."

Alcuina saw a lovely girl whose back was covered
with the red weals of a recent lashing. She pointed to
the girl. "Are they often rebellious?"

Sarissa shrugged. "Perhaps. Or perhaps someone de-
sired the pleasure of giving her a good flogging." She
sipped at her own wine. "I may have done it myself,
but I do not recall it."

At another time Alcuina might have been horrified at
this statement, but just now she was curiously unable to
feel anything except an idle interest. She raised a pale,
shapely leg, hardly aware of the other's smiling, watching, and examined it. The welts left by the carnivorous
plant were quickly fading to faint pink marks. Soon
they would be gone entirely. She ate from the proffered
trays of sweetmeats until the edge was taken from her
ravenous appetite, and soon the whole world took on a
sort of rosy, restful glow.

The two women left the bath and were dried by
slaves with thick, soft towels. Never had Alcuina dreamed
of such luxury. This seemed to be the correct way for a
queen to live. She wondered how she had lived for so
long without this. Still nude, they returned to the outer
chamber, which was Sarissa's sleeping-place. The bed
it contained was larger than the bower that Alcuina
shared with her maids at home.

"Now, we must have you properly attired," Sarissa
said.

She fired off words Alcuina could not understand,
and the slaves began to open chests and bring forth
scarves and jewels and cosmetics.

Under Sarissa's direction, Alcuina was adorned and
painted, her nails lacquered and her lips stained red.

She was draped with necklaces and bracelets and anklets and waist-chains of gold studded with gemstones, far more delicate and subtle in design than the massive northern jewelry she was used to.

"Now, look at yourself, my dear." Sarissa, still naked, took her to a tall glass.

Alcuina's eyes widened at the transformation wrought in her appearance.

She was richly draped with precious metals and stones, and her face was subtly painted to highlight her great beauty. Something seemed to be missing, though. In an abstracted fashion she realized that, except for waist-chains and a large, glowing red jewel in her navel, her body was still entirely bare. Every bit of the jewelry seemed designed and placed to frame her full breasts and rounded buttocks, to emphasize the curves of thighs and hips. She appeared more naked than if completely unclothed, and every inch of her was flaunted brazenly.

"Perhaps," Alcuina said hesitantly, "some garments now?"

"Not necessary," Sarissa said. "Just one more item."

She took something from a slave and fastened it around Alcuina's neck. So slow had Alcuina's reactions become that it was some time before her eyes widened in horror at the broad iron collar that had been clamped around her slender white neck.

"My new toy," Sarissa purred.

Seven

The Hell-Scorpion

"How can you be sure of your direction in this accursed place?" demanded Conan. He and the old man had been wandering through the Shifting Land for three days, and its bewildering changes of terrain had the Cimmerian utterly baffled.

"The first lesson in this place," Rerin said, "is never to trust the evidence of your senses. Here the voices of the trees and the animals tell me where we are and where we must go."

"I would not trust *these* trees to tell me my name, even if I could understand their speech!" Idly he lopped a branch from a nearby tree with his sword. "Trees that eat people should not be trusted."

Rerin laughed: a rare thing for him. "Is it so strange that plants should eat men? After all, in the world we come from, men eat plants. Why should the green things not enjoy a turnabout here?"

"It is not natural," Conan maintained. "Man-eating animals I can put up with. I have even encountered cannibals, but plants should stay rooted properly in the earth, not go about in search of prey." They had spent wakeful nights avoiding the alarming flora of the Shifting Land.

"The beasts here can be worse," Rerin said. "I am surprised that we have encountered so few."

Conan's stomach growled. "I wish we would encounter one soon. I have neither spear nor bow, but I am hungry enough to chase down a deer with nothing but my sword."

In the mild climate Conan had removed all but his wolfskin tunic and leggings. The rest of his clothing and armor was bundled in his cloak and tied across his back. Sword and dagger were belted at his waist.

They were headed toward sunset, whatever that might mean in this place. They were crossing a deep cleft in a mountainside with a stream at its bottom. This stream flowed uphill, as did some others they had seen. Others flowed downhill, and they had even encountered one that had an uphill current on one side and a downhill current on the other. Conan had been in many strange places in his life, but this was the oddest of them all.

"Be still!" Rerin hissed.

Conan did as he was bidden. He listened hard, and soon heard a rumbling, slithering sound. His eye caught a hint of movement upon the ridgeline they had just crossed. He thought he could make out something like a scaly back, sliding just above the crest of land. The bulk of the thing was below the crest, but from what he could see it looked as if half a league of the thing was going by.

"Crom!" he said when the thing was out of sight. "What was that? It looked like the grandfather of all serpents."

Rerin shook his head. "I know not, but I do not think it is native to the Shifting Land. What called it hither I dread even to contemplate."

"Just as well we got into this valley when we did," Conan said. "If we had been slower crossing the ridge, it might have seen us. If it has eyes, at any rate. If there are more like that hereabout, we may be in for trouble."

"*May* be?" said Rerin. "We have been in mortal peril since we crossed from the world of men."

With a slight rustling noise, an animal emerged from a clump of bushes. It was piglike, with a snout for rooting, and small, hoofed feet. For a moment it stood and squinted at them nearsightedly, its nostrils quivering at their strange smell. In that moment Conan grabbed up a jagged rock and threw it, all in one motion, almost too swift to see. The stone struck the beast between the eyes with a loud crunch, and it fell over on its side, stone dead.

Conan grinned. "There's our dinner!" He drew his knife and advanced on the dead creature.

"You are as handy with a rock as with a sword," Rerin observed.

Conan began butchering the carcass. "Cimmerian lads are expected to find much of their own food after they have learned to walk. I've spent many a night on a cold mountainside watching over the clan's cattle on short rations. Woe to the rabbit or mountain goat that came within range of my throwing-arm during those lean days. I am even better with a sling, but a simple stone will do."

"So I see. I shall build us a fire, though I fear to attract attention."

"I would rather die fighting than starve," Conan

said. "In any case, I would like to speak with the inhabitants of this land, so let them come."

Soon the joints of the "pig" were sizzling and smoking on spits over the flames. As the meat was lightly cooked Conan carved away chunks and stuffed them into his mouth, thrusting the joints back over the flames to cook some more. Rerin ate somewhat less ravenously, but he managed to put away a goodly portion of the meat as well. From time to time Conan took up his sword and hacked at a hairy root that kept creeping toward them from the nearest tree line.

"It may come from this demon land," Conan said, waving a rib, "but it tastes as good as any wild boar I have eaten in the world of men."

"Pray we find other things as agreeable," Rerin said gloomily.

"Cheer up, wizard. We are alive, we are free, and we are on the track of the lady to whom we both owe allegiance. There are worse things than that." He picked up a large rock, one of a pile he had gathered by them, and threw it. It crushed a small bush he did not like the look of. "We could be dead," he went on, "or in chains."

"I envy your ability to be calm in the midst of the unknown, young man."

Conan shrugged. "I have never found any advantage in worrying about things before they happen. If danger threatens, I can fight it or run from it, but until it is before me there is little I can do about it. Does that not make sense?"

Rerin sighed. "Of a sort." He stared into the flames, and his expression went blank. Conan knew that this meant the old man was in one of his trances, so the

Cimmerian applied himself to his eating until Rerin should come out of it.

After several minutes Rerin blinked and was once more aware of his surroundings.

"Well?" said Conan eagerly, "did you learn aught of Alcuina?"

"She is in some manner of danger, but it is not mortal peril, as if something were about to slay her."

"Eh? What do you mean? Either she is in danger or she is not."

"It was not clear to me. From what I could learn, she has escaped from her captors, and they search for her. She has fallen in with others, and these mean her no less harm."

"That does not surprise me," Conan said, "in this place. Do you know yet where she is?"

"There was a veil between me and her whereabouts, and I fear that she has fallen in with magic-practitioners of no mean order. However, before I was cut off from her I saw a great building, like a castle. I think she is in that place."

"A castle," Conan mused. "I have dealt with castles before, and border forts, strong-houses, temple treasuries, and the like. Any strong place made by men may be broken into, and its treasures despoiled."

"You speak as if from much experience," Rerin said. "However, I fear that this place may not have been made by men."

"That is bad, as is your talk of magic-practitioners. But, we can only do our best." He tossed a bone over his shoulder into the dark beyond. They could hear something pounce upon it. Conan lay down with his head pillowed on his cuirass and drew his wolfskin cloak over him. "You take first watch. Keep the plants at a distance.'' He placed his hand upon his sword hilt and was soon snoring peacefully.

Rerin closed his eyes and raised his palms in a gesture of prayer. ''Father Ymir, for all mankind I am grateful that you did not make many like him, but on behalf of Alcuina and myself, I thank you for sending him to us when you did.''

In a high tower of the great castle, in a chamber filled with strange instruments and the sounds and smells of stranger beasts, Hasta stood over a brazier, inhaling the fumes from blossoms that blackened and crisped upon the coals. His silver eyes revealed nothing, but his body twitched spasmodically, and the mirror he faced revealed not his reflection but a writhing nest of multi-colored smokes. Inhuman sounds emerged from his lips in a mumbling stream.

Behind him a door opened quietly, and Sarissa entered. Now she wore a caped robe of sheerest material, which molded itself to breasts and buttocks and thighs, concealing nothing and enhancing everything. She waited quietly, not daring to disturb her brother in the midst of his trance. There were limits to her power, but none to the painful and humiliating ways he could express his displeasure.

Below in her chamber she had at last tired of her new toy, who was now sobbing and exhausted, and had become aware that some important spell was being cast within the castle. As earthly beings know instantly the sound of a loved one's voice, so Sarissa recognized the vibrations of her brother's spell-casting and decided to go investigate. Her people's abiding burden was boredom, and they spent much of their time in search of new diversion. She knew that this spell her brother was casting was something different, and she was hopeful that it might prove amusing.

With a shudder Hasta emerged from his drugged and entranced state. He became aware of Sarissa's presence, and she embraced him from behind, her chin resting upon his shoulder. "What have you found, brother?"

"Our new slave is the object of a considerable search, sister. It seems that some foolish sorcerer from the world of men has set events in motion that could prove destructive in both worlds."

"How fascinating. For my new little pet? Is she really a queen as she claims?"

"She is. At least, as such things are defined in the world of men. A very small and petty queen even by the standards of that world, but a true queen withal. Has she proven to be interesting?"

"Enthralling. She is far more haughty than you would believe, even while she is being bent to my will. Breaking her is surely going to be a more engaging task than taming a fractious horse. Already it has provided . . . amusement."

"I must try her myself," Hasta said, momentarily distracted from his sorcerous pursuits.

"But who searches for her? We could send the huntsmen out and arrange a thrilling ambush!" The prospect of violence was always welcome to the castle folk.

Hasta gestured toward the mirror, and images formed there. "These minions of the Lord of the Demon Land had her, then lost her." They saw the half-animal creatures searching through the forest, stooping to the ground and sniffing, as if trying to pick up a trail by scent.

"Just those?" Sarissa was disappointed. "Those creatures are too stupid to be interesting. No wonder she escaped from them.''

''I think that the Demon Lord may be sending one of his hunters,'' Hasta assured her. ''That will be more interesting. And, there are others.'' The picture changed, and they saw two men, one young and one old, tramping across a field. ''The old one is a wizard from the world of men. Like the queen, he is a minor figure even in that world.''

''But what of the other?'' Now she was all interest. ''Such a creature as that comes our way but seldom!''

''By all the tests I can apply from a distance,'' said Hasta judiciously, ''that is a genuine hero. Why he searches for her I cannot interpret. It may be for some feeling that has no equivalent in our own world.''

''What a pair the two of them would make!'' Sarissa exclaimed. ''A queen and a hero! We would have the only such matched set in all the collection.''

''Perhaps,'' Hasta said skeptically. ''However, our data are incomplete. Some testing really should be done first.''

''Oh, by all means,'' Sarissa agreed. ''What shall we send?''

''I have been considering that. Shall we call forth a hell-scorpion?''

''That would be perfect,'' she said enthusiastically. ''If he can survive that, then he is indeed a hero.''

''Then help me set up the ritual.''

For the next few hours they prepared and performed a rite to call forth a creature from the far recesses of their world. During this ritual they performed several acts that would be considered abominations if performed between two human beings. Among their people these were deemed right and proper, a source of power.

*   *   *

Rerin and Conan were in an open field, tramping toward far mountains, when they were struck by a dizzying sense of disorientation. It was like a combination of taking a long fall and standing in an earthquake. Yet, when it passed, they were standing as they had been and the nearby trees did not sway. It was not the first time they had experienced this sensation, which was commonplace in the Shifting Land.

"What's changed now?" Conan asked irritably. "Anything in our path?"

"I fear so." Rerin pointed to a deep cleft that had appeared in a hillside before them. In the cleft was the entrance to a great cavern. It looked like a feature of the landscape that had been there forever, yet it had not been there a few minutes before.

"I do not like this," Conan said. He opened his bundle and buckled on his cuirass. Clapping on his helmet, he fastened its chin strap. "Let's skirt that cave at a good distance," he advised. "It has the aspect of a demon-haunt."

"I agree," Rerin said. "It has appeared too conveniently before us, and I fear some hostile power has taken an interest in us."

They edged away from the ominous cave mouth, keeping a wary eye on it. They were just past it and beginning to relax when the attack came. With an inarticulate cry, Rerin grasped Conan's shoulder and pointed. From the mouth of the cave a thing of pure nightmare was emerging.

"Crom!" Conan said in a choked voice.

The creature was the size of an elephant, and it stood upon innumerable, jointed legs. It was covered with a horny carapace and bore before it a pair of huge pincers on massive arms. From its rear protruded what appeared to be a cluster of snakes, arching high over its back. Between the pincer-tipped "arms" was a tiny head bearing two antennae, which waved about as if under their own volition.

The two men stood absolutely still, knowing that the slightest movement or sound might give away their position. Whatever unearthly senses the monster might possess, ordinary vision did not seem to be among them. For several heartbeats the situation remained static, then the antennae ceased their random motion and pointed straight at them. Slowly, the thing began to creep in their direction.

"I think," Rerin said in a most unwizardly and strangled voice, "that it is time to run." He proceeded to do exactly that, and any watcher would have been amazed to see how his skinny old legs kept him ahead of the fast-leaping Cimmerian.

Conan ran for his life, but he heard hideous sounds growing closer behind him. Surely the ungainly thing could not run as fast as a Cimmerian mountaineer? He looked back over his shoulder and saw to his horror that the monster was scuttling after them on its multiple legs, faster than any man could run.

With the instantaneous decision that so characterized him, Conan halted in midstride, whirled about, and drew his sword. It was not that he thought he stood a chance against so formidable a creature, but that any slight chance he might have would not be improved by further, tiring flight. He could just hear the old man's pattering footsteps receding into the distance, then he had no attention to spare for anything but his immediate concern.

The monster bulked huge as it bore down upon him.

As always, the part of Conan's mind that controlled his fighting worked with lightning speed, cataloguing the thing's strengths and weaknesses.

There were alarmingly few of the latter. Its armored body looked as invulnerable as the walls of a strong castle. Its tiny head with the crucial antennae might be attacked, but it was wedged between the powerful arms, and to attack it meant coming within reach of the pincers. The snakelike multiple tails were as yet an unknown quantity. All this went through his mind between grasping his hilt and the moment when his sword point cleared the sheath. That left the legs, which were relatively spindly. Having made all the calculations that might do him any good, Conan charged.

At first his path took him directly toward the monster, which reached for him with its terrible pincers. With timing so precise that few men could have matched it, Conan dove to one side just as a pincer almost touched his cuirass. He went into a forward roll and came up in a crouch by the thing's flank, swinging his sword with both hands. The nearest leg gave way beneath his blow, but it was no easy task. The legs looked thin against the monster's bulk, but each was still as thick as the arm of a strong man and armored with horny chitin.

By striking at the joints he was able to cripple two of the legs before going into another dive and roll. He knew that it would be death to stand in one place for more than a moment. This time he managed to hew away a single leg before some instinct made him look up, just in time to see one of the serpentine tails plunging down at him. In the instant that he saw it he also noted its bulbous tip from which protruded a transparent, needlelike fang dripping some green, viscous fluid.

He dropped aside and rolled away just as the tail passed through the space where he had been standing. A cloud of stinking smoke erupted from the grass where the fluid was splattered.

Conan ran, and the thing whirled to chase him. He was gratified to note that, fast as it was in running, it was somewhat slower in turning upon its own axis. This gave him time to get a score of paces away and ready himself for his next attack. He knew that it would take a long time to disable enough legs to stop the thing, but he could see no other method open to him. He repeated his first tactic, crippling two more legs and dodging the tails, but this time the monster sent three tails plunging at him, and he was saved from them more by chance than by his own speed. The creature had anticipated his tactic this time. Apparently then, it had a form of intelligence. His original tactic had worked well, but he dared not try it again.

Once more he charged at the beast, with his sword gripped in both hands. Now it held its pincers wide, expecting him to dodge to one side or the other. Instead he came straight in, hacking at the tiny head. He felt his sword connect jarringly, then he was beneath the creature, rolling and chopping at its legs, careful to attack the legs on the same side he had started working upon. Thus, he had to disable only half as many legs as by working on both sides. As he rolled from beneath it the thing sent the whole cluster of tails darting at him, but he was well clear before the ground exploded in smoke and steam from the action of the acid venom.

This time as the thing turned and charged him it was noticeably slower, and it sagged a bit to the wounded side. That was all to the good, but what could he do next? If the thing was capable of learning, then it would be prepared for the tricks he had used ere now and would counter them. This was a difficult puzzle, and one he had a terribly short time to solve.

There was one way he had not as yet attacked it. He could see little way to do it damage, but it might buy him a little time. As it neared he waited until the pincers made their grab for him, then he leaped, got one foot atop a pincer, and launched himself upon the thing's back. He made an experimental chop at the backplates, only to confirm that the stuff was as impervious as steel armor. The footing was treacherous as well. The tails were not able to reach so far forward, but he dared not stumble back toward them. He jumped off to one side, planning to hack at a few legs before running once more.

As he landed, an unseen stone in the grass turned beneath his foot, and he went sprawling on his back. Before he could rise, one of the tails came down like a meteor. It smashed against his breastplate, and his nostrils were assailed by the chemical fumes of the disintegrating bronze. Then he saw another about to strike his face. Even his quick reflexes were not swift enough to save him, but something batted the swollen poison-gland and fang aside, splattering his face with a fine dew, which burned fiercely but was not strong enough to kill. Instantly he was on his feet and running, and old Rerin was at his side.

They stopped at some distance from the monster. It was turning, once again seeming to be slowed by its injuries.

"It's good to know your staff is good for something besides leaning upon, old man," Conan said.

"Get your armor off quickly," Rerin urged. "The venom will eat through and start on you!"

Conan ignored the buckles and cut the straps of the cuirass with his dagger. The once-fine bronze lay smoking upon the ground, slowly collapsing as the venom ate the metal away. He fought the urge to wipe at the spots where the stuff had splashed him. The pain was bearable, and it would only mean a few new scars among the many he already had. The thing was bearing down upon them once more.

"If it had eyes," Conan muttered, "I could reach its brain with a thrust."

"It may not have a brain as we know such things," Rerin said. "But its antennae serve it for eyes and ears. If you can disable those, perhaps you may finish it at leisure."

The thing was almost upon them. "Have you a spell to aid me, old man?" Conan asked.

"No."

"Ah, well," said Conan.

To get at the antennae he must reach the head. He had done that once before, but the thing must be ready for such a move. Besides supporting the antennae, the little head bore on its bottom a set of sideways-working jaws with which the thing ate. It occurred to Conan that if he could not get close to the head by his own efforts, perhaps he could persuade the beast to convey him thither.

This time the creature did not simply bear down upon Conan. Instead it halted and reached for him with its clawed pincers. He dodged from side to side, and it brought its own rear around, to menace him with the deadly, whiplike tails. As it made a pass with its pincers he leaped onto the arm, straddling it in the "wrist" just behind the pincer. It was a matter of some anxiety to him that the thing might raise him within range of the tails, but to his relief it instead brought him toward the jaws.

The instant he was within sword range, Conan hacked at the base of the nearest antenna. A shudder went through the whole beast, shaking him violently upon his precarious perch. He hacked again, and the antenna fell away. The thing went into a paralytic tremor. Conan leaped down from the pincer; the other made a slow, uncertain grab at him, but he evaded it easily. With both feet braced he hewed off the other antenna with a single chop.

As the antenna fell, Conan turned and ran. The beast behind him made clacking, chittering noises, but Conan did not look back until he was once again with the wizard. He was in time to see the creature's spasmodic jerkings cease as it collapsed upon the sward. Smoke rose from it, and it began to collapse in upon itself, much as had his cuirass as the acid had eaten it away. Soon there was little more than a smoking hulk left of the frightening creature.

"It was not a natural part of this place," said Rerin. "With its vital principal gone, there is nothing to hold its component matter together, and it melts into the aether."

The old man was breathing hard, and Conan was more than a trifle breathless himself. "That was a brave thing you did, wizard. Had you not knocked that stinger aside with your staff, I would have died over there. I thank you. There is a warrior's heart inside that withered old carcass of yours."

"I accept the compliment," Rerin said, "in the spirit which you no doubt intended."

Conan closely examined his sword for traces of the volatile venom, which might damage it. To his delight he found none. He sheathed the weapon at his waist and went in search of his other belongings.

Sarissa turned excitedly from the mirror. "Was that not wonderful? He is all I had hoped! This is a true hero. How may we capture him?"

"There are any number of ways, sister," said Hasta, smiling. "But why bother? Since they are searching for our slave-queen, they must come here. Let them come to us. I am curious to see how he will try to take her back."

Sarissa smiled as well, in dawning anticipation.

Eight

The Castle of Giants

On their fifth day in the demon land they encountered the first of the searchers. Conan raised a hand in warning, and old Rerin halted. The old wizard could hear nothing amiss, but by now he knew how preternaturally keen were the ears of the barbarian.

"Someone is trying to sneak close to us," Conan said, "but they do not know how."

"Human or other?" asked Rerin.

"They go on two feet, whatever that means in this place. There are many of them."

"Too many?"

"That we shall know when I have tested their mettle." Conan loosened his sword in its sheath.

He chose a little glade as a good place to meet potential foes. For the last two days they had been traveling through woods where the trees and shrubs preferred to keep their roots properly in the ground. This made for more peaceful sleep, if nothing else.

Shadowy forms began to materialize at the tree line.

They were man-shaped but not human. Their fingers had too many joints and their ears were long and pointed. Their bodies were gaunt and their movements furtive. Conan's sword whispered from its sheath as they came closer.

"You are close enough now," he cautioned them. "State your business."

"We want the woman," hissed one. Its tongue was not apt at forming human speech, but it was understandable. "The woman from the world of men. Our master wants her. If you have her, surrender her to us or die!"

Conan smiled grimly. "We want her too. You are the ones who took her. How did you lose her?"

The demon who had spoken only hissed in hate. Conan could hear Rerin muttering spells behind him. There were a dozen of the things, but they were not large and did not look strong. None of them appeared to be armed. Abruptly the speaker made a complex gesture and chittered out some formula, which Conan took to be a spell.

He was about to split its skull when Rerin stepped forward holding his staff horizontally at shoulder height. He was casting a spell as well, and the demon fell back, covering its face with its arms, as if reacting to a blinding light.

"Had you killed it in the midst of its casting," Rerin said calmly, "the full force of its spell would have fallen upon you. You would have rotted where you stand."

The leader growled out an order, and the demons turned and fled into the brush.

Before it disappeared, the speaker turned and said,

"We shall have you and the woman yet. A hunter comes!" Then it was gone.

"That does not sound good," said Conan as he sheathed his sword. "Who is their master?"

"One of the great powers of the demon world, I doubt not," said Rerin pessimistically. "If such a one takes too close an interest in us, I fear that my paltry magics must be of little value to us."

"Between your magic and my sword we have done well enough so far," Conan contended. "We may yet win through and find our way back to the real world. I have always trusted in my own strength and skill; you should do the same."

"Oh, for the confidence of youth," sighed the old man.

By evening they were within sight of the castle. It hulked upon its mountainside like a dragon, and Conan studied its strange battlements and turrets with the eye of a man accustomed to spying out the weaknesses of such places. "We'll have to get closer," he said at last. "This air is too thick to see small things. It is the small things that let you into a place like that. Are you sure she is in there?"

"I am certain. You may not sense it, but that place sends forth an aura of evil and sorcery that I can feel in my bones."

"What kind of people dwell there?" Conan asked. "It looks like a place built by giants."

"It may well have been. Many peoples live in the demon land, and many more dwelled here in the past. Some of them were giants, and that place has the look of the homes of the ancient, giant peoples. I think, though, that those who dwell there now are somewhat like us, in external appearance, at least. Within they are as inhuman as those demons we saw.''

"Are they mortal?" Conan asked. "Can they be cut with steel?"

"I believe so. No inhabitants of this world are truly immortal. Many are hard to kill, as witness that scorpion-thing you slew."

Conan looked about restlessly. "What do the folk up there eat? I see no cultivated fields, no sign of villages or commerce. Even the strongholds of robber-chieftains must have a few peasants dwelling nearby to grow food."

"Life here does not follow the same rhythms as in the world of men," said old Rerin. "Whatever concerns occupy the people of that great hall, getting their daily bread is not likely to be among them. Their bodily needs may be satisfied by their command of the dark arts. They could even be vampires, battening upon the blood of human victims."

"Nonetheless," Conan said, "if they huddle behind stone walls they must fear something. If they fear, then they can be hurt. But, we'll know nothing until we get closer. Come." He set off at a mile-eating stride, and the old man followed after.

It was just after nightfall when they reached the base of the cyclopean walls. Strange, many-colored stars gleamed overhead, and the great, green moon shed a malevolent radiance through the thick, waterlike air. Conan ran his fingers along the stone in search of the joints and cracks between the blocks that might afford a climber a secure handhold.

"Crom," he muttered. "It's all of a piece! There are no joints."

"This pile was raised by magic, not by human hands," said Rerin. "I know a spell that would raise us to the top of the wall, but surely those inside would feel the working of an alien mage so near."

"I need no magic to climb a wall," Conan said. "This stone, if stone it be, is rough and pitted like lava. If it is like this all the way up, I can climb it."

Rerin felt the wall and shook his head doubtfully. "Perhaps one who is half ape and half mountain goat can climb this, but I fear that I cannot. Had we a rope, you could climb and haul me up after you. As it is, I must abide here until you find one."

"You had best stay down here at any rate. Hide yourself somewhere beyond the tree line until I return with the queen. In that place, full as you say it is with wizardly people, you would be of little help, and there is no sense in both of us dying in there should I fail. If I come not back by dawnlight, you may see if your wiles can prevail where my sword could not."

"May Ymir aid you in your task, Cimmerian," the old man said with deep feeling. "I say again, the queen wrought well in accepting your service."

Conan scratched his chin. "I am not sure that Ymir looks into this place. I am sure that Crom does not, for he takes no note of things outside Cimmeria, and little enough there." He clapped Rerin upon the shoulder. "Now, get you gone, old man. Find a safe place, and be ready to help us when we come down, for I've no doubt there will be those who will pursue us."

Conan turned back to the wall and reached up to the full extent of his arms. He felt until his fingertips lodged into minute depressions, and slowly, painfully, he drew himself upward. Scrambling with his feet, he found a precarious lodgment for his toes and reached up another foot with one hand. Thus, a foot or less at a time, he ascended the wall.

His progress was slow, but it was steady. Few men could have made such a climb save at the expense of great exhaustion and limbs trembling with fatigue, but Conan reached the top of the wall with no outward sign of wear. He found himself to be standing atop a battlement that was fully equipped for battle, but which was utterly devoid of inhabitants. He saw no passages into the interior in his immediate vicinity, so he picked a direction at random and began exploring.

There was no courtyard within the wall, but instead the whole castle seemed to be a single structure, with strange towers and other architectural features protruding from it here and there. At intervals he saw sculptured creatures with strange and repellent aspects, some perching atop the battlement, others seeming to rise up through the wallwalk itself. It all appeared to be the work of an utterly demented sculptor.

All was strangely silent, and from time to time he paused to listen, but no sound came to him. His nostrils flared, but the air carried no hint of woodsmoke. He wondered how the inhabitants went about their cooking and heating without fires. His wandering brought him to the base of a hulking tower, with a squat, conical roof. A door flanked by a pair of cadaverous, sculpted guards stood open, yawning into the black interior of the tower.

Slowly and suspiciously Conan entered with sword bared. His free hand touched the wall while his feet slid slowly forward, testing his path into the gloom. Two paces within the doorway his feet found an abrupt drop-off in the floor. He tested it cautiously and found it to be the beginning of a descending stairway. A warm breeze came up from below, and upon it he could faintly discern the strains of wild, bizarre music, thick with the sounds of drum and cymbal. Now he also smelled smoke on the air, but it was incense, not the wood of a cooking fire.

He descended at least one hundred steps before he first caught a glimmer of light. Moving as silently as a ghost, Conan made his way to a doorway, through which the light shone. He was gazing into a lavishly furnished chamber that was strewn with cushions and carpets of what seemed to be woven gold. The light came from odd candles burning in niches, casting an eerie radiance from their circular flames.

As he swept the room with his gaze Conan saw a woman lying amid a tangle of golden coverlets and exotic furs. She wore only elaborate jewelry, and his breath caught at the voluptuous, pale-fleshed beauty thus displayed; full, round breasts and generously curved buttocks. Her face was turned away from him, and he saw no sign of awareness, as if she was asleep or drugged. His feet made no sound as he stepped into the room. Alert for attack, he crossed to the woman and tapped her beneath the jaw with the flat of his sword.

"Wake up, woman. I have some questions in need of answers." Groggily the woman's head turned and her eyes opened. Conan's own eyes widened in amazement. "Alcuina!"

It took a few moments for Alcuina's eyes to focus, and in that time Conan saw that she wore a wide collar of iron about her neck and that it was connected to a ring in the floor by a short length of chain.

"Conan," she breathed at last. "Have you truly come for me, or is this another of the dreams these hellish people inflict with their drugs and spells? If so, it is a more effective torture than any they have tried thus far."

"I am real, though I've no idea how to prove it." He grasped the chain in both hands and tried to pull it from the floor. "First let's get you free from this place, then we can think of some way to prove that I am real."

He pulled on the chain until the veins swelled upon his brow, but even his great strength could not break chain or ring. He muttered a curse, and Alcuina, with the drugged fog clearing from her head, became aware of her extreme state of undress.

"A liege man should not see his queen thus," she said, hiding her embarrassment. She made no futile effort to cover herself; there was too much flesh exposed for two hands even to make a beginning.

Conan shrugged. "In the South they are not so fussy about clothes. Even queens sometimes wear little more than you are wearing now." He looked her up and down with frank admiration. "Have no fear, you've nothing that other women do not have. Perhaps a closer look is in order, just to make sure."

"We have more important things to concern us," she said impatiently. "Can you not free me of this chain?"

"We shall see. I had hoped to do this quietly, but—" With a full-armed overhead swing, he brought his sword down upon the chain. There was a mighty clang and a few sparks, but the only other result was a nick in his blade. "Cursed hard steel they make hereabout," he muttered, studying the damaged edge in annoyance.

Alcuina's sharply indrawn breath was the only warning he had, but it was sufficient. He ducked and whirled in a single motion, bringing the sword around in a horizontal swing that halved his attacker at the waist. Blood exploded into his face as the man fell, but he saw more entering the room through a doorway he was sure had not been there before.

The men were all identically dressed in white silken loincloths and iron collars like the one Alcuina wore. They bore a variety of swords and spears, and some carried small shields. A man thrust at his belly with a spear, but Conan grasped the shaft and yanked him forward, crushing his face with a blow of the sword hilt.

Now others were coming into the room, these with silver eyes and rich, colorful clothing. They took no part in the fight but merely stood by, enjoying the spectacle. Conan dropped to one knee, and a sword whistled above his head as he gutted its wielder with an upward rip.

"Flee, Conan," Alcuina cried. "They are too many for you."

Conan's teeth were bared, and his eyes were reddened, at the moment quite devoid of sanity. "I'll leave here with you or dead, by Crom! I'll feed steel to these dogs all day, if I must."

The colorful spectators seemed to take great delight in these words, but Conan was lowering the number of their servants at an alarming rate, and one of them began to chant and gesticulate. From somewhere overhead a heavy net descended upon the Cimmerian, and he was quickly entangled in its meshes. In a rage he struggled and tried to cut through the net with his sword, but the tough cord was impervious to steel. The net grew tighter until Conan was totally immobilized, able only to curse, which he did with great fervor.

One of the spectators, this one a woman, stepped close and leaned forward. From her upturned palm arose a puff of smoke, and Conan had no choice but to inhale. His last thought before losing consciousness was that this woman was stunningly beautiful.

When he awoke he found himself lying upon the cold floor of a dungeon. It was not a new experience to him, but this time the precautions taken to keep him confined seemed to be excessive. As he sat up he saw that his clothing had been taken from him, and a heavy iron collar had been fastened around his neck. From the collar, four heavy chains went to rings in the four corners of the cell. It seemed to him that so much ironmongery was not needed, since he had been unable to break the much lighter chain that held Alcuina.

For lack of any better employment, he tugged at the chains. They were all dauntingly solid. He could move only a foot or two in any direction, and there was not sufficient slack to use a chain as a weapon should one of his captors come close enough.

Except for a few bruises, he felt well enough. The drug that had rendered him unconscious seemed to have no aftereffects, and he felt perfectly alert. And hungry.

"Feed me, Erlik drink your blood!" he bellowed at the top of his lungs. There was no immediate response. He tried again. "Are you going to starve me, since you could not kill me with steel?"

Once again he drew no response. He examined his surroundings. The room was an irregular cube, seemingly carved directly into the stone of the castle. A small window high on one wall admitted a faint light, and there was a single, circular door made of heavy timbers. He had never seen a round door before, and he wondered how it opened, since he could see no hinges.

He lay on his belly and chose a link of one of the chains to work on. He was able to get enough slack to rub the link back and forth along the floor for at least a foot. It seemed futile, but given enough time he might wear a few links down enough to weaken them. At the moment he had nothing but time in any case.

After what he judged to be an hour of this monotonous activity, he examined the link. The side he had rubbed was a bit shinier, but that was the extent of it. This could be a lengthy task. His work was abruptly interrupted when the round door rose into the lintel above it. At least that mystery was solved.

He heard approaching footsteps, and a woman bearing a tray entered the cell. He had expected a neckringed slave, but this was one of the spectators of his fight. Unless he was much mistaken, it was the same one who had rendered him unconscious. He could not be sure, as the ones he had seen looked much alike.

"Come over here, you silver-eyed trull," Conan said affably. "I'd like to wring your pretty neck."

To his surprise she answered in a tongue he understood. "Ah, but then you would not be able to eat this splendid dinner I have brought you."

Conan smelled the proffered viands and his mouth watered. "Well," he grumbled, "I agree. Give me the food, and I'll not kill you."

"First, a small precaution."

There was a rumbling sound and Conan looked down in stupefied puzzlement as two clamps grew from the floor of the cell and fastened securely about his ankles. Then something writhed about his arms, and they were jerked behind him and strongly pinioned. He was trussed like an ox in a slaughterhouse.

The woman sat directly before him and set the tray between them. She wore a gown so sheer that it might as well have been altogether absent. The generous curves of her were almost as mouth-watering as the food, despite his hunger and the circumstances. She took a small piece of grilled meat on a skewer and inserted it daintily into his mouth.

"My name is Sarissa," she said. "You may address me as mistress."

"Not likely," Conan assured her. "How about some of that wine?"

"Disobedience can be a painful experience here." Nonetheless, she gave him a drink from a crystal goblet.

"I am used to pain. You cannot persuade me that way."

She continued to feed him. "You have never experienced the kind of pain I can inflict. I have developed some truly exquisite varieties." Her trilling laughter was musical, and chilling. "But, no, pain is for ordinary slaves. You are special, and I have no wish to break you. You shall be the prize of my collection."

"What kind of collection?" Conan growled.

"Why, my collection of unique human specimens." She pushed a small morsel of bread into his mouth. He was uncomfortably aware of her delectable smell. "I have never had a true hero to experiment with. Life grows terribly dull here. You shall furnish us with endless pleasure. You fight like a wild beast, and you have such a superlative body." She ran her hands freely over him, taking visible delight in the hard muscles and heavy limbs. Conan bore this in stoic silence.

"What manner of entertainment do you expect from me?" he asked, thinking that he knew already.

"Things that shall test your mettle as a hero. It is so rarely that we see exciting spectacles of strength and courage." She kneaded the massive musculature of his shoulders and neck.

"I can believe that, after seeing your men keeping their distance from me while slaves did their fighting for them."

"You were magnificent," she said, punching him lightly in the midsection to test the resiliency of his abdominals. It was like hitting a tree trunk. "I would not have believed that a single man could wreak such slaughter. It was most gratifying."

Conan snorted. "Untrained slaves are no challenge, however willing they might be. If that is your idea of entertainment, you should find an abattoir more to your taste than a battlefield."

"Then we must find some challenge more worthy of you." She closely examined a sturdy thigh and seemed to be satisfied with its evident strength and symmetry.

"Why do you not just let me go? And Alcuina as well. You have no right to hold us here."

"Right? We have you, and you are ours; that is the only right. My little slave-queen is so amusing, too. Why are you so anxious to have her? I am far more beautiful than she."

"I could dispute that. I am her sworn liege man and I followed her here to rescue her from those abominations who came in the night to steal her away."

"I do not understand your silly loyalties. Here we live for our pleasures, and for other things you would not understand. Rest assured that you are in our power, and must do our bidding. Submit, and life will be most interesting for you.''

Conan's vocabulary had never included such a word, and he let her know it in no uncertain terms. She smiled at his command of profanity and rose to her feet after one last caress. She paused at the door of the cell, and said, ''Your destruction will give us all great satisfaction.'' Then the round door slid back down into place.

''They are all mad,'' Conan muttered to himself. His limbs were released, and he fell once again to rubbing the chain link upon the unyielding stone.

Nine

The Games of the Masters

Conan was asleep, snoring upon the cold stone floor of his cell, when a sound awakened him. He sat up, straining his ears, and became aware that the collar was no longer about his throat. The collar and its chains lay upon the floor. He examined the collar, which now lay open, but he could find no trace of any fastening.

"More wizardry," he muttered, dropping it to the floor. It had been the sound of the thing clanking to the floor that had awakened him, no doubt.

He arose and began pacing tigerishly about the cell, stretching the stiffness out of cramped muscles. He had been released from the chain for a reason, and he wanted to be ready for whatever might befall him. With a rumbling sound the door rose.

Conan crouched, facing it, and waited for whatever might enter. He was unarmed, but he had hands and feet and teeth, and he was prepared to use them. A time passed and nothing approached. Cautious as a hunting wolf, Conan went to the door. He leaped through and spun through a full circle. He was in a featureless corridor and there were no enemies in sight. In one direction there were a few more of the round doors and then a blank wall. In the other direction the corridor was shrouded in gloom.

With a clank the door to his erstwhile cell dropped shut.

"Did you think I would go back in?" he shouted to those he knew must be watching.

He started down the dark corridor. A few paces along the stone hall he found his sword lying upon the stone. He snatched it up, and the rough feel of the grip immediately raised his spirits. All he needed now was somebody to kill with it. Preferably someone with silver eyes.

"I could use my tunic as well," he shouted. There was no response. "Ah, well," he muttered to himself, "better naked with a sword than in full armor with no weapon."

He continued his exploration of the corridor. The fact that his sword had been returned to him meant that he would be needing it, and soon.

He came to a stairway leading upward and began to climb. Although there was no visible light source, the air was suffused with a faint, twilight radiance, which was just sufficient for him to make out his way. At the top of the stair he found another round door. Somehow he was sure that this did not merely lead into another dungeon cell. Slowly the door began to rise.

Conan did not wait for it to open fully, but as soon as the gap was large enough to admit his body he dove to the floor and rolled under it, springing to his feet the moment he was on the other side.

There were two fully-armored men in the circular

room beyond the door, and they were startled by his impetuous entrance. Conan attacked immediately. He had no friends in this castle; anyone he encountered here except for Alcuina was an enemy. He chose the man on the right as the more exposed to assault and lunged with his sword extended in both hands. The point slid between the breastplate and steel gorget, and Conan jerked it out immediately, whirling to face the second man. The first, dead but unaware of the fact, advanced a step and then collapsed, blood spurting from beneath his gorget.

The second approached cautiously. Both men were wearing the most elaborate plate armor Conan had ever seen. It was made of innumerable small plates, cunningly jointed to allow free movement. There were few weak spots, and this man would not leave the gorget-breastplate joining exposed as the other had. Conan circled, sword held at full extension, point threatening his enemy's eyeslots. He preferred to use the edge, but he knew that the point was usually superior against armor such as this. Besides, this way he could keep the man at a greater distance while he sought out a weakness to exploit.

The armored man held a long, slightly curved sword in both hands. It was single-edged, and that edge looked decidedly keen. Naked as he was, Conan wished to avoid that edge. Behind him the door descended into its slot.

The foeman slid in, incredibly swift for a man in full armor, cutting at Conan's flank. Conan crossed his wrists and brought the sword around to block the opposing blade with its flat. Steel rang on steel, and he brought his blade up and around in a broad circle to smash into the man's shoulder. The man was staggered, but his armor was strong enough to withstand the blow. Both men took up their guard stances again.

Once more the armored man attacked, confident in the protection of his harness. This time Conan did not counter with his sword, nor did he dodge. Instead he dropped his own weapon and stepped inside the range of the other sword. Gripping the other man's forward wrist in both powerful hands, Conan wrenched the hand loose from the hilt and twisted the arm down and back.

Futilely the man sought to cut at Conan with the sword held in his left hand, but by this time Conan had stepped around almost behind his enemy and was wrenching the arm up along the spine. An audible snapping sound told him when the shoulder joint gave way. It was pointless to strike at a man in such armor, but an armored man could be wrestled as well as one without artificial protection. Releasing the arm, Conan took the helmet between his palms and rotated the head until it was facing almost directly backward. This time he could hear nothing through the steel, but unless the man's neck was flexible as an owl's he was dead. Conan dropped the lifeless hulk to the floor with a clatter.

Now he had the leisure to examine his surroundings. The circular room was perhaps ten paces across, and looking up he saw that a gallery ran around its periphery, about ten feet from the floor. Just now the railing of the gallery was thronged with gaily dressed people, their silver eyes alight with delight at the spectacle below.

"Well done, hero," said the one he knew as Sarissa. "Was that better than fighting untrained slaves? Those were elite bodyguards of a lord of the Shifting Land."

A man clad all in cloth of gold called across to her,

"Let me try three. Surely he cannot defeat three of my men at once!"

"No," Sarissa answered, "next we must try something different. What shall it be?"

As a hubbub broke out among the watchers, Conan saw Alcuina kneeling in their midst. She still wore only jewelry, and he was infuriated to see that her fair body was covered with the inflamed welts of the lash. Her wrists were secured to the railing by the ever-present chains. The fury writ upon her face matched his own.

"Can you not at least let him have some garments?" she demanded.

"What for?" shouted Conan defiantly. "I've more to be proud of than most men."

"How refreshingly primitive," said one of the silver-eyed men. "Can he do anything besides fight?"

Conan beckoned to him. "Come down here, popinjay, and I will show you how I gut fish."

This was answered with delighted laughter. Conan eyed the railing. It was a high leap, but he just might be able to get a hand on the railing and haul himself over. Then it would just be a matter of hewing down this mob of degenerates and releasing Alcuina. Then they could worry about finding a way out of this place.

The plan had great appeal, especially the part about killing all these silver-eyed devils who were not content merely to kill a victim, but must humiliate him as well. He decided to kill the one in the golden robes first. He thought of going for Sarissa first, but a certain native squeamishness had always made him reluctant to kill women, however evil they might be.

Without warning, Conan ran straight for the wall with the speed of a tiger, and like a tiger he leaped for the railing. His sword was too large to grip in his teeth, so he had only one free hand, and with it he barely got a sufficient grasp upon the railing and began to haul himself up. He heard a collective gasp and his blade was darting for the surprised man the instant his arm cleared the railing, but it never reached him. Conan felt a massive shock run from his hand through his whole body, and he jerked back, away from the railing. It was unlike anything he had ever felt before, and he fell crashing upon his back onto the cold, bloody stone floor.

When he regained consciousness Conan was still in the circular room, but the spectators were all gone. He sat up, sore in every muscle. He knew that the fall could not account for this pain, and that it must be an aftereffect of the terrible, unseen blow that had come through the railing he had grasped. He tasted blood in his mouth and spat upon the stone floor.

The two men he had killed had been taken away as well. There was a pile of objects on the floor, and he went to investigate. To his surprise it consisted of his clothes and possessions.

He quickly donned his garments and strapped on his other accoutrements. Even his ornaments had been returned, including the massive arm-ring Alcuina had given him. Despite his earlier bravado, he felt far better after resuming his clothes. He rammed his sword back into its sheath and clapped his helmet upon his disordered black locks. He now had everything he had come into the castle with. His heavy cloak and winter clothes were somewhere in the woods with Rerin. Now to find a way out of this pit.

Clearly they did not intend for him to stay here, else how could they have any fun with him? None of the pit's several doors stood open. He eyed the treacherous railing. Was it dangerous all the time? Many of the spectators had been leaning against it, and Alcuina had been tethered to it. Perhaps it had worked its spell only after he had grasped it. There was only one way to find out.

For a second time he ran to the wall and leaped. This time, with his sword sheathed, he was able to grasp the railing with both hands. He hauled himself over it in a single motion, and this time there was no crippling, paralyzing jolt. He found himself upon a circular balcony and near a door. Without hesitation, cradling his sword in one hand, he went through the door. It was as good a course as any. He did not plan to leave the castle without Alcuina, if it meant searching every room.

As before, he had the unmistakable feeling of being watched. He wondered what these people did for amusement when there were no errant wanderers to torment. Civilized people were all the same; they had no warrior virtues of their own and thus had to admire them in others. Well, he would show them something worth admiring before he killed them.

"What will it be?" he called out. "I've killed your hell-scorpion, and I've killed your men. What do you want to see die now, you gutless eunuchs?"

He continued down the corridor he had chosen. He passed many doors, none of them closed. He saw nothing of interest to him in the rooms and halls he passed. At another time he might have explored more closely, for they were full of treasures, but for once he was not interested in loot. He wanted Alcuina, he wanted out of this place, and he wanted to get back to the real world, in that order.

His explorings brought him to a great hall from

which many corridors branched. In the center of the room lay Alcuina, naked. Her ornaments had been taken from her, and her wrists and ankles were closely bound. She did not move.

Conan halted without the room. He knew a trap when he saw one. He would be assaulted upon entering the room or trying to leave, he had no doubt. Now, while it seemed he had a little leisure, was a good time to decide upon his next move. The woman seemed to be unconscious. She did not appear to be tethered to any solid object, but merely lying upon a pile of silks that nested her own silken nudity. What was their game this time?

Then he smiled. For certain, none of his blades would cut the cords that bound her. That meant that he would have to carry the queen to safety. It also meant that he would be deprived of the use of one arm and a good deal of his mobility. Well, if they thought that would stop him, they knew little of Cimmerians in general and himself in particular.

Like a man without a care in the world, he stepped into the room and crossed to where the queen lay. He scooped her up, threw her across his left shoulder, and gave her shapely bottom an affectionate pat. "Fear not, Alcuina, I'll have us out of this place shortly."

"I shall believe that when it happens," said her voice, somewhat muffled by the wolfskins covering Conan's back. "And a mere swordsman is not entitled to touch his queen in so unseemly a fashion."

"Regained your senses, eh? And your tongue as well. I swear by Crom, you are the touchiest wench I ever pledged my sword arm to. I follow you to the demon land, I kill monsters and men in your service, and all you can do is complain about a little pat on your royal backside. On top of all those stripes it should feel soothing.''

"Put me down, you hulking ape!" She began to wriggle about on his shoulder.

"If I do that, how can I carry you away from here?"

"Then at least carry me so I can see and breathe instead of smelling your mangy wolfhide!"

"That would be inconvenient." He gave her bottom a harder slap, one that cracked loudly. "Now, be still and allow me to rescue you." Despite her writhings he held her easily.

"Rescue! You idiot, you have walked into a trap any child could have anticipated!"

"I know that, woman," said Conan with unwonted patience. "I have walked into many traps in my time, and I have walked out of all of them. Or crawled at any rate. Now, tell me, where do these people assemble to practice their magic?"

"Assemble? Do you not want to get us away from here?"

"You weary me with your questions. They want me to try to escape. Any way that I choose is sure to be fraught with perils. I hate to leave living enemies behind my back in any case. Where may I expect to find them?"

She released a gusty sigh. "You are a brave man and a great fool. Ymir curse me if I ever employ a hero again. You must climb the large central tower. That is all I know of the place. It is there that Sarissa and her friends like to ply their whips and other instruments. I think it is the place where they amass to perform their abominable rites as well. It is full of strange wizardly things, and there is a great thing on the wall, like a looking glass, in which they can see all that goes on in the castle."

"That sounds like the place we want. Let's be off." With Alcuina across his shoulder, Conan scanned the doorways leading from the room. His splendid sense of orientation told him which one led toward the center of the castle, and he dashed off through it at a fast trot.

"Where have they disappeared to?" asked one of the ladies impatiently.

"They must appear soon," Sarissa assured the assembled lords and ladies.

They stared into the great spyglass as it peered into the various passages of the castle, spending a few moments on each before going on to another. The barbarian had taken an unexpected exit from the chamber where Sarissa had left Alcuina. No doubt he was disoriented from his captivity. They had not seen him since.

Each person in the room had been given charge of one of the possible escape routes to the outside of the castle. Each had expended a great deal of ingenuity upon guarding and laying traps in the route he had drawn. There was much wagering over which of them would get the Cimmerian, and how far the man would get, and how long it would take him to die.

Certain basic rules had been laid down, of course. Venomous gases could not be employed, nor any spell against which a mere human would be powerless. He must have at least a semblance of a chance of fighting his way through, since that was what he did best, and what they found most entertaining about him. Should he be able to survive each challenge in turn and win his way to the outside, then Sarissa would have the privilege of killing him in whatever manner she chose. He could not be allowed to escape, with or without Alcuina. That would spoil the game.

"I wish he would appear soon," said a lord, stifling a yawn. "I begin to tire of this." The glass flashed onto a corridor blocked by an obscene, tentacled thing, which waited hungrily for prey.

"Is it me you search for?"

The assembled people whirled to stare at the main entrance. There stood Conan, with the nude Alcuina still slung over his shoulder. As they boggled, speechless, Conan set Alcuina down in such wise that she could attend to the proceedings.

"Now you have spoiled our game," Sarissa said, pouting.

"I was tiring of your games anyway," Conan told her.

"I might as well kill him," said Hasta. He raised a hand and began a complicated gesture.

Before he could properly begin, Conan closed the distance between them, and his sword was buried in Hasta's skull. He wrenched the blade loose and it blurred through the air twice. The two lords to either side of Hasta fell screaming.

The others seemed to be stupefied, unable to comprehend that they were actually being physically attacked by a lower life form. He killed three more before some made a break for the exit. He slaughtered with such speed and precision that his earlier fighting had been slow by comparison. Those who managed to escape the room he left alone. The others he slew without mercy.

One of them did not flee. Conan was wiping the strangely colored blood from his sword when he returned to the center of the room. There sat Sarissa, cradling the mangled remains of her brother. "You've slain him," she said tonelessly.

"So I have," said Conan without pity. "It is a great shame that you were so preoccupied with sorrow. You missed a fine show." He gestured at the grotesquely sprawled heaps of bodies, the faces upturned, silver eyes fast losing their gleam.

"I must see to my brother's funeral rites," Sarissa said.

"You can do that later," Conan said, his voice like stone. "If I let you live."

He grasped Hasta's corpse by the front of the garments. With a powerful motion of his arm, he cast the body directly into the great mirror, which shattered with a noise that shook the whole castle to its foundations. He yanked Sarissa to her feet.

"Show us the quickest way out of here if you would live, woman!" he demanded.

Numbly Sarissa staggered toward the room's entrance. As he passed the door, Conan picked up Alcuina, this time holding her cradled so that she could see where she was going. For once she was too shaken to taunt him.

"Make her release my bonds," was all she said.

"For now," Conan answered, "I prefer you the way you are."

Sarissa led them to a portal in a wall and down a long, winding staircase. Not for a moment did Conan relax his guard. He was alert for treachery. He knew that the woman would try to kill them; it was only a question of when.

Much to his surprise she led them to a tiny portal leading onto the sward outside the castle walls. He pressed the point of his sword into the cleft of Sarissa's spine.

"Now you will walk over into the trees, and we shall follow close behind you. I am keeping close watch on your hands, woman. At the first sign that you are casting some spell with your voice or your hands, I shall serve you as I did your brother."

With her spine rigid and her hands close at her sides, Sarissa led them toward the forest. The trees closed about them, and Sarissa slowed, but Conan kept her going for several hundred more paces, pricking her back when her pace did not suit him.

"Now you may stop," said Conan when he deemed they were sufficiently far from the castle.

A dark, cowled form emerged from the woods, bearing a bundle of goods. "Alcuina!" cried Rerin in delight. "He has indeed brought you safe from that place."

"After a fashion," Alcuina said. Conan had set her upon the turf, where she sat fuming. "If you have something in that bundle to cover me with, I would be most grateful, old friend."

Conan himself did not take his eyes from Sarissa, who had shown no sign of emotion and had spoken no word since the shattering of the mirror.

"I am at a loss as to what to do with this one, old man," Conan said. "If we turn her loose, she'll work some mischief against us with her spells. Yet, we cannot keep her with us."

"You need not fear," Sarissa said in a dead voice. "When you destroyed the great mirror, you killed me and all my people. The group-soul of my race dwelled in that ancient artifact. You, in your barbarian ignorance, smashed it."

"Ignorance!" snorted Conan. "If I had known that

was the way to slay you all, I would have destroyed the thing at the first opportunity. It need not have happened, woman. If you had shown Alcuina kindness, if you had not tried to use me for your entertainment, we would be on our way home, and you would have your brother and your castle and your accursed amusements.'' Conan was not one to waste much pity upon those who brought their misfortunes upon themselves.

"It is true, what she says," confirmed Rerin. "All the magical aura is gone from her."

"Let me return to the castle, so I may perish with my people," said Sarissa.

"Very well," said Conan, sheathing his sword. "I have no further use for you." He paid her no more attention as she turned and began to walk, slowly and dejectedly, back toward her castle.

When she was gone, Alcuina turned to Rerin. "And now, old friend, have you some spell to loose these magical bonds?"

Rerin bent forward and studied the cords that bound Alcuina's wrists and ankles. "Have you tried a knife?" he asked.

"I never thought of that," said Conan. He drew his dagger and slid it across the bonds, which parted easily.

"Never thought of it!" Alcuina screamed, her face turning scarlet that flooded to her breasts. In her anger she seemed to have forgotten her nudity for the moment. "You deliberately left me like that so you could handle me at will and do as you liked in the castle!"

"There is much to be said," Conan assured her, "for a queen who is immobilized when there is warrior's work to be done."

"You fool! What would I have done if they had killed you while I was helpless! Did you think of that?"

"I am sure that you would have done your queenly best and managed affairs as well as you have so far."

"Look!" said Rerin, anxious to forestall what was about to erupt into civil war between queen and warrior.

They looked to where he was pointing. The castle, which had been so solid, was beginning to melt, or rather collapse in upon itself, its outlines becoming wavery, as if all within it had grown soft, shrunken, and diminished.

"It is like a jellyfish cast upon the seashore," said Conan, scratching his beard-stubbled chin.

"Their magic must have been all that held that unstable place together," Rerin mused. Then he noticed Conan's growth of whiskers. "How long were you in that castle?"

"It must have been some three or four days," Conan said, puzzled.

"No," protested Alcuina. "It was nine or ten days at least."

"And yet I spent only a single night out here since Conan ascended the wall. Even time is strange here in the demon land."

"We must find our way home, and that swiftly," insisted Alcuina. "This place terrifies me, and I am concerned for my people at home. What may be happening to them?"

"I am hungry," Conan said. "Rerin, get a fire started. I shall be back soon with game." With that he darted off into the underbrush.

Rerin sat by Alcuina when the fire was crackling. She wore his cloak as a temporary garb. "What think you now of your champion?" he asked.

"He is like something from an old tale. I have never seen a warrior like him, yet he is so wild and self-governed that I wonder whether he serves me or his own whim.''

"And yet he has possibilities. You need a king to sit beside you in the hall, and none of the neighbor kings suits you. You could do worse than this Cimmerian. He has no kingdom to swallow yours up, and with him leading your war-host you need fear no enemy.''

"It might work for a while," Alcuina said, "but some night as he lay sleeping I would probably kill him.''

Ten

Court of the Winter Kings

King Odoac of the Thungians, his rotund bulk swathed in rich winter furs, stood blowing on his hands. Behind him stood a band of his picked warriors, and beside him in the snow was thrust a hunting spear. They awaited the great stag that the huntsmen were to drive past them. There came a sound of crashing brush from the right.

"The stag comes!" said the king's nephew.

"I can hear that, you young fool," said Odoac.

He picked up his heavy javelin and made himself ready. According to ancient custom the king had the first cast, and after him each warrior in order of rank.

With a cloud of erupting snow the splendid beast broke from the brush. Its eyes rolled and its tongue hung from its mouth in exhaustion and panic. Behind it the huntsmen yelled and clattered, driving it toward the waiting noble hunters.

As it lumbered past, the king stepped forward and, with a straining grunt, cast his spear. The cast was

134

powerful but far wide of the mark. The spear glanced from the wide-spreading antlers of the beast, and the beast halted, startled by the unfamiliar impact.

While Odoac cursed in futile rage, the stag turned to face the hunters. With its head lowered, it began to trot toward them, presenting the most difficult of targets. The king's nephew, young Leovigild, stepped forward as his arm flashed back. He took three paces and cast his javelin. It sped unerringly to the stag, slipped below the antlers and beside the head, and pierced the juncture of chest and neck. With its neck artery cut and its heart pierced, the great animal collapsed and died almost instantly.

The young man stood smiling, and the others clapped him on the back, praising the superb cast. Then they all fell silent as the king strode up to his nephew, rage upon his face. With a powerful buffet of his open palm, he struck the younger man to the snowy ground.

"You insolent young puppy! I would have had him if you had not jostled my arm! Do you think your forwardness has escaped my notice! You have taken my stag just as you would like to take my throne!"

The warriors remained silent at this outburst. They all knew that no man had stood near the king, and that he had missed his cast through his own clumsiness, but none would give him the lie. These insane rages were growing more common with Odoac, as he felt his powers waning through the ravages of age and overindulgence.

"You are unjust, my liege," said Leovigild. The youth's face was pale with mortification, but he made no move against his uncle. "I cast because it was my turn, and all men know how loyally I have always served you."

"See that it remains so, puppy," said Odoac with

unbearable contempt. "It will be many years before Ymir takes me into his hall and you may sit upon the throne."

The king whirled and stalked off. He would have liked to kill his nephew, as he had killed all other rivals, some of them his own sons. But custom decreed that he must have a designated heir, and Leovigild, his murdered brother's only son, was the last remaining male of the royal line. Had he slain the boy, his nobles would have felt free to rid themselves of Odoac and make one of their number king in his place. As an infant and a boy, the lad had been no threat. Now that he had reached man's estate, something would have to be done about him.

Some of the warriors would have aided Leovigild to stand, but he shook off their helping hands. "I should not have allowed such a blow, even from a king," he said, fearful that he had lost respect in the eyes of the warriors.

"What could you have done," said a grizzled nobleman, "save sharing the fate of your male kin? You must bide your time, youngling. It cannot be much longer." Mollified, he walked back to the hall in the midst of the warriors.

That evening, after the feasting, Odoac dismissed all from the hall save his noblest warriors and champions. With drinking-horns filled, they waited to hear their master's words. His obese bulk filling the great throne, Odoac looked around at them, his piglike eyes almost buried in the fat face. His gaze halted for a moment upon Leovigild, and the young man stared back, unafraid. He was handsome and yellow-haired, a short, soft, blond beard framing his firm jaw. His eyes were clear and blue, in contrast to Odoac's muddy, bloodshot orbs. Odoac envied the boy's youth, strength, and fine looks as much as he feared his ambition and the way the warriors were increasingly turning to Leovigild for advice and approval.

"My warriors," the king began, "it is time we made plans concerning the future of the kingdom. For years now we Thungians have been menaced by two enemy peoples: Queen Alcuina and her Cambres, and Totila and his Tormanna." He almost spat out the last words, trying to hide his fear of Totila with a mask of contempt. If the truth was known, he secretly envied the way Totila, a mere bandit-chieftain, had built his warband into a powerful kingdom while he himself, who had inherited a kingdom from his father, had barely been able to hold it together with murder and treachery. "Of course, I would have destroyed both of them long ago had it not been for their accursed wizards, Rerin and Iilma.

"Let it not be said that I am an unreasonable man. I offered Queen Alcuina my suit, in honorable marriage. With her lands and people annexed to mine, neither of us need have feared any enemy. But did the slut eagerly accept, like my first three wives?" He glared around him and pounded on the arm of the throne with his fist. "No, she did not! She behaved as if I, King Odoac of the Thungians, were some humble crofter, instead of a mighty king whose forebears can be traced back to Father Ymir himself!" The king calmed himself with a visible effort before going on.

"I have borne this humiliation and insolence, with patience, for as long as any man could be asked. The time has now come to act. Word has come to me that, some weeks agone, Alcuina disappeared under uncanny circumstances." A murmur of conversation broke out at this news. "I doubt not that this is the work of Totila's pet wizard, Iilma. Alcuina's men are shut up inside their stockade, and they are leaderless. They have no one of royal blood to command them, so they huddle together waiting for their queen to return. I think they will have a long wait. Now is the time to strike and swallow them up, before Totila does!"

There was a savage growl of approval from the assembled warriors. Whatever their doubts concerning his erratic behavior and waning powers, they had no such doubts concerning his acquisitiveness and his predatory instincts. Of these things, they all approved. Odoac had been a decent battle-leader in his younger days, and perhaps he was showing a flash of his old power in this plan. After all, kings lived by preying upon rival kings, and better the Thungians should absorb the Cambres than the hated Tormanna.

"I am not so certain that this is the best course, Uncle," said Leovigild. The old king stared at him with undisguised hate, but the youth went on fearlessly. "It seems to me a shabby thing to attack Queen Alcuina's people while her fate remains unknown. This is not the way great people should deal with one another."

"Is that so?" said Odoac in a dangerously mild voice. "And yet, it is the way we have always dealt among ourselves, high and low, here in the Northland. The weak are swallowed up by the strong. That is the way of it, as I learned from my sire and he from his, and so it has always been since the wars of gods and giants."

Many nodded at these words, for custom was the only law among them except for might. Yet others plainly wanted to hear more of what Leovigild had to say.

"I think that this way is unwise. I grant that it is

good to be strong and fierce, for how can a people survive otherwise? But I think it is also good to be wise and behave with forethought. Here is my counsel: If we war upon the Cambres at this time, both peoples will lose warriors and will be the weaker when the inevitable war comes with Totila. Instead why do we not send heralds to the Cambres in their fortress and propose an alliance against Totila until Queen Alcuina returns? This can have only two outcomes, both of them good: If Alcuina comes not back, then the Cambres must in time acknowledge you as their king, having no king of their own and having followed you in war. Should Alcuina return, how can she again reject your suit, since you will have been the salvation of her people. In truth, her folk must demand it, since she has to wed soon.'' There was great approbation at words of such maturity and wisdom from so young a man.

Had it not been for those sounds of admiration, had the boy come in private to Odoac with this plan, then Odoac might have adopted it and claimed it as his own. As it was, the words threw him into another towering rage. ''What womanish, weakling words are these? Could the fierce Thungians ever follow such a simpleton? No such coward could be born of our royal line, and I am minded to cut you from it!'' So saying, Odoac lurched to his feet and began to draw his sword. His men rushed to restrain him, and forced him back into his throne.

A senior counselor turned to Leovigild. ''Best get you gone, lad. We'll not let the king harm you, but you cannot stay here now.'' Ashen-faced, Leovigild strode from the hall. After a time, Odoac grew calm enough to be released.

''That boy tries me beyond my patience,'' said Odoac

at length. "Best that he is exiled. He is treacherous as well as cowardly. I thank you for restraining me," he said piously. "I should never wish to shed the blood of a kinsman, be he never so disloyal." The warriors let this pass in eloquent silence.

"What of the custom, my liege?" asked a grim-faced man. "Now you have no heir. The people must have an heir to the throne, or there must be trouble."

Odoac shifted uncomfortably in his seat. "Think you I am so old that I may not set this matter aright? As soon as we have settled the problem of the Cambres, then I shall take a new wife, be it Alcuina or some other. Then you shall have an heir within the year, I vow."

"That is good to hear, my king," said the same man, and Odoac was not sure that there was no mockery in the voice. "Now, what of this black-haired champion of Alcuina's that we have heard something of? Is this fellow likely to cause us trouble?"

Happy to be off the subject of the succession, Odoac said, "I have spoken with the trader Dawaz about this man. He is a mere sellsword, an adventurer from afar with neither kin nor friend here. He seems to possess some small skill with his weapons, and with a bit of luck he managed to slay Agilulf. I have also heard that he disappeared on the same night as Alcuina, as did the wizard Rerin. All the more reason why we should move now. The Cambres have lost queen, champion, and sorcerer. When shall we have such an opportunity again?" He looked around and saw only battle-lusting faces. "See to sharpening your weapons, then." He turned to a trusted retainer named Wudga. "Go you to all the outlying steadings and summon the warriors. It has been many years since there has been a winter hosting, so remind them that every man must bring as much preserved food as may feed him for at least a fortnight. After that we should be feasting upon the stores of the Cambres!''

A ferocious cheer went up at these words, the unfortunate Leovigild forgotten for the moment. Odoac sat back and smiled with satisfaction. Few problems, however thorny, were not to be solved with a little warfare and prospect of loot.

Leovigild rode for many hours, unsure where he might go. No man had pursued him from the hall, none had sought to molest him as he bundled his few belongings onto a packhorse and rode from the garth. Immediate death at the hands of Odoac's men might have been preferable. He was an exile, driven from hearth and hall, denied the protection of his family. In the North, a man without clan or kin was under virtual death sentence.

His small, shaggy mount pushed patiently through the snow, twin jets of steam streaming from his nostrils. Mane and tail swept almost to the snow as the surefooted beast picked its way among the serried drifts, its hooves crunching musically through the hard crust left by the great freeze.

Where could he go? He had his two horses, his sword, helm and cuirass of finely worked bronze. On the packhorse were his hunting clothes and his feast clothes, two long spears, a short javelin, and his shield of painted wood and leather. With the clothes he now wore, these were his total resources. It never crossed his mind to take the protection of some landholder and serve as a peasant farmer. Starvation was preferable. An armed warrior of good blood could always join the war-band of some chieftain. That was at least honorable, but it would have to be far from here, and a lone man was not likely to survive the journey. Besides, he was rightful heir to the lordship of the Thungians, and he had no intention of relinquishing his claim.

His gloomy thoughts turned to Alcuina of the Cambres. If the reports were true, she now was in some form of exile as well. If the loathsome Iilma was behind it, Alcuina's situation was far more dire than his own. He had never met her, but rumor had it that she was a great beauty. The thought of such a lady wed to his uncle was repellent, although honor and loyalty forbade his expressing the thought while in the garth.

He wished to avoid the men of the Tormanna and of the Cambres. Times were even more unsettled than usual, and there was no law to protect lone wanderers. Captors might wish to make sport with him before killing him, and many a man who was laggard on the battlefield made up for it by fiendish ingenuity in the treatment of prisoners.

He remembered a small valley in the hills to the north. He had found it years before when hunting alone. It was uncultivated and snaked along the ill-defined border between the lands of the Cambres and the Tormanna. If he could pass between the two nations unseen, he might find a place to hide, perhaps taking service with a petty chieftain until he might return to claim his birthright. Surely Odoac could not live much longer.

That evening he bedded down on the level ground near the mouth of the valley. It was a wild place, frequented only by hunters or herdsmen in search of strayed stock. With the flint and steel from his belt pouch he kindled a fire. There was scant likelihood that he would be seen in this wild spot.

As he was about to bed down in his warm cloaks, he was startled to see ghostly lights flittering among the trees within the narrow valley. His hand went to the protective amulet that hung at his neck, and he chanted out a quick spell to ward off evil. The lights came no nearer and seemed no more menacing than the fire, which was now a small heap of coals before him.

"Ymir!" he muttered in a near whisper, "am I a child to hide my head for fear of will-o'-the-wisps?"

With a short, forced laugh he bundled into his cloaks and was soon asleep. Nothing molested him, but his sleep was fitful, troubled by vague, menacing dreams.

The next morning, remounted, Leovigild peered into the narrow, growth-choked valley. Little of the snow lay there, but the density of the tree canopy could have explained that. Still, it was an ill-looking place. It took some urging on his part to force the horses into the tangled draw. When he had visited this place before, he had been on foot. That had been in the days of high summer, but even then the darkness of the valley had oppressed him. He had spent a morning in halfhearted pursuit of a wounded stag, and turned back hastily when its tracks ended in a welter of blood and broken brush. Some dire predator dwelled in the valley, but he was older and better-armed now.

The air was still and warmer than that outside the valley. The growth of plants was different as well. Here, instead of pine and fir, broad-leafed oak predominated. The trees were stunted but of luxuriant growth, and once he was well into the valley the undergrowth thinned, and the traveling was easier. The valley floor was uneven, a tiny stream meandering over a gravel bed in its center. The heavy growth of stunted trees and thick vines, the great mossy boulders, all lent the valley a certain wild beauty, marred by the gloomy dimness.

Leovigild watched for game to supplement the scant rations in his saddlebags, but he saw little sign of larger animals, and the smaller ones would be passing the winter in sleep. Still, he kept his bow strung, its handle of hide-wrapped yew comforting to his hand.

He was beginning to regret his decision to travel by this route. The men of Totila and Alcuina would never accost him in this place, but it had the aspect of an abode for dragons and giants. His imagination peopled the copses and caves with witches, and behind the mossy boulders he thought he glimpsed ragged dwarfs ducking from sight. He tried to shake off the uncanny mood.

"Tales to frighten children," he muttered. "It is men I must be wary of, not goblins from old stories."

Having thus reassured himself, Leovigild urged his horse forward. There was a tiny clearing in the overhead cover, and a heap of snow lay before him. It was the first sizable drift he had encountered since entering the valley. Then a great many things happened at once. As he guided his horse around the drift the heap of snow burst upward, flinging white clumps far and wide.

Leovigild's mount reared screeching, casting the youth to the ground with enough force to half stun him. Towering above him was a creature of nightmare—its wedge-shaped head reared high upon a sinuous trunk as thick as a man's body. Its unblinking, slit-pupiled eyes fixed malevolently upon the helpless Leovigild, and he knew that he had no chance against this thing from the earth's youth.

"Snow serpent!" he gasped.

Travelers claimed to have seen the giant, white-furred

snakes in the lands north of the forest belt, where the sun rose not for half the year, nor fully set in the other half. Never had he heard of such in the woodlands of his people.

His packhorse bolted toward the upper end of the valley, but his mount fidgeted, too paralyzed by terror to pick a direction and run. With Leovigild motionless, the primitive brain of the serpent was distracted by the terrified beast. Its jaws gaped, and yellow slime dripped from its fangs to hiss upon the snow. It lunged forward, and Leovigild heard the doomed beast's shrill neigh cut short by a horrible sound of crunching bones.

With a wrenching, painful effort, the youth raised himself enough to see a writhing, white-furred coil from which protruded the twisted legs of his mount. Horror thrilled his spine as the serpent's head reared from the writhing mass, its jaws grotesquely distended. The horse's head and part of its forequarters had already disappeared into the gaping maw, and he realized that the monster intended to swallow the horse whole.

Now, he knew, was his chance to escape. Even so immense a monster must need some time to swallow an entire horse. He tested his limbs and found them all relatively sound. It would be some time before he was hale enough to run, but he could creep painfully upon hands and knees.

As Leovigild began to drag himself away the serpent turned to fix its eyes once more upon him. It shook its head, trying to rid itself of the carcass, but its backward-curving fangs would not release it. It had to swallow the horse or die with the carcass in its jaws. Gradually it lost interest in the lesser prey and went back to its task.

Leovigild was gasping with a mixture of pain and

relief when he pulled himself to his feet with the aid of a small sapling. He bled only from small scrapes, although he felt as if King Odoac's hall had fallen upon him. As he made his slow, halting way up the valley he took stock of his situation.

If he had felt poor and abandoned upon setting out, he was in far worse condition now. He had the clothes he wore, his sword and knife, and a relatively undamaged body. His packhorse with his other belongings was somewhere ahead. With luck, he might recover them. Only the thought that he might have ended as snake food himself kept him from cursing his luck.

He paused to catch his breath. Painfully he bent and touched the earth. "Father Ymir, I thank you that I have escaped as cheaply as I did." He suspected that Ymir took no interest in his doings, but it did no harm to keep on good terms with the gods.

"A pious sentiment, for so young a man."

Leovigild whirled at the sound of a human voice, causing himself great pain in so doing. He saw nobody. "Show yourself!"

"I am here before you."

Leovigild peered into the gloom and saw a lump of mossy stone a few paces before him. It had an oddly regular look to it, a semblance of a human face below the long strands of lichen hanging from its crest. In deep-shadowed pits he saw a pair of unmistakable eyes. At another time it might have sent prickles of horror up his spine. So soon after his encounter with the snow serpent, it was a mere curiosity.

"What manner of creature are you?" he asked.

"I might ask the same of you, O foolish one."

Leovigild could now see that it was a small, gnarled man sitting atop the boulder. So twisted and irregular was his shape that he seemed more a part of his surroundings than a living man, and whether he was covered with ragged garments, hair, or moss was equally uncertain.

"I am Leovigild, heir to the lordship of the Thungians. My pack-beast was slain by a great white serpent, and I now search for my mount."

"And what brings you hither, to a place avoided by men since your breed first came to these wooded hills?" An oversized, knobby hand emerged from the rags and scratched at a bark-brown cheek.

"My business is my own. I but seek passage up this valley and intend to leave it two days' journey to the north. That at least was my intention. The loss of my horses may cause me to tarry here a while longer."

"You may stay here far longer than you had intended," said the ugly little man.

Uncomfortably Leovigild thought of old tales he had heard as a child, of places outside human ken. There were said to be barrows and hills where unwary travelers were drawn by mysterious lights or music, to spend a night feasting with the small people, only to emerge with the dawn and find that twenty or more years had passed.

"Would you seek to ensorcell me?" His hand went to his sword hilt. After his battering he was far from his best fighting form, but he had little doubt that he could defeat this homunculus.

The creature laughed, a sound like two boulders rubbing together. "The pause of death is the longest delay of all. You men are a short-lived race." The creature spoke slowly, as one who never felt the press of passing time.

"I must find my packhorse," said Leovigild impa-

tiently. "This is your valley, and I would be grateful
for your aid in tracking the beast. But if you will not
aid me, then at least hinder me no further." Painfully
and stiffly he turned to trudge off.

"Be not so hasty, youth."

Leovigild turned back to see the dwarfish figure rising from its rock. Standing, the creature stood no higher
than Leovigild's waist, but it was easily twice as broad
through the body. The long arms were roped with
heavy coils of muscle, and the youth was no longer so
sanguine about besting the little man in combat.

"Let us go and find your animal. I warrant you
would not live long alone in this valley."

The dwarf picked up a club and shouldered it. The
bludgeon was a knobby-headed oaken cudgel as long as
Leovigild's leg, old and hand-polished. The creature
handled it as lightly as a willow-wand. He set off at an
easy walk, his stubby legs adjusting to the irregularity
of the footing with the effortlessness of long custom.

"What manner of man are you?" Leovigild asked
once more. "I have never encountered your like, though
you live so close to my homeland."

"I am no man at all. I am a *Niblung*, and my people
lived in these Northlands long before men arrived with
their long legs and their short lives. Your kind have
encountered us seldom because we wish it so. This
valley has such an aspect that few wish to venture
hither, and those who camp nearby are troubled with
strange dreams. Those who enter soon turn back, bothered by strange fears they cannot explain."

"Such was my experience," Leovigild said, nodding. "I persisted only because I had no safe route
through the lands of my foemen." The words were out

before he could stop them. He had not intended to reveal his fugitive status.

"It may be," said the little man, "that we of this valley shall help you. I am Hugin. Follow close behind me, young Leovigild. There is danger for you in much that seems harmless in this valley."

"I have already encountered some of the peril of this place," Leovigild said.

"Aye. And if you failed to see a thing as huge as the snow serpent, how will you see the things that are small but just as deadly?" His shaggy, mossy eyebrows flapped up and down like the wings of a bat.

"How came that creature to this small valley?" Leovigild asked. "They are figures out of our oldest tales and are said to live only in the lands of eternal snow in the farthest north." They scrambled over a litter of fallen logs, a legacy of some mighty storm of years past.

"Such of the breed as are left inhabit those lands," Hugin agreed. "Yet once they were numerous and widespread. Far back in the mists of time, longer ago than you humans can remember, the world was covered with unending snow and great sheets of ice. Then the land was ruled by such as the snow serpent, and the great hairy tuskers, and the giant white apes. The ice retreated to the north, and the great snow-beasts with it. Once in a great while, though, some ancient instinct stirs in the brain of one of those fell creatures, and they are driven to wander south. In time they return to the north, unable to bear the heat or to find food to suit them. The serpent would have returned soon, but your horse has provided it a good meal, and it will sleep for many days."

It seemed incredible to Leovigild that no more than an

hour's walk to either hand were the familiar pine forests of his homeland. This was a slice from another time and place set amid his accustomed surroundings.

Not all its dangers were as outlandish as the snow serpent. Silently Hugin pointed to a writhing nest of vipers in a hollow beside the little stream. They were of a breed Leovigild had never seen before. Unwarned, he might have trod in their midst. From time to time tracks in the mud assured him that they were still on the trail of his packhorse.

At midday they picked their way gingerly around a thicket from which came regular snortings. Leovigild could not keep from peering within, despite Hugin's silent urgings to leave well enough alone. To his amazement he saw a sleeping boar, large as a full-grown bull. Its curling tusks were longer than his forearm. The sight made him long for his boar-spear, but he knew that all the boar-spears and nets in Odoac's hunting lodges might not suffice to slay so terrific a beast. There would be great carnage among the huntsmen, at best.

Something occurred to Leovigild. "Hugin, a few days ago, the queen of the Cambres disappeared. Her name is Alcuina, and she is said to be a woman of great beauty. It may be that she is accompanied by her champion, a huge black-haired outlander, who I have heard is more than commonly handy with his sword. Have they passed hither?"

"Nay," Hugin said. "I would have heard had they come to this valley."

"That is unfortunate," Leovigild said, disappointment etched upon his brow.

The shaggy brows flapped once more. "It sounds important to you, the whereabouts of this beautiful queen."

"In truth, I would give much to know where she is, if she still lives. It is important to our peoples."

"And to you, as well," Hugin said with a rasping chuckle. "I take you to one who may be able to tell you about your lost queen, and it may be about much else besides. Just follow old Hugin."

"Whom do you lead me to?" Leovigild asked. But Hugin would say no more.

As they trekked northward, the valley widened and trees grew larger. Without warning, they came to a small clearing, and Leovigild saw his packhorse standing at the base of a large oak, placidly cropping dry, brown grass. Then he saw that the beast was tethered to a sapling.

"Who has caught the animal and tethered it?" he asked.

"You'll see soon enough." The small man waddled to the base of the tree, where an untidy bundle of objects rested by the trunk. Leovigild examined the bundle and confirmed that it contained all his belongings that the packhorse had carried. At least he was no longer quite so destitute.

"Who have you brought me, Hugin?" Leovigild looked around, seeking the source of the voice. He was growing mighty weary of disembodied voices. "Up here," said the voice. It was a woman's voice, and it came from the tree above him. He leaned back to scan the tree over his head.

In the thick lower branches a hut perched on a small platform. Thin smoke rose from a fire-hearth he could not see. Of the speaker he could discern nothing.

"Show yourself," Leovigild called.

"Come to my house if you would see me, youth."

He thought he caught a thin edge of amusement in

the voice. That was all to the good because he would otherwise have suspected treachery to lurk in such an invitation. Among his people, a man coming to another's home stood in plain view and announced himself loudly if his intent was honest. The house holder was then expected to come outside and greet the visitor, unarmed or at least with hands well away from his weapons. The inhabitants of this valley lived by odd customs, or so it seemed. He was comforted by the fact that it was a woman's voice, a consequence of his youth and inexperience.

A series of limb stubs jutted from the trunk at heights convenient for climbing. Despite the awkwardness of the sword at his waist, Leovigild climbed nimbly to the little bower. One who hunted boar and bear in the northern woods had to be adept at scrambling swiftly into trees. When he saw the woman who sat cross-legged in the doorway of the tree-hut, he nearly lost his hold on the tiny platform before her. Only a quick scramble saved him from a bad fall and worse loss of dignity.

He had half expected a female version of the gnarled, ugly little Hugin. What he saw instead was a young woman of great beauty. Not only was she not clad in the rough garments of the *Niblung,* she was clad in nothing at all. Confusion warred with excitement in his somewhat disordered mind.

"Come sit with me," said the woman, now sounding even more amused than before.

Leovigild complied, unable despite his strongest efforts to keep his eyes from staring at the woman. Aside from her state of nudity she was a woman such as he had never before seen. Her hair was raven-wing black, a great rarity in the North, but her skin was fair to the point of near translucency. Her face was triangular, with wide cheekbones and large, tilted eyes the color of emeralds. Her body was small and slender, but her breasts were full and firm, and her hips swelled ripely below her tiny waist.

He had to swallow a few times before he regained control of his voice. "I, ah, thank you for your kind invitation, my, ah, lady."

Never in his life had he felt so foolish. It occurred to him to wonder how she kept from freezing. True, the valley was somewhat warmer than the forests outside, but it was nonetheless cold enough that even a toughened northerner felt the need of a heavy cloak.

"You seem to be ill at ease," she said.

"I fear so, my lady. In my homeland one does not often come upon unclothed women." The art of gallantry was little practiced in the North.

"Oh, I see. Have no fear, my kind are not bothered by the cold, as are you."

Leovigild felt a violent urge to change the subject. "Hugin told me that you might be able to help me with certain questions that trouble me. I do not wish to impose upon you, but I would be most grateful for any assistance you might afford me."

"And what form might this gratitude take?" Her green eyes were unfathomable. He knew not whether she made sport of him or meant her words seriously. Her expression was grave, but that might easily hide mockery.

"As you can see, I possess little," he said, "but what I have you may ask of me."

"Fear not," she said. "I shall ask nothing you would be loath to give."

She took some shreds of bark from a withy basket at her side and cast them upon the coals that glowed upon the small stone hearth before her. A cloud of fragrant smoke ascended and hung before them both. She inhaled deeply.

Leovigild was aware of a stinging in his nostrils as he breathed the smoke, then an unaccustomed dizziness assailed him. He blinked smoke-tears from his eyes and saw the woman with a new sharpness and clarity, as if the light had somehow grown stronger.

"What is your name?" he asked bluntly.

She had closed her eyes, but now the lids rose, and her emerald gaze had a distant look. "My true name you may not know, for it would give you power over me. You may call me Atalia. I come of a race as ancient as Hugin's. Where his folk are of earth and water, mine are of air and fire. Secrets of past and future are disclosed to us. Ask me now what you would know."

Leovigild had heard of witch-women and spaewives who told fortunes and performed small magics, but he had always been half convinced that most of them were mere posers or deluded half-wits. This woman was different. Though her face and form were as beautiful as any he had ever imagined, she was as alien to him as the dwarfish Hugin. She might truly have the gift of prophecy. But what could he ask her? He was curious about the future, but the tales and poems of his people were full of heroes and kings who received some prophecy of doom and did all in their power to circumvent catastrophe. Inevitably the actions they took to avoid doom were precisely those that brought it about.

The gods, then, did not like for mortal men to know too much about the future. The past did not concern him. There was much that was confusing about the present, though. Perhaps Father Ymir and the lesser gods would not resent his arming himself with some knowledge of how things went outside this little valley.

"Where is Queen Alcuina of the Cambres?" he asked.

Atalia's eyelids drooped, and she breathed deeply of the smoke. After a long silence she began speaking, very slowly and in a voice somehow more hollow than that with which she had spoken earlier.

"She is in a place that is neither this valley nor the world you know."

This was a disappointment. The woman spoke in riddles, like the dragons of old tales. "Are you saying that she is dead?"

"No. There are—other places. Some of them are open only to sorcerers, others may not be entered by mortals at all. She has been taken to one of those places by the working of dark forces."

"Iilma," he half whispered. "Is she alone?"

"My sight cannot penetrate to the other worlds, but she was followed by two men who crossed over close after her. One was an old man, a wizard. The other a huge man with hair as black as mine. He is no ordinary man, but one with the mark of a strange destiny upon him. He is a sojourner, for his fate lies not in these northern forests."

"Those will be her wizard, Rerin, and her foreign champion, whose name I know not. It may be that her plight is not wholly desperate, then. And what of her people, the Cambres?"

After another pause, she said, "They are leaderless and despondent. Should they be set upon now, they would fall easy prey, for the heart is gone from them."

He chose his next words with great care. "I do not ask what I should do, nor whether I shall die upon the morrow or many years hence. But where would lie my wisest choice of action?''

She smiled. ''You are cautious. That is good, for cautious men frequently live longer than rash ones. I give you advice, then, not prediction. Go to the Cambres and their queen. For good or ill your fate lies with them, and no man does well by striving to avoid his fate.''

''The Cambres it is, then.''

Leovigild felt as if a great burden had been lifted from him. A decision had been reached, and he need trouble his mind no further. When he left here he would climb from the valley and make his way to Alcuina's holding in the field of great stones. Even that uncanny place would seem familiar after his strange day in the valley.

''There is still the matter of my payment,'' Atalia said, and now her green eyes glowed with a different light.

''And what might it be?'' Leovigild asked.

She rose from where she sat and seemed to flow into his arms. Even through his clothing he felt the heat of her naked body, warmer than was natural to any human woman. ''As I told you,'' she gasped, ''it is a fee you will not be sorry to pay.'' Slowly she drew him back into her hut.

It was a frosty morning, and Siggeir was on watch. As he often had these last few weeks, he kept especial watch upon the stone circle out on the plain, in futile hope that he would see Alcuina returning from the place where she had disappeared so mysteriously. He had tried to urge the others to make an expedition against Totila, to slay that king and seize his wizard Iilma. Like most of them, Siggeir was certain that Alcuina's disappearance was the work of the wizard, and he felt that Iilma might be persuaded to return their queen to them. A few had wanted to go, but most were too fearful of both Totila and Iilma, and Siggeir's urgings had come to naught.

It was with some interest that he saw the lone figure mounted upon a small horse approaching from the west. Few were the travelers upon the ways at this season. Was it a messenger, or perhaps a wandering bard come to sing for a few meals and a night's lodging? He saw as the man drew near that it was a handsome youth in fine clothing.

"Who might you be?" Siggeir called down.

The young man looked up and grinned at him. "I am Leovigild, once a prince of the Thungians, now an exile. Who is in charge here in the absence of Queen Alcuina? I have some words that may be of interest to her people."

King Totila was bored. Winter life was a weary round of eating, sleeping, gaming, and trying to pass the long, dark hours until the return of spring. Then would resume the exciting pastimes of fighting, hunting, and raiding, which were the proper amusements for a man of good blood. The rare winter hunts helped, but now they were past the great midwinter feast, and game was scarce. Unless his huntsmen turned up an incautious stag or boar, they would be reduced to smoked meat and dried fish until spring brought the beasts from their winter dens.

It could be worse. He had seen winters when he and his warriors had had to subsist on cheese and porridge, just like the thralls. He shuddered at the thought. A clean death in battle was better than a life such as that. He had heard of the great kings of the South, where the land enjoyed spring all year round, where there was always sparkling wine instead of sour beer that had been in the cask too long. That was the way for a king to live, and that was how he intended to live as soon as he had settled with his neighbors. Then he would push his borders southward and establish a southern capital near the Zamoran border.

That was for the future, though. The problem now was how best to subdue those neighbors. He had come to depend upon the wizard Iilma. He was not sure that this was a good thing, but what else could he do? A king needed a counselor, for a king's true vocation lay in war-leadership.

As if on signal, Iilma came rattling into the hall. A few of the warriors looked up from their game boards, but they gave the mage no more than passing attention. He was a common sight, and in winter men developed the ability to ponder their moves in a game with awesome intensity and patience.

"I bring you news, my liege," said Iilma.

"I could use diversion," Totila said. "I trust that it is about Alcuina. Have you come to tell me that your vaunted allies in the spirit world have delivered her to me?"

"It is not that, my liege. As I have told you, time in the spirit world is not the same as time here. While many long weeks have passed among us, no more than a day or two may have passed there."

The wizard was uncomfortable with this questioning. What Iilma said was true in general, but he knew that something must have gone seriously wrong in the spirit world. He could not imagine what factor might have been introduced to throw his plans awry. He was not sure how much longer he could keep Totila waiting. Now, though, he had a distraction.

"The burden of my news concerns your neighbors, the Thungians and the Cambres."

"Say on." Now Totila's interest was aroused. Idly the king picked up his helmet and turned it in his hands, admiring its workmanship. Like all the northern warriors, he loved fine metal work.

"I have found that King Odoac has driven forth his heir, young Leovigild. He rode from the king's hall some days ago, and no man knows where he has gone."

Totila barked a short laugh. "That makes a clean sweep of the family, then. That foolish pig Odoac rushes to his own doom. With no heir of their own blood, the Thungians shall be all the more willing to acknowledge me their king when I have slain him."

"You have no heir either, my liege," said the wizard.

Totila glanced at him from beneath lowered brows. "I shall have, as soon as you produce Alcuina for me. Besides, I am far younger than Odoac, and no man doubts my ability to produce an heir. And I am a proven war-leader. I am of royal blood. Thus, Alcuina's people as well as Odoac's can have no objection to my overlordship. Once I have wed Alcuina, who comes of an ancient line, our son must be an heir satisfactory to all concerned. Is that not so, wizard?"

"That is so, my liege. It is also of the Cambres that I bear news. Since Alcuina's abduction by my allies, they have been shut up within their garth on the plain of the Giants' Stones. I have found out that Odoac plans to take advantage of their leaderless state and attack them within a few days."

"A winter hosting!" said Totila eagerly. "Who would

have thought that old Odoac would show such enterprise? It is more like him to doze away the winter in a drunken stupor.'' He fell to pondering, and his shrewd mind turned over the various ramifications of this stunning news. ''But, yes, I see now what his thinking is. He has exiled his heir. Now he must quickly prove that he is still a good war-leader, lest his own men slay him and send to young Leovigild to return and be their king. He dare not attack me, but the Cambres are a tempting target.''

Iilma nodded at these words. Once again he knew that he had chosen well in picking Totila to groom as a mighty king. The man had a quick mind as well as a strong arm and a ruthless will.

''So tempting are they in fact, that I think I shall go conquer them myself,'' said Totila. ''I shall swallow up both peoples at once. Such an opportunity must not escape me. Warriors!'' He bellowed the last word at the top of his rafter-shaking command voice. ''Gather your gear and summon your kin! Prepare for a winter hosting!''

A mighty cheer greeted these words, and another northern nation prepared for war.

Eleven

A Hunter Comes

"Are you certain that you know where we are going, old man?" asked Conan. He forged ahead of the other two, his eyes alert for solid, fightable enemies, while Rerin kept his senses open for sorcerous danger.

"As certain as one may be in this place, which is not all that certain. A gate lies in our path somewhere up ahead, and it is one through which we may return to our world, somewhere near where we left it. Beyond that, I know little."

They were traversing a forest of towering trees, the ground almost devoid of underbrush. Great winged forms were to be discerned from time to time, soaring above the treetops, but creatures on the ground were for the most part small and shy, avoiding the approaching humans.

"I pray to Ymir we get there soon," said Alcuina.

She now wore Conan's tunic and trews, which she had roughly altered to fit her smaller form. The Cimmerian retained his wolfskin overtunic and leggings. Alcuina had fashioned crude boots from the excess of Conan's fur cloak. The relatively mild climate here made these makeshift garments adequate.

They had not eaten that day and had only had the carcass of a small beast slain by Conan to share among themselves the day before. Still, they were northerners and used to extended periods of deprivation.

"Black Erlik's throne, but I hope we find some game soon," said Conan, his stomach growling loudly.

"Wait," interjected Rerin.

"What is it?" Conan asked.

"I feel—I am not sure. Something has come near us, and it is charged with the evil of this world."

"Know you anything of its nature?" asked Alcuina.

"I cannot say. It is nothing I have ever seen in the spirit-trance. It is not like the folk of the castle, nor is it like the demons who bore you hither. More than that I cannot say."

"I hope it is not another of those scorpion things," Conan said. "One of those was enough."

"No," Rerin said, "I think not, but—" Then he looked upward, beyond Conan. "Look!"

The others followed his pointing finger. Far ahead, on a high ridge of ground beyond the trees, was a mounted figure. Its long cloak billowed in the wind as it stared down at them. Its features were masked by a shining, silver helm, but a baleful red glow shone from within its vision-slots. Of its arms they could tell nothing from so great a distance, but its warlike aspect was nonetheless apparent. Conan was minded of what the demon he had questioned about Alcuina had told him: "A hunter comes."

"If it's a man," Conan said, "then it's a bigger man

on a bigger horse than the common run. And I think it means us no good.''

"Do you think it is human?" Alcuina asked Rerin.

"I do not think that there are any true humans here," Rerin said, "save for ourselves and perhaps captives brought here from the world of men. But what it is I cannot say."

With no warning, the creature whirled its mount and sped across the ridge, away from them. In an instant it was lost to sight.

"I like not the look of that rider," said Alcuina.

Conan shrugged. "I could tell little in this accursed thick air. It looked like a giant, but that might be some trick of the light or the air."

Inwardly he was not so sure. He saw no reason for communicating his unease to his companions, though. If this thing boded ill, which he did not doubt, then time enough to worry about it when the danger was directly upon them.

They proceeded through the great wood, which gradually gave way to a more sparsely vegetated upland where stands of smaller trees predominated, separated by small valleys and meadows. It looked to Conan much like the area where he and Rerin had originally entered the demon land. He felt slightly more comfortable here, as visibility was somewhat improved in these surroundings. There was little he feared, even in a place such as this, as long as he had a clear field of view and time to ready himself against attack by an enemy.

That night they camped in a clearing, and grilled cuts of meat over a smoky wood fire. Before stopping for the night Conan had brought down a vaguely deerlike animal by casting a makeshift javelin consisting of a straight sapling trimmed of its branches, its thicker end whittled to a point by Conan's dagger. It proved sufficient for a short cast, and they all ate well for a change.

"We shall reach the gate early tomorrow," Rerin said. "I can feel its nearness much more clearly now. It is not far."

"What of that rider we saw today?" asked Conan. "Can you feel his presence now?"

Rerin concentrated for a few moments. "I cannot tell for certain," he said at last. "Everything magical casts a certain aura, and this may be detected by one who is trained in these arts. However, some auras are stronger, and a weaker one may be masked by a stronger, as the light cast by a candle is hidden within that cast by the sun. Here there are so many magical auras that it is difficult to separate one from another. The signal sent out by the gate is very strong and is unmistakable. The rider"—he shrugged—"his aura is not so strong, although it is intensely evil."

"Conan," Alcuina said, "think you that you can best this weird horseman?"

"If it is mortal, I can slay it. And it must be mortal."

"How can you be sure of that?" she asked.

"Because it wears a helm," he said imperturbably. "Immortals have no need of armor. It wears a helm because it does not want a cleft skull."

"I hope you are right," said Rerin. "I feel we shall know upon the morrow, at any rate."

The next day found them trekking through the upland into a high valley of great stone formations and scattered, low trees. The air was still dense and waterlike to vision, causing shapes and shadows to waver subtly. Once, distantly, they seemed to hear a pounding of great hooves. They moved warily, for their enemy was sure to strike before they could gain the gate.

"There!" shouted Rerin as they crested a small hillock. Before them, in a depression of the ground, was a stone gate such as the one they had come through. It stood in a grassy glade that seemed to be devoid of animal life. They approached it cautiously, ready for anything.

"How much time will you need?" Conan asked.

"An hour, perhaps two, but no longer," said Rerin. From his pouch he took plants he had collected on their way, and bits of stone, animal bones, and the like. "Alcuina, help me gather fuel and kindle a fire. I must work quickly, but I dare not risk rushing through the spell too rapidly. If so much as a word or a gesture is left out, I must begin all over again."

"Is there aught I may do to help?" asked Conan. He hated taking part in sorcerous doings, but he was willing to overcome his distaste to save their hides.

"Nothing except to keep watch. If our pursuer arrives, he must not be allowed to interrupt me."

"I'll try to keep him away from you," said Conan, smiling sourly. "Get to work. I shall go to the top of yonder mound to keep guard."

So saying, he walked to the indicated elevation. From its crest he could see nothing except more of the landscape. Who was the rider, and what might be his powers? Conan found himself regretting the loss of his cuirass. Although he rarely let himself depend on armor, Conan knew that the extra protection could be crucial in a close-fought combat. As it was, he had sword and helm, but no shield. He had fought with considerably less, and he was yet alive. He sat and waited.

Much smoke and chanting came from where Rerin and Alcuina sat by their fire before the great stone gate.

The colors of the smoke changed from moment to moment, and within the gate the view shifted and wavered. The old wizard's voice came sometimes as a high-pitched wailing, at others as a deep rumble. Such things set Conan's teeth on edge, and it was almost with relief that he heard the pounding of great hooves.

Conan rose from his cross-legged position and drew his sword. Idly he thumbed its edge as he awaited the coming of the rider.

From the tree line it came, a man-shape mounted upon a horse-form. But as it neared, Conan saw that rider and mount were neither man nor horse. The two seemed to be clad in gleaming armor, although much of the man-shape was hidden by a voluminous cloak. The horse-thing walked slowly forward, and its gait was not quite that of a natural beast. Its eyes gleamed red, as did those of its rider, through the smooth, featureless helm.

"That's far enough," Conan called out. "State your business. Do not attempt to interfere with these people." He jerked his head in the direction of his companions, never taking his gaze from the rider.

"I am a hunter." The voice rang hollowly from within the thing. "I have come to fetch you all for my master."

"And who might that be?" Conan asked. He really was not interested in the answer, but every second he kept the thing occupied was more time for Rerin to complete his spell-casting.

"I serve the Lord of the Demon Land. Come with me."

"If we wished to visit your master," Conan said, "we would not be here. Now be on your way. If you wish to live, do not seek to hinder us."

With no further negotiation, the hunter charged. Conan

was almost caught off-balance. A natural horse rears back slightly, digging in its rear hooves before springing forward. The hunter's mount did no such thing. All four hooves dug in as one and the beast was coming forward with blinding speed. The rider made no motion to draw weapon, but suddenly there was a blade in its right hand, and the long, narrow length of keen steel was descending upon Conan almost before the startled Cimmerian could react.

Conan sidestepped the whistling blade, and it but sheared away a piece of wolfskin from the shoulder of his tunic. Reflexively Conan swung a backhand blow against the side of the beast, seeking to chop off one of the rider's legs. The blade rang hollowly against armor, and Conan darted a few paces away. Not only had he failed to cripple the rider, there had been nothing beneath his sword that even *felt* like a leg.

Mightily puzzled, Conan awaited the thing's next move. He seldom fought defensively, but he knew that it would be unwise to carry the fight to the enemy until he had some slight knowledge of that enemy's strengths and weaknesses.

The thing charged again, the rider leaning forward along the neck of the mount, blade at full extension to skewer Conan like a bird on a cooking spit. This time Conan was ready for its instantaneous charge, and he dodged to the left, planting his feet for a powerful blow to the rider's left side. He barely began to bring his sword from behind his shoulder when suddenly a four-foot blade appeared in the rider's left hand, coming down to split Conan's skull. Desperately Conan stopped his blade in midswing and turned the chop into a block, interposing his sword at an angle sufficient to deflect his enemy's steel from his head, but receiving a painful cut on his left shoulder.

"Crom!" Conan shouted as he darted away once more. "Where did that blade come from?" He ran to where Rerin and Alcuina seemed to be finished with their rites. "How much longer?" he growled.

"Just a few more moments," Rerin said. "The spell is finished, but its effect requires some small time."

"Try to speed it up," Conan urged. "This thing fights like nothing I've ever encountered."

Then the thing was charging again, and Conan ran to meet it. He knew that it was not human and flight might be more sensible than battle, but he was duty-bound to keep this hunter away from his queen while he had breath and blood. It charged with arms spread wide, the great blades glistening to either side, ready to strike. Conan halted and braced himself, sword slanting back over his right shoulder. If he could not dodge to the side, then he would split the mount's skull. He had never encountered armor that would not split when he struck with his full force.

When the hunter was no more than ten paces away, a yard-long horn sprang from the frontlet between the mount's eyes, and it began to rotate, transforming the jagged, saw-toothed steel into a silver blur. Conan stooped, picked up a heavy rock, and cast it at the rider. It struck full across the vision-slots, and for an instant the mount broke stride and the blades wavered. Conan dove forward into a tumble as the spinning "horn" was within a handsbreadth of his chest. He sprang to his feet at the rider's side and hewed at his shoulder joint. The rider wavered slightly, but the blade made little impression on the steel armor.

As the rider went by, Conan grasped his cloak and

hauled back, hoping to unseat him. The heavy cloth ripped loose from its fastenings, and for the first time Conan got a clear look at what he was fighting. The smooth helm surmounted a series of flexible neck-rings. Similar rings covered shoulders and arms. A series of broader, interlocking bands covered chest and midsection, and a complicated joint covered the place where the human torso was merged with the horse-body. The mount was likewise made up of steel bands and plates. Not man and beast, this, but a single creature. So far his weapons had not left so much as a mark on it.

As it prepared for another charge, Conan sought for any kind of weakness in the thing. Its armor joints seemed to be tight enough to repel a needle, but there had to be some access to its vulnerable innards. The only possibility Conan could imagine was the vision-slots. There might not be eyes behind them, but he was willing to wager that they would be less impervious than the steel encasing the hunter.

As it came toward him Conan readied himself. He had a sense of its timing now, and he sidestepped the horn and ducked the right-hand sword as it came whistling down. He grasped the hunter around the waist and swung himself up behind it, dropping his sword and drawing his dagger as he did so.

He was about to embrace the thing closely and seek its eyeslots with his dagger point when a row of viciously-edged blades erected itself along the thing's spine. Instantly Conan tumbled over the crupper of the horse part, and not a second too soon, for a similar row of blades, but much longer, shot up from the spot where he had been sitting. He snatched up his sword and wondered when this nightmare would end. He hated the feeling of helplessness.

"Come!" shouted Rerin. "The gate opens!"

Conan ran for it. In the midst of the stone gateway, the air flickered and boiled with movement and color. Alcuina was urging him onward, and he did not dare to spare an instant's glance to see how close the hunter followed. He ran up the mound and shoved Rerin and Alcuina through, then he whirled to face the hunter. He could not leave their vulnerable backs exposed to the thing.

It was bearing down upon them swiftly, but there was still enough distance for him to stride a few paces backward, beneath the lintel.

First there was a whirling disorientation, then a sense of cold, and he realized that he was standing in ankle-deep snow. The air was chill and blessedly thin. He continued to back away from the gate, and he was aware that they were surrounded by people. He risked a quick glance around and saw that they were on the field of Giants' Stones, surrounded by Alcuina's men, and more people were coming across the field from the garth.

"Back!" Conan shouted. "Away from the gate!"

There was a collective shout of awe and terror as the hunter burst from the gate. For a moment it stood, seemingly disoriented. Slowly its head turned, as if searching out its prey from among this mass of mortal flesh. Desperately Conan scanned the crowd as well. Then he saw the weapon he wanted. A man stood by with a twelve-foot spear, the kind used by footmen against mounted men.

"Reccared!" Conan called. "Give me your spear!"

Not taking his boggling eyes from the hunter, the man tossed the spear to Conan. With the weapon in his hands Conan quickly examined the point; it was long and narrow, just what he needed.

The hunter had turned its head at the sound of Conan's voice, and now it dug its steel hooves into the snow for a charge. This time wide, curving steel blades sprang from the flanks of the horse-body and a pair of barbed spears shot forth from the chest between the forelegs. Its movements did not seem to be quite so swift or sure as before.

There was an awed sigh from the encircling crowd as the seemingly unstoppable monster bore down upon the relatively small form of Conan. How could mere flesh and blood stand up to such a terrible machine? They looked for him to be minced upon the instant.

Conan stood fast, gripping the spearshaft. He would have one try, then he would be victorious or dead. He made sure that the spear-blade was turned flat. The eyeslots were narrow, and a vertical blade would jam without penetrating.

In the very moment when the hunter came within range, Conan thrust. Unerringly the blade went into the left eyeslot, crunching through something, then the forward momentum of the hunter thrust Conan backward. He tightened his grip on the spearshaft, although an unearthly tingle shot through it. It would do him little good to slay the thing only to fall beneath its toppling, razor-edged bulk.

Sparks and smoke shot from the damaged eyeslot, and a strange odor filled the air, as when lightning strikes near. The hunter reeled and thrashed wildly, swinging Conan on the end of the shaft like a boy swishing a wand, but the strong ash held. Abruptly a great gout of blue flame shot from the eyeslot and smoke burst from the armor joints. The rider sagged while the horse stood and trembled, then was still.

Conan loosed his stiffening grip. The form of his opponent stood unmoving, as if its glittering metal were frozen. The thing was dead, if it had ever been truly alive.

"What was it?" asked Alcuina wonderingly. She had come from somewhere to stand beside him. The others were closing around as well.

"We saw the lights coming from the stones, my lady," said Siggeir. "We came to see if it was you and the wizard returning to us. Come back to the garth now. We are all in danger here in the open."

"Danger?" Alcuina said. With the passing of the hunter, she could not imagine anything representing a danger.

"Our enemies are on the march," Siggeir insisted. "Let us get behind the walls, where we can meet them on equal terms."

"Look!" said someone.

They all looked at the metal hunter. Red rust was spreading across it with unearthly speed, and it began to groan and creak from inside. An arm fell off, then the horse-legs gave way, and the thing came crashing down. It split open, and out poured a spill of gears, levers, wheels, and other things no one there could put a name to. These, too, began to rust or crumble.

"This was not its place," commented Rerin.

"I rejoice to see you safe, my lady." They looked up from the pile of rust to see a handsome young man with yellow hair and beard. "I am Leovigild, nephew of King Odoac of the Thungians."

Alcuina glared at him, but her interest was obvious.

"Has my garth been taken by enemies that Odoac's heir sits among my men?"

"I am his heir no more," the youth assured her. "And I swear that I am not your enemy. Come, let us return to the garth, where you may find more suitable raiment, and where we may discuss these matters fully and in comfort."

Nodding regally to the young man, Alcuina set out for the garth. The others fell in behind. Last of all was Conan, feeling a little put out that the glory of his recent monster-slaying had been eclipsed by these new political developments. Rerin came up to him and surveyed the remains of the hunter, now little more than a pile of reddish powder. "Come, Conan. There will be warmth and food inside. If you wished eternal glory, you should have arranged for a bard to stand by during your battle."

"Does she hold my services so cheap?" Conan demanded. "That downy lad will need a few years before he's any kind of warrior."

"Warriors come and go," Rerin reasoned as they walked, "but Alcuina is a queen, and has the welfare of her people to think about. Actually, I had discussed with her the possibility of selecting you for her consort—"

"Hah!" Conan broke in. "I'll be on the first ship heading south come spring. If I want a kingdom, I'll conquer it, by Crom! I'll not marry one."

"It may be just as well, then. He is of royal blood, as is she. Between them, they may save their peoples."

Twelve

Blood on the Snows

Conan sat brooding into his ale cup as the queen of the Cambres and the exiled heir of the Thungians held counsel. Much as he hated to admit it, the boy spoke wisely and forthrightly, if somewhat too cautiously for Conan's taste. He noticed that Alcuina's men regarded the Thungian with respect, something he would not have expected from people as clannish as this. Of course, royalty was never treated in quite the same fashion as the lower classes. Kings and queens virtually had to wed with foreigners, lest the stock grow degenerate.

"Alcuina, we face two enemies," Leovigild explained. "First, the Thungians, led by my uncle. Second, and far more dangerous, Totila and the Tormanna. Odoac is a murderer and grown a bit crazy in his old age, but Totila is a great warrior in his prime, and he has not allowed his men to grow soft through inaction. The Cambres are not numerous. You might hold off either one of your enemies here within your stone wall, but not both."

"Need it come to that?" asked Siggeir. "Perhaps the Tormanna and the Thungians will fight one another instead of come against us."

"Both kings want a queen," Alcuina pointed out. "They want me. Soon they shall know that I have returned and will move all the more quickly. They will settle with one another after we have been dealt with."

"That is so," Leovigild concurred. "And I think I know how it will happen: Totila will propose to Odoac a temporary alliance. Between them the two armies will attack this place. Once that is accomplished, they will contest between themselves for Alcuina and her lands and people. My uncle, who is a fool as well as a madman, will probably agree.

"Totila did not build a kingdom from nothing by being a fool. Sometime during the fighting he will murder Odoac. The Thungians, without a king and with me exiled or dead, must turn to the only available war-leader: Totila." There were nods and murmurs of admiration for this sagacious reasoning.

"You speak with great wisdom for so young a man," said Rerin. "Now we must make our plans. How may we avert this disaster?"

"Let's march out and meet Odoac," said Siggeir. "He and the Thungians will be easier to deal with than the Tormanna. We can defeat them, then march back to meet the Tormanna from behind our walls."

"Even should we defeat the Thungians," Alcuina said, "we would be severely weakened. In any case Totila might take the garth while the warriors were away."

Conan smiled to himself. Nobody even proposed the solution that to a southern queen would be the most obvious: to agree to marry the weaker of her two enemies, who could then be murdered at leisure, while he slept. In the North a queen would only do such a thing in order to accomplish an extraordinary vengeance. Since Alcuina had nothing personal against either king, she would never even think of it.

"I do not feel competent to advise in matters of tactics," Leovigild said, "as my experience of warfare has been limited. Also, although I am exiled, I cannot take arms against my kin, though I shall be more than happy to do battle with the Tormanna. However, one among us has not been heard from. Queen Alcuina's champion is not only a great warrior, he has served in many armies in far climes. I suspect that he can see possibilities that would not occur to us. Conan, will you give us your counsel?"

Conan wiped his mouth with the back of his hand. In the North a warrior of high standing was as valued for his wise counsel as for his sword arm. This was another matter in which the northern war-bands differed from southern armies. "In open battle we have a slight chance against either enemy, and none at all against both. This we all agree. I know of a way we may seriously weaken both armies before it comes to a battle or a siege. It will take skill and daring. First you must summon all your huntsmen."

"My huntsmen?" Alcuina said. "Why?"

"Because they know this land far better than any warrior. When Odoac and Totila come they will have great, straggling war-bands slogging through the snow. We shall have huntsmen stationed near all the forest roads to inform us of their movements. Instead of a single army we shall divide into many small bands, with every man mounted. Without warning we must strike them on the march, kill a few, then turn and run, to hit them at another point. The minute they band together to make a shield-wall, we return to our camp, to strike one enemy or the other on another day. Even if we only kill a few, they will be more than half defeated before they arrive here. The bravest of warriors lose their edge when they face unfamiliar tactics.''

"Who ever heard of such fighting?'' Siggeir said doubtfully.

"It is certain that Odoac and Totila never have,'' Leovigild said. "I think Conan has given us our only chance.''

"We can use this tactic many times against Odoac,'' Conan cautioned, "but only once or perhaps twice against Totila.''

"Why is that?'' Alcuina asked.

"Because of those damned magpies!'' Conan growled. "Totila will soon understand what is happening, and Iilma will have the birds high overhead, searching for us. Who can hide from a flying enemy?''

"We could hide beneath the densest trees until it was time to attack,'' Leovigild suggested.

"They would see our tracks in the snow,'' Conan pointed out.

"I think I could help,'' Rerin said.

"Speak on,'' Alcuina urged him. "We need all the help we can find.''

"I have never been able to fight Iilma or his magpie-familiars,'' the old man admitted. "His wizardry is too powerful for me. However, I have mastered a spell by which, in winter, I can cause a brief but dense snow-fall. Once we are in position in wait for the marching Tormanna, this snowfall will mask us from the birds.''

Conan grinned and took a long swallow of his ale.

"Old man," he said, "you may have won the war for us."

The queen's huntsmen were short, sturdy men for the most part, clad in leather and rough homespun. Most of them were darker than the warrior class, and Conan judged that their people had been native to these parts long before the fair-haired folk had wandered hither. They had charge of the game in the forests and were expected to guide the aristocratic hunters to the best sport. As such, they enjoyed privileges far greater than most commoners and could be expected to be loyal to their queen.

"Some of you," Conan began, "will be detailed to lead the raiding bands to secure camping places. Others will keep track of the two armies heading this way." His breath steamed on the chill air. "Still others will be guiding the thralls who will be bringing fodder for the horses. When you move, keep out of sight, but keep to the ridgelines and other high ground. That way the armies will not see your tracks. They will stick to the low roads where the going is easiest. You'll operate in small bands, with some always keeping watch on the enemy while others come back to report. If they chase you, run. Do not try to fight; that is the task of the warriors. Now go to the warrior Siggeir. He will assign each of you to your tasks."

The huntsmen left, and Conan turned to a far more difficult task: He had no more than a day, or at the most two, to teach these men the rudiments of fighting from horseback. He was grateful that they needed only to learn how to hit and run. He would need months to teach them anything more complicated. Their swords were too short to be wielded effectively from horseback, so he was teaching them to use their spears from the saddle. Armorers were cutting down their shields to make them more wieldy from horseback.

Straw dummies had been set up on posts outside the garth, and the men were riding down on them, stabbing wildly with their spears. They all laughed uproariously every time one of them misjudged his thrust and toppled from his horse.

"This is not sport!" Conan yelled in exasperation. "This is war! Stop thrusting so hard! All that does is unbalance you. You don't need to pin a man to the ground; just thrust a few inches of steel into him. Thrust too deep, and you lose your spear. Sit easy in the saddle, and brace yourself only as you thrust. These are not trained warhorses, and you don't want to confuse them." Another man fell off and there was a gusty roar of laughter. Conan sighed disgustedly.

That evening as the men and the horses trudged exhaustedly back into the garth Alcuina took Conan aside. "Do they have a chance?" she asked bluntly.

"They are improving," he answered judiciously, "and the enemy have never dealt with horseback raiders of any kind. That is a great advantage. We mean to weaken them, not defeat them."

"I suppose that is the most I can hope for, then. Perhaps with you and Rerin and Leovigild we may come through this."

"Will the boy be of that much value?" said Conan, nettled at her obvious attraction to the youth.

She looked back at him coolly. "Of course. When Odoac dies, the Thungians may give their allegiance to him without dishonor. We may then form an alliance with them against the Tormanna."

"And a royal marriage," Conan said, "followed by a merging of the peoples?"

"Of course," she said. "That is how it is done among royal families. If we slay Totila, the Tormanna may elect to ally themselves with us as well. He has no heir."

"So be it then!" Conan barked. He whirled on his heel and stalked away.

"Conan!" she called.

He turned, his anger draining away. Against the hulking stone wall she stood, small but regal. He prepared to endure another royal dressing-down, but when she spoke, her voice was gentle.

"When a queen plans for her future, it must not be as a woman following the desires of her heart, but as a ruler who must do what is best for her people. I would that it were not so." Saying no more, she turned and started back for the hall. Conan stared after.

That night in the hall they feasted well, but Alcuina was careful to ration the ale. They would be riding out before first light to try their first foray against the enemy. Conan hoped to have the morrow for further training in their first encampment before splitting up into raiding parties, but there might not be time. He was glad that he had battle to look forward to. It took his mind away from Alcuina.

The younger men talked nervously of the adventure to come. Win or lose, this fight would be remembered, if only because it would be so unorthodox. The older men were less voluble. Many of them were extremely doubtful of such outlandish tactics. How could men fight properly if they could not feel the ground beneath their feet? At least none of them seemed to be downcast or gloomy. It was nearly impossible for northerners to be cheerless when battle was in the offing.

Conan tore at a joint of veal with his teeth. They were not a trained and drilled army, but he had little liking for armies in any case. He had led far worse men into battle. These were brave and loyal, however unsophisticated their warfare might be. He felt a touch at his shoulder and looked up to see Leovigild standing beside him.

"Conan," the younger man began, "I think you may have been the salvation of our people. Your services will not go unrewarded. When this is over, you could be a great earl, with wide lands, and peasants and thralls to work it. When I come into my inheritance, I shall not be known as an ungrateful king."

Conan grasped Leovigild's arm and hauled the young man down to sit on the bench beside him. He leaned close and spoke slowly and steadily. "Three things, boy . . ." He held up a single, greasy finger. "One, I serve Alcuina, not you. Any rewarding is for her to do, not you. Two"—he placed a second finger beside the first—"never congratulate a man for a victory that is yet unwon. The gods don't like it and have been known to punish such presumption. Three"—the third finger went up beside the other two—"I sail south with the springtime. Land is difficult to take on shipboard in any quantity, so I'll take my reward in gold, if Crom and Ymir grant us the victory."

To Conan's surprise Leovigild grinned broadly at his words. "Truly, the Cimmerians are as grim and gloomy as legend has it. I thank you for words of wisdom. We'll talk of reward later. For now, you are the greatest champion in the Northland, and I am a penniless outcast who rejoices to follow you into battle. Let the victory fall where the gods wish it.''

Conan smiled thinly. Despite all his best efforts, he could not keep from liking the boy. "However it befalls,'' he said, "there will be blood on the snow soon.''

Conan surveyed his little army. They had been granted an extra, precious day to train in their encampment. This had been invaluable, for it gave him a chance to drill them in the art of remaining hidden among the trees, then charging down upon the enemy at a signal. The men had been divided into six squadrons, three to each enemy army. It had taken Conan all day to get them coordinated enough that he could count on the squadrons to strike the head, center, and rear of each enemy army simultaneously. He was not so sure that they would break off engagement as reliably. However, he saw no choice. The best way for a smaller army to engage a larger was to catch the greater force in marching order.

As they dismounted at their campfires to prepare for the night, he felt that they were now as ready as he could make them. It was just as well, because he saw a party of huntsmen coming from the tree line. They ran up to him, and one of them, a tousle-headed youth who carried a boar-spear, reported.

"We've found the Tormanna, lord. When we left, they were eight hours march from here, as slowly as they were walking. They will be bedding down about now, perhaps six hours away.''

"Have they an advance guard out?'' Conan asked.

The youth shook his head. "No. All together, with a

few mounted men at the head of the lot. We saw King Totila. Him we knew by his cloak of men's hair.''

"Good," Conan said. "On the morrow, before first light, you shall lead one of our force to a good place on their route of march for an attack." Within the hour another little band of huntsmen came in to report that the Thungians had been spotted, coming by a more southerly route. If all went well both of Alcuina's forces should spring their first ambush about midday upon the morrow.

It had been agreed that Conan would lead the group to attack the Thungians. Leovigild would lead the attack against the Tormanna. This disturbed Conan because he was certain that Totila and his Tormanna were the more dangerous enemy, and he would have preferred to lead the attack himself. The warriors had insisted, though, that the band not led by the queen's champion must be led by a man of royal blood, and Leovigild would not fight his fellow Thungians. In spite of Conan's reputation those in Leovigild's party counted themselves lucky, for they would have a chance to show their prowess and loyalty before the man who was likely to be their next king.

They arose before the tardy winter sun and readied themselves. Before parting, Conan took Siggeir to one side. The man was to ride beside Leovigild as his second in command, charged with giving the signal to attack. "Siggeir, do not let Leovigild try to fight Totila himself. From what I've heard of that man, it would be death for an untried lad to challenge him."

Siggeir was silent for a moment. "I shall do my best, and advise against it, but how may any man keep a spirited youth from snatching all the glory he can? He'll be wanting to show Alcuina he's brave as well as wise.''

Conan clapped him on the shoulder. ''Just do what you can. In the end he must face the same dangers as the rest of us, I suppose.'' Conan turned to his following. ''Mount up! We ride now!'' He swung into the saddle of his little, northern stallion and faced Leovigild. He raised an arm. ''Good hunting, prince!''

Leovigild returned the salute. ''We'll meet again, warrior. In Alcuina's hall or Ymir's!''

There was a brief thunder of hooves, a flurry of churned-up snow, and the two bands split up, one to the west, the other to the south.

Conan stood beside his horse, holding the cloth that covered its eyes. He and his men were well within the cover of the trees, but with a good view of the road below. The Thungians were coming, and they were already well past the first two squadrons. Conan's own force would strike the head of the column. His hand gripped the sword at his waist.

He had scoured Alcuina's armory to find one long enough to use from horseback. At length he found one, Aquilonian by the look of it. It had probably been a gift from one chief to another in years gone by. It might never have been used, since it was unsuited to the local style of combat.

Conan judged that the Thungians were close enough. ''Mount,'' he said in a quiet voice.

The men stripped the covers from their horses' heads and hooves. They all wore wide grins of anticipation. They readied their spears, and Conan's sword rasped from its sheath. He nodded to Hagbard, who sat his horse beside Conan. The man raised a hunting-horn to his lips and winded a long, loud blast. With a shout they spurred their mounts down the long slope.

The men below looked up in amazement at the little band of horsemen who bore down upon them. Surely this could not be an attack. Why were the men mounted? Why did they not get off their horses if they wanted to fight? Where were the customary boasts and taunts that always preceded combat? Then they had no more leisure for speculation as the horsemen collided with them.

Conan leaned far out and swung his blade down over the edge of a shield. The man he faced was unused to such blows and failed to raise his shield high enough. The steel sword opened a gap in his bronze helm, and he fell with blood pouring from the rent metal. Conan glanced about and saw that his men were making a good account of themselves, thrusting their spears over the shields of the foe. A few had given in to the temptation to cast their spears, something he had specifically forbidden them to do, and now had nothing to fight with except their swords.

A man thrust at Conan with a spear, and he flicked the shaft aside before chopping into the man's shoulder. The man fell, cursing, and Conan noticed a tight knot of men who surrounded a fat, gray-bearded man in fine armor. This must be Odoac and his household warriors. Conan tried to force a way to him, but his horse was unused to the clamor of war and would go no farther.

"Hagbard!" Conan called. "Sound your horn!"

Hagbard broke away from his fight and raised the horn. At the signal, most of the men drew away from the battle and rode up to the trees. Conan waited for a moment to see how well they were obeying the signal. As he had feared, several were fighting on in a berserk fury. Quickly, those were overpowered and slain. He even saw one leap from the back of his horse onto an enemy and grapple on the ground briefly before being cut to pieces.

Amid the trees the horsemen regrouped. Conan made a quick count and found that they had lost ten men. He had expected to lose more. Henceforth, their losses should be fewer because now the berserks and the fools were dead.

"Shall we try them again, Conan?" called a man who had blood running from beneath the rim of his helm.

"Not today," Conan answered. "It is too late for another sally, and the horses are too excited. We'll find a good camp and hit them early tomorrow, then once or twice more before nightfall."

That night the men sat around their campfires talking happily among themselves, as if they had won a great victory instead of a trifling raid against their enemy, with no more than a score of the foe slain or wounded. Conan smiled grimly. They would not be so exuberant by the next night. By then they would have learned that this kind of fighting was long, hard, dangerous work with little glory in it.

"What do you think, Conan?" asked Hagbard. "Did we not do well today?"

"Aye," Conan said. "Most of the men performed better than I had hoped."

Hagbard grinned. "The Thungians huddled like sheep. They will be no stop to us."

"Today they were surprised. Tomorrow morning they will be a little less so. After that it is only a matter of time until they find out how to fight us and how easy it is for men behind a shield-wall to deal with horsemen, especially when they are not mounted on trained animals.''

"Is it so easy?" asked Hagbard, crestfallen.

Conan gave a curt nod. "Today, out of habit, they struck at the riders. Soon they will realize that it is much easier to kill the horses. When we see spearmen lunging for the mounts while others engage the riders, we'll know that it is time to ride for the garth.''

Totila cursed the dense flurry of snow that had begun to fall. The horsemen had struck them twice the day before, and once this day. The magpies flew close by his head to perch upon Iilma's shoulders.

"Saw they anything?" Totila demanded.

"No, my king," Iilma answered. "The snow is too dense." He hesitated. "I feel some wizardry in this snow. It is not of natural origin.''

Totila spent a brief moment in thought. After the first strike the day before, the horsemen had attacked in the midst of snows such as this.

"Band together!" he shouted. "Form a shield-wall here! They'll be back soon!"

The column of marching men closed up quickly and stood shield-to-shield. They were grim and impatient for combat. The will-o'-the-wisp horsemen had struck and run without giving them any target for their wrath. This time the king was getting them ready to fight before seeing or hearing the hated horsemen. They waited in tense silence.

Leovigild waited nervously at the edge of the trees. They could hear the marching men below, but they could not see them. He had not thought of this when the old wizard had suggested this plan of action. The snow blinded the birds, but it blinded the horsemen as well. He turned to Rerin.

"I do not like this. We had an advantage when we could see them. Perhaps this was not so good an idea."

"It was the only hope," Rerin told him. "And it did give us two undetected ambushes." He looked around him at the falling snow. "You had best make your move. The snow will thin soon."

"They've stopped," said Siggeir, who sat his mount at Leovigild's side.

Leovigild thought on this for a moment. "Totila is no fool. We hit him twice in the snow. Now he expects us to strike while it is snowing." He came to a swift decision. "Siggeir, ride quickly and bring the other two squadrons here. If they are no longer strung out in line of march, it will be useless to strike them in three small groups. Best to pick one spot on the shield-wall and throw all our force against it."

"That was not Conan's instruction," said Rerin doubtfully.

"Conan is not here," said Leovigild. "I am."

"Stick to your spells, Rerin," Siggeir advised. "Leave battle to the warriors." He wheeled his horse and was off. The many dents and nicks in Leovigild's armor testified to his willingness to get into the thick of the fight. That was enough for the Cambres.

"Do not worry," Leovigild assured Rerin with a smile, "I think this is the course Conan would have advised had he been here."

Before the snow had begun to thin, the rest of the men had ridden up to form a group around Leovigild. "We'll find them in a shield-wall down there," he called out. "This time we must not split up, but strike as a single force against one part of the wall. Those we do not engage can do nothing but watch. Do not try to seek out a champion to fight, but help your comrades to break the wall. We can hurt them sorely that way. When I order the horn sounded, break off and rally in the trees."

"Where do we hit them?" asked Siggeir.

"Where Totila stands," Leovigild answered. "You have all seen him by now. Follow me. When I see him, I'll ride for him. If we can slay Totila, the war may be won at a stroke. Now, let's ride!" With a ferocious roar, the men charged off after Leovigild, leaving Rerin to wait worriedly.

"Here they come!" Totila shouted, grinning between the cheekplates of his helm. He drew his sword. "Let's see how well they fight against men who are prepared!" His men shouted their approval.

The horsemen turned when they were within spear-range and began to ride along the face of the shield-wall. Totila knew they were looking for him, and he made no effort to hide himself. His helm and cloak were famed throughout the Northland, and he was anxious to try their best men.

In the van of the attackers was a handsome, fair-haired young man he had marked before for his bravery. He had little doubt that this was young Leovigild, cast out by Odoac. He wondered where the black-haired champion might be. He longed to test himself against that man. On the other hand, killing Odoac's heir would be a fine political move.

Leovigild saw Totila standing in the forefront. This was no man to huddle in the midst of his housecarls like Odoac. The sight of Totila standing there so fearlessly caused Leovigild to forget the wise advice of Conan,

Rerin, and Siggier. He pointed with his spear and charged straight at Totila. Just before he collided with the shield-wall, he heard Totila shout to his men: "Hold your places and thrust at the horses! They are helpless without them!"

Then he was within spear-thrust of the man with the splendid helm and the cloak of men's hair. He thrust strongly, but Totila cut away his spear point with contemptuous ease. Had he followed Conan's advice Leovigild would have withdrawn to let another spearman have a chance at Totila. Instead he drew his sword and cut at the magnificent helm. Totila blocked easily with his shield. Leovigild could only reach out with the tip of his sword. In frustration, he leaped to the ground and attacked Totila shield-to-shield. With a fierce grin, Totila met him savagely. His blows rained down so swiftly that Leovigild barely had time to ward them, much less to send blows back in reply.

In desperation, Leovigild cut low at Totila's knee. With an agility that was amazing in so large a man, Totila leaped over the cut, leaving Leovigild bent far over with the follow-through of his blow, his shield lowered. Totila's first blow smashed against the younger man's helmet. His second split the tough bronze of his cuirass.

Totila was preparing the deathblow when a pack of Cambres rode up, pushing him back with their spears. The biggest of them leaned from his saddle, grabbed the youth by the collar of his backplate, and hauled him across the saddle. Then Leovigild's rescuer set a hunting-horn to his lips and sounded it. With a flurry of churned-up snow, the horsemen rode off.

Totila accepted the praise of his men for his fight with the youth. Then he surveyed the enemy dead.

There were at least a dozen. "How many did we lose?" he called.

"About half a score," said a grizzled warrior who was binding up a cut arm.

"No advantage to them, then," Totila said triumphantly. "So, when it is clear, Iilma's birds will tell us they are coming. When it is too snowy for the birds to fly, we will know that they are coming! We've nothing to fear from them, so let's march to Alcuina's garth and finish this matter!" With a shout of joy, the Tormanna followed their king.

Conan and his men were encamped on their homeward ride when the rest of the Cambres caught up to them. A huntsman came running up to Conan's fire to give him the news, and the Cimmerian stood to receive them. He knew that the news was not good when he saw the inert form across Siggeir's saddle. He helped the lad down and saw the wounds on head and chest. His practiced eye told him that the boy had taken these wounds while on his feet facing a bigger man.

Conan looked at Siggeir and Rerin. "Totila?" he asked.

Siggeir nodded. He reported to Conan on the day's doings while Rerin got out his herbs and began tending to the young man's wounds. Conan shook his head when the recitation was done.

"To mass for an attack against a shield-wall was a wise move," Conan said. "But to dismount to fight—especially against a man like Totila—that was foolish."

"What would you have a man of good blood do?" demanded Siggeir. "He saw Totila standing there before his men like a true king. Could he in honor do less than meet Totila on even terms?"

The other Cambres nodded and agreed. They wanted a warrior king and if Leovigild was willing to risk certain death to live up to their ideal of such a man, they honored him for it.

Conan smiled at their grim faces. "Northerners. What headstrong fools you all are. Well, I am a northerner, too." He looked down at Leovigild's recumbent form. "He'll make you a good king, if he lives."

Rerin looked up at them. "His wounds are grave, but I can heal them if we can get him back to the garth. In my hut I can do far more for him than I can here."

Conan summoned a party of the huntsmen and ordered them to fashion a litter. "They can carry him through these woods far faster than a horse-drawn litter," he told Rerin. "The rest of us will ride after, staying between you and the enemy."

"How fared you against Odoac?" Siggeir asked.

"We killed many," Conan told him. "We struck them five times before they took to making a shield-wall and trying to spear the horses. But Odoac stayed in the midst of his men; we had no chance to kill him."

"That is unfortunate," Siggeir said. "Perhaps we've whittled them down enough to make a good fight of it when it comes to the siege."

Conan nodded, but held his counsel.

Alcuina saw the man being carried on the litter, and her heart sank. Since the men had ridden to war, she had spent most of every day here on the wall above the gate, waiting for word of what was happening out in the forest. Her greatest fear was that they would bring Conan or Leovigild back dead. She knew that she needed both of them if her people were to survive, and she was sure that this was one of them now. If it was, which did she want it to be? She pushed that question aside as she ordered the gate to be opened and ran out to meet the little party.

She released a long sigh when she saw that it was Leovigild's pale face above a mass of bandages. She felt a great relief, and she was not certain if it was because it was not Conan, or because Leovigild was not dead.

"We must get him to my hut," Rerin said from the back of his horse.

Alcuina gave orders to the thralls, and Leovigild was carried inside to Rerin's hut, where the old wizard dismounted stiffly.

"Bring him inside," he ordered curtly. While Rerin tended to Leovigild's hurts, he reported to Alcuina. "We were successful," he said when the report was finished. "But I do not think we hurt them as badly as Conan had hoped."

"And now poor Leovigild is out of the fight," she said.

"His value was not as a warrior," Rerin said, "but as a leader. In that he did well. Any who had doubts about the lad lost them when they saw him fighting the Tormanna and taking on Totila man-to-man. They'll fight as fiercely for him now as they would were he fighting in the forefront of them."

"Do you think he would be a good king?"

"An excellent one," Rerin assured her.

She nodded. "Then that is what he shall be."

Conan and the others rode in as the sun was setting. Wearily they dismounted and turned their horses over to the thralls. The wounded went to Rerin's hut for treatment. Alcuina came from the hall and crossed the yard to Conan.

"How many did we lose?" she asked.

"A score, and as many wounded, although few are sorely hurt. We cost them three times that many. Most of the men we lost were in the first assault. In the second and third, our men knew better what they were doing. After that the enemy learned how to defend themselves."

"Was it enough?"

"Perhaps. We shall know soon. At any rate, we're in a better position than we were a few days ago. How is the lad?"

"Speak more respectfully of the future king of the Cambres. Rerin says he will recover, although it shall be many weeks before he is fully fit."

"I rejoice to hear that he will be well and that your tongue has lost none of its edge."

For once, she smiled at him. "It does no good to let a liege man grow too familiar, even a black-haired outlander who craves to head south for the hot climes and the sweet wine. Come, Leovigild has been demanding that you be brought to him as soon as you arrive here."

"Picked up kingly ways already, has he?" Conan pretended to grumble. Indeed, he was happy to know that the boy would live.

They went into the hall, where a huge meal was being prepared for the returning warriors. Behind the arras at the end of the hall they found Leovigild on a bed of bearskins and other furs. His head and chest were heavily swathed in bandages, and his face was pale, but he managed a weak smile of welcome when he saw Conan.

"I fear I did not do well on my first command, champion. I hope you fared better."

"You were a purblind idiot to try to fight Totila," Conan said, earning a venomous glare from Alcuina. "But aside from that you did well. Your men will have no cause to regret that you lead them in battle. You'll have some fine scars to show for it, too."

"Do you think the men hold me the lesser man because I could not defeat Totila?"

"If any say so," Alcuina hissed, "I'll have the hide off their—"

"No," Conan interrupted, "only a fool would expect a young man on his first blade-wetting to slay a man like Totila, no matter how high his blood. You did well, Leovigild, and your hair is not decorating his cloak."

Rerin came in to check on his patient. "You must not tire him. He needs rest."

Conan grinned crookedly. "Physicians are the same everywhere. We'll speak tomorrow, Leovigild. Your shield may guard my right side in any battle." He made to go but turned back at a last word from Leovigild.

"Conan, you must slay Totila. You are the only man in the North who has a chance." His eyes grew haunted. "It was like fighting a mountain."

Conan's face became most grim. "He'll not have my hair either."

After the feast, where each man had had his chance to boast of his feats in the late fighting, Conan sat working a few nicks out of his sword with a whetstone. He looked up to see Rerin standing by his side.

"How goes it, Rerin?"

The old man sat on the bench beside him, shaking his head. "I am most apprehensive. It is three battles we face."

Conan raised his sword and sighted along one edge. "Why three?"

"There will be a battle of armies, and a battle of kings, and a battle of wizards. To survive, we must win all three."

Conan turned the sword over and checked the other edge. "Do you think we will not?"

"My greatest fears are for the wizard-duel. I know my craft, as you have seen, but Iilma has traffic with powers I dare not even contact. They must destroy him in the end, but until he is overwhelmed by the fruits of his ambition, he may wield powers far in excess of any I command."

Conan put the sword back in its sheath and hung it from its peg. "Few things are worse for an army than too much talk of defeat before battle can even be joined. Thus, you are defeated ere you fight. If you have already lost in your own mind, Iilma need do nothing at all."

"That may be true of warriors, but I can make a ready evaluation of my strength and his, using neither optimism nor despair. As of now, he has the upper hand."

"So much for now. The fighting will begin tomorrow or perhaps the next day. How may we arrange matters more to our advantage in the meantime?"

Rerin smiled slightly. "You are not merely the simple warrior you seem."

Conan lifted his horn and swallowed a heavy draught of ale. "When it comes to fighting, I prefer to meet my foe man-to-man and sword-to-sword. Wizardry is different. I have no liking for it, and if I must endure it, I want to have every advantage I can get. Now, what is your suggestion? You did not come here to exchange idle talk.''

"Be sure of it. Do you think that you can defeat Totila?''

Conan shrugged. "I have met no man yet who was my match. That means nothing. Totila is a great warrior, by all accounts. When we meet we shall know which of us is the greater.''

"Odoac is of no account as a man," Rerin said. "How the Thungians fight shall depend upon who kills Odoac first, we or Totila. They will probably join his slayer for lack of a king. The deciding factor must be Iilma, and he is in bad odor with Totila now.''

"How so?'' asked Conan.

"He has failed a number of times, despite all his powers. His walking dead men could not defeat us; his demon-abductors failed to bring him Alcuina; even my poor snowstorms prevented his magpies from helping them on the march. By now he will be desperate to regain favor with Totila. In this desperation we may find his fatal weakness.''

"Say on," urged Conan, intrigued. Wizard and champion talked long into the night.

Thirteen

Demon Birds

A section of the great hall had been curtained off as an infirmary for the men sorely wounded in the late fighting. With the stoicism of the North they made light of their wounds, although they knew that some of them would not live to see the coming of spring. Leovigild was in such pain that even breathing was an agony, but he felt that he was fortunate to be among such men, and did his best to pretend that he was not suffering.

His game of knucklebones with a man who had lost an éye and two fingers was interrupted when an arras stitched with the deeds of a warrior dead two hundred years was pushed aside, admitting a small group of the senior warriors, along with Alcuina, Rerin, and Conan.

"I trust you are on the mend, Leovigild," Alcuina said.

"I have seldom felt better," he said bravely, fooling no one, "and I hope to raise my sword in your cause soon."

Alcuina smiled, and such was her beauty that he

found Atalia slowly vanishing from his memory. Indeed, the fantastic day and night he had spent in the little valley now seemed as insubstantial as a dream, and was fading from his memory as a dream fades upon waking.

"I'll not call upon your sword arm until you are fully fit," Alcuina said. "However, there is a bold plan afoot to weaken Totila somewhat, and I deemed it meet that you should have a part in our counsels."

"I am honored that you so value my counsel, my lady," he said. He managed a weak smile at Conan. "And I warrant that, if there is a bold plan brewing, this great, black-haired rogue is in the midst of it."

Unceremoniously Conan propped a foot on the edge of Leovigild's rude cot and leaned forward, crossing his arms upon his knee. "We grow weary of Totila's tame spell-caster, Iilma. Our good Rerin, here, thinks he knows a good way to strike at him."

"That would be a fine deed," Leovigild said. "But how may a plain warrior deal with one who has dark powers in his hands?"

"Rerin," said Alcuina, "tell Leovigild and these warriors what you told me this evening."

The old man stood forth and stroked his gray beard. "I have now observed much of this man, Iilma, far more than I ever wished. His form of wizardry is something far, far different from my own. I seek to use the properties of the plants, stones, and beasts of our land to aid my queen for the good of us all. I use my spells to gain the help of the gods and spirits of the forest and the streams. These supernatural beings are not hostile to men if they are given the proper respect, and by my spells they may be persuaded to help us by moderating the cold and snows of winter, making the beasts of the forest plentiful to the hunters, and causing the streams to teem with fish for the nets of fishermen. They cause the cattle, sheep, swine, and horses to be fruitful and bear many young. Others of these benevolent spirits help me to stop the onset of pestilence and speed the healing of the injured, such as these warriors, whose honorable wounds have brought them to this place." He waved a hand gracefully to include all the bloodied, bandaged, but uncomplaining men who occupied the cots and the pallets in the straw.

"Iilma, the Hyperborean, is a different breed of wizard." His mien became solemn and baleful. "He does not seek to help men to prosper amid the dangers of nature. He seeks power for himself. He knows, though, that knowledge and skill may gain him only so much. True power over men is wielded by the arms of warriors, and for this reason he has attached himself to a king—a rising battle chief—who must give Iilma much of the credit for his ascent to power.

"For such power as this wizard wishes to control, the small gods and spirits are of little use. Some time, long ago, Iilma struck a dreadful bargain. He trafficked with the great powers of the worlds beyond ours. Until recently these were worlds I had only glimpsed in trance state. The beings of these worlds can grant great puissance to a mortal man, but at a terrible price. His mind, his very soul, are forever changed. When such a dark bargain is struck, there is an exchange. The wizard of this world gives some part of himself, some crucial part of his soul that is forever accursed. In return he receives one or more spirit helpers, familiars that greatly expand his powers and act as go-betweens in his dealings with the other worlds."

"The magpies!" Leovigild said.

"Exactly," said Rerin solemnly. "Of course, they are not true magpies. They are demons of another world, but they could not maintain their true form in this world, nor would they want to, for one of the tasks of such familiars is to spy and bring knowledge back to their master, and it is best for them not to attract attention. In all the lore I have studied, birds or bats have been the favored forms that familiars take. This gives them wide-ranging powers, all the great sky as their field so that they can bring back to their master whatever he needs to know. Of all birds, the scavenger birds such as magpies, crows, and ravens are most favored, for whoever takes notice of them? A hawk or eagle always draws attention. A wren or sparrow looks out of place in certain areas, and owls are not seen in the day. But the scavengers are everywhere."

Conan broke into the lengthy recitation. "Tonight, I go on a magpie hunt."

"If Iilma is deprived of his familiars," Rerin said, "he must lose much of his power."

"I hold," Alcuina said, "that Conan should take other warriors with him. It is not meet that one man should venture into such peril alone."

"Some of us are willing to go with him," said Siggeir. But there was a hesitation in his voice that said that his heart would not be in such a venture.

"Nay," said Conan, "if it were a fight with men, the more the better, but I go against two birds and a wizard. There is no advantage in numbers in such a fight. Besides, it will be done at night, and none here except me have any skill at night fighting."

"We fought the liches at night," Siggeir said, "although it is true that we built up fires so we could see to ply our weapons. What manner of men choose to fight at night, when one cannot tell friend from foe, and no one can witness the deeds of the valiant?''

"Picts," said Conan with a grim smile.

"Picts?" Leovigild said. "Who are they?"

"They are a folk who love to fight at all hours," said the Cimmerian. "And they have a rare skill at night-battle. There are others who are good in the dark—Afghulis, Himelian hillmen, the pygmies of southern Kush—but the Picts are the best. I have fought them and lived among them."

"It is no manner for men to fight," said Siggeir haughtily.

"Nonetheless," Alcuina said quietly, "someone must carry out this task, and it is Conan who has this skill. And if it is to be done, my champion is the one who deserves that honor."

"I wish you well, Conan," Leovigild said. "If any can defeat Iilma's familiars, it must be you."

The sliver of a crescent moon was rising over the hills to the east when Conan betook himself to the walk atop the palisade. The small band gathered atop the wall stared in wonder at the Cimmerian's bizarre appearance. He was dressed all in black wolfskins, and he had blackened his face and arms with a mixture of wax and soot. The buckles and metal fittings on his swordbelt had been wrapped in dark cloth to hide them and to muffle any sound they might make. A strip of leather about his brow held his shoulder-length hair in place.

"It is time," he said.

"Father Ymir watch over you," Rerin said.

Conan grinned without mirth. "Crom is my god. It is said that he and Ymir are not on the best of terms. When the fighting begins, I trust to my sword arm."

"The huntsmen say they are not far," said Alcuina, with her sure grasp of practicalities, "but moving slowly, as you predicted. Good fortune, Cimmerian, but use caution. This is but a sally to weaken Iilma. The true battle is yet to come, and I shall have need of your services at that time."

"Fear not, Alcuina," said Conan, "I'll not deprive you of my services untimely." He sprang to the top of the palisade, hesitated for a moment, then leaped outward, ignoring the rope that had been hung from a post. There was always a possibility that Totila had sent a scout to watch the gate, so it had been decided that Conan should leave from the opposite wall.

He landed lightly, taking the shock on bent knees, with the assurance of perfect balance. The faint moonlight transformed the snow-covered field into a mantle of cloth of silver. In the distance, he could barely discern the standing stones.

The huntsmen had said that Totila's force was coming through the eastern uplands. Conan set off in that direction, traveling at a mile-eating trot that he could maintain all night. Within minutes he was in the forest, and he moved amid the pines with as much assurance as he had upon the plain, his eyes as keen as an owl's in the dimness.

At the end of four hours Conan was still not breathing heavily. He slowed, knowing that Totila's force could not be far. It was the smell of smoke on the still air that told him he was near his destination. The smell of smoke led him toward the glow of banked fires in the distance.

A rough count of the fires gave him an estimate of the enemy's strength. The war-band was larger than he had anticipated. Totila must be a man of force and ability to have mobilized so many men in the depths of winter.

Conan scouted the periphery of the camp, probing for weak points and the location of the leaders. As he had anticipated, there were no sentries posted. A hardened robber-band such as Totila's would consider such precautions to be weak and effeminate. After a full circuit, he had seen no tent or bower set up within the camp. Apparently Totila slept upon the ground, wrapped in his cloak the same as his warriors. He led by example. That was another thing to remember.

This night, though, Conan's quarry was not Totila. The wizard Iilma would be somewhere close by, and Conan would wager that the wizard was not sleeping in his cloak like a common warrior. The air was nearly still, but there was the faintest of breezes apparent to the Cimmerian's sharp senses. He crept a short distance downwind and sat with his back to a tree, his eyes closed and, to any casual observer, asleep. He was not asleep. He was sorting through sense-impressions with the concentration and attention to detail of a Zamoran inquisitor.

There were few sounds to study, but the smell of smoke lay heavy in the air. Most came from the low-burning embers of the warriors' fires, and it had the sharp tang of common pine wood. Soon, though, he sorted another smell. It was smoke, but not that of pine alone. This smoke had other smells he did not recognize, possibly herbs and bark. It was for this that he had been searching.

Conan rose and began to follow the scent-trail. It led him upwind of the camp, into a small fold between two low hills. Now he could hear sounds as well, strange rattlings and croakings. He spied a large clump of brush on one slope and made his way toward it. Dropping to his belly, he crawled the rest of the way beneath the overhanging bushes. A few minutes of this slow progress brought him to the source of the sounds and the strange smoke.

In the narrow fold between the hills was a tent of reindeer hides, and before it sat a man clad in identical skins, with the horns of that beast crowning his headdress. He was chanting softly, shaking a rattle in odd patterns over a tiny fire, which burned in a multitude of unnatural colors. Conan searched for the source of the clacking and croaking sounds and soon found it.

A few paces from the fire stood the magpies. In the past he had spied them flying high above Alcuina's garth. Then they had behaved like ordinary birds. Now their actions sent a chill of fascinated horror through the Cimmerian. They were croaking and making other, less nameable sounds in time with Iilma's chant, and their heads bobbed rhythmically. Occasionally they stepped to right or left, as if in some primitive dance. Most uncannily they moved in perfect lockstep, as if both were controlled by a single will.

What hellish wizard-craft was the Hyperborean brewing now? It would be some devilment to strengthen Totila's hand, or to undermine Alcuina's position. Perhaps even an attempt upon his own life. It was a temptation simply to dash into the clearing and cut the wizard down in midspell. Rerin had warned him against any such foolhardy act. Iilma, he had said, was a

sorcerer who dealt with dark forces and would as-
suredly have provided elementary safeguards for his
own security. A wizard had trouble enough protecting
himself from the demons he manipulated without having to worry about mere mortal men striking them
down. They were at their most vulnerable when in the
midst of spell-casting, a task that demanded all their
concentration. Like other men, they were vulnerable
when asleep. Vulnerable did not mean defenseless. His
speculations ceased as he saw a dim, insubstantial form
appear above the fire. What might this be?

As Iilma chanted and the birds croaked, the figure
gained apparent solidity, although it remained suspended
over the colored flames as if it had no weight. It had the
appearance of a man. The face was indistinct, but it
looked to be a young man, with long, yellow hair. It
looked, Conan thought, almost like Leovigild. Was the
wizard spying upon the youth? That could not be, for
this phantom was unbandaged and was dressed in the
type of clothes worn for hunting or fighting.

Abruptly Iilma's chant broke off, and he waved his
hands in a gesture of dismissal. The wraith faded out,
and the fire ceased to burn in unnatural colors. As the
flames reverted to normal hues, Iilma said something to
the birds. Conan did not recognize the language, but he
heard the note of triumph in the words. Shrewdly, the
Cimmerian guessed that the wizard was testing some
spell that he would use at a later time, and now he was
confident of his mastery. The magpies bobbed their
heads as if in agreement.

Conan's blood chilled as one of the birds turned, its
eyes burning brighter than the embers of the fire. Its
stare was directed straight toward him. In an instant

both birds and the mage were glaring toward him, as if their eyes could penetrate the intervening brush and gloom.

"Who dares to spy upon my rites?" hissed out the wizard.

Without hesitation Conan sprang to his feet and strode into the clearing before the hut. His sword slid from its sheath in a blurring motion, and the sorcerer flinched back, his hands beginning an arcane gesture.

But Conan's blade was not aimed at the Hyperborean. Instead it flashed in the firelight as a blur before striking one of the magpies. The Cimmerian had expected the bird to turn instantly to a mass of blood and feathers, but he was shocked at the solid impact that shook his arm from palm to shoulder. It was as if he had squarely struck some far larger creature.

He wrenched the sword back and whirled a cut at the other bird, but the creature had darted back and was beginning to transform itself into something other than an earthly being. The Cimmerian watched in dread as Iilma began a rapid chant and the feathered wings grew. Feathers became glittering scales as the wings grew leathery. The legs lengthened as well, becoming a perversion of human limbs but retaining birdlike feet with bronze talons tipping the hooked toes.

Conan knew that he was seeing the creature's true form now; a hideous combination of man, bird, and reptile, standing a head taller than himself, with a gaping, fanged beak from which a black, serpentlike tongue lolled and writhed and seemed to have a life of its own. Only the burning, hate-filled eyes were the same, freezing Conan with a basilisk stare as it reached for him with the claw-tipped upper joints of its wings.

The action shook Conan from his brief paralysis, and he leaped to the attack. Darting between the outstretched claws, he hewed at the shoulder-joint of the left wing. Rerin had said that these creatures, if they were to live in the world of men, must obey certain basic laws of that world. This meant that they could be injured and killed. The sword struck with a meaty crunch and foul-smelling fluid splattered Conan. He wrenched the blade free and struck like lightning at the opposite shoulder. Unexpectedly he was struck a vicious blow across the face just as his sword sliced into the unnaturally tough flesh. He staggered back, dazed and unaware from where the blow had come. Then he saw the thick tongue lashing back and forth, stained with his own blood.

The demon-bird wailed continuously in an ear-shredding shriek, its wings sagging on their injured shoulders while Iilma kept up a demented chanting. Abruptly the creature sprang toward Conan, its taloned feet outstretched like those of a falcon stooping upon a victim. Conan thrust at the thing's belly and felt the blade sink in as claws struck his chest and bore him backward to the ground. The wide-spread toes tightened, and he felt talons begin to sink into his shoulders and back as he pushed and twisted his sword, now buried deep in the beast's entrails.

The demon-bird leaned forward; its beak gaped wide as the snake-tongue lashed forth. A numbing impact struck Conan's shoulder, and there was a sizzling sound accompanied by a sickening stench of burning hair. The tongue drew back and poised over Conan's face. It was tipped with a circular mouth, rimmed with tiny, jagged teeth, and oozing a foul fluid. He knew

that only his heavy furs had saved him. For that mouth
to touch his flesh would be death.

Desperately Conan wrenched his sword from the
thing's belly. His shoulders were too constricted to
swing the weapon effectively. As the gaping beak
came forward, he jammed the blade between those
jaws, turned so that the double edges were against
upper and lower beak. Instinctively the demon-bird bit
down. The keen edge of the sword sheared through the
deadly tongue and the obscene member fell away to
writhe upon the ground.

The demon-bird's grip upon Conan loosened as it
shrieked out its agony. The Cimmerian wrenched himself free and scrambled away from the thing as it writhed
on the ground, its ''blood'' pumping from its mouth.
Gradually the thing began to lose its shape as its strength
faded, melting into graying slime that liquified and was
drunk by the earth.

Then Conan was struck a heavy blow from behind.
Instead of sprawling, he rolled as he hit the ground,
springing up to face the direction from which the blow
had come, sword outstretched to meet the new danger.

The other demon-bird! In his desperate fight he had
forgotten the other. It was severely injured, its transformation incomplete. Its right side was cloven, and the
dangling right wing still bore the glossy plumage of the
earthly bird. It hissed and lurched to the attack.

Conan felt weakened from his ordeal and did not
want to contest with the thing's powerful talons and
deadly serpent-tongue. As he backed away he heard the
continuing chant of the Hyperborean. Holding the creature at a distance with the point of his sword, he risked
a glance at the wizard, who stood a few paces behind

him, his eyes shut in concentration as he wove his spell.

Conan continued to back away, his steps taking him toward Iilma. When he judged his distance to be right, he whirled and struck out at the mage, continuing the movement into a full spin that ended with him facing the demon-bird again. The move was too swift for the thing to take advantage of his momentarily turned back.

The desperate blow had not severely injured the mage. The distance had been too great, so that only the tip of the blade gouged a superficial cut across the wizard's cheek. But his concentration was broken. The chant faltered as the wizard's eyes widened in amazement, and his hand went to his injured cheek.

As the chant slowed and stopped, the demon-bird sagged in weakness. This was all the advantage Conan needed. Instantly he dashed in, hacking at the thing with swift, powerful blows, which it was now too weak to avoid. He hewed at neck, shoulders, and legs as the beast squalled and began to collapse. As it fell forward he dived out of its way, and then he was on his feet again, slashing at its spine. He continued to rain blows upon the creature until it was a quivering mass of not-flesh that was beginning to change color.

Then he stepped back and looked for Iilma. The Cimmerian's chest heaved like a bellows from the exertion of the ferocious battle. It would be good if he could finish things now by slaying the Hyperborean. Without the birds, the wizard had lost much of his bodily protection. But Iilma was nowhere to be seen. Conan searched the snow for fresh tracks, but he could discern none. Cursing, he cleaned his fouled blade and sheathed it.

Wishing to be away before the sun rose, he set out

for the garth. At least the wizard was greatly weakened now. He had lost his far-ranging eyes as well. Rerin said that Iilma would have to journey to some accursed place and perform long rituals before he would be able to acquire new familiars. Best of all, he was now vulnerable to the swords and spears of other men.

Fourteen

When Kings Meet

Totila stretched in his saddle and looked back at the long file of his warriors winding along the forest road. They were in good spirits, for the gadfly horsemen had not struck at them since the day before. He did not think that he would see them again until he reached Alcuina's garth. That had been a weakening tactic, and they had given it up as soon as the Tormanna had come up with a good defensive tactic. Where had the Cambres learned to fight in such a fashion? He suspected that Alcuina's new black-haired champion was behind it. The more Totila learned of the man, the more he longed to come to grips with him.

Iilma rode up beside his king. "My birds tell me that the Cambres are huddled in Alcuina's garth like sheep in a pen."

Totila turned upon him with a look of little favor. "Your damned birds have been of little use so far."

Iilma shrugged, hiding his feeling of inner doubt. "A fluke. Who would have expected a poor magician like

Rerin to show such imagination? In any case, they have brought me further word, which you will find of great interest."

"Speak on," said Totila patiently.

"About a mile from here this road merges with another, which comes from the south. On that road are King Odoac and his Thungians. We shall reach the fork about the same time that they do."

Totila stroked his chin and smiled. "Odoac, eh? It is high time that I had words with that Thungian pig."

"At this point an alliance might be—"

"Stick to your wizardry," Totila broke in abruptly. "Leave statecraft to me." They rode on in silence.

As the sun rose higher the king of the Tormanna scanned the cloudless sky. "Where are your magpies, wizard? I've not seen them all this day."

"I have—sent them upon a mission, my lord. It is a matter of importance, concerning a stratagem that will be of great help to you in taking Alcuina's fortress." He dared not admit to his new weakness. It was imperative that the king think him as powerful as ever. He thanked his dark gods that he had made his preparations for the phantom-spell before he lost his familiars.

"Has it aught to do with the noises that came from your camp last night?" the king asked. "Men complained of it this morning. They said they were wakened by hellish sounds, as if giant serpents and boars and eagles were battling."

"Your men," Iilma said stiffly, "have no business concerning themselves with my arts, however clamorous they may be."

The Tormanna reached the fork in the road first, and Totila ordered the men off the road for a rest, cautioning them that they were soon to receive visitors. Every man must keep his weapons handy. Before an hour had passed, they saw the Thungians slogging up the southern road.

Odoac's heart jumped into his throat when he saw the army seated upon the ground before him. An ambush by the Cambres? But these men were making no effort to hide themselves. Then he saw the towering man who wore the cloak of many-colored hair and the eagle-crested helm, and he felt even more trepidation. He had hoped to find the leaderless Cambres easy meat. Totila and all his warriors primed for battle made a daunting prospect. There was nothing he could do except put the best face on it if his men were to follow him.

"It seems as if we are not the only ones minded to mount a winter hosting against the Cambres," Odoac said. He managed to get the words out steadily, although sweat came from beneath the rim of his helmet. His men's expressions grew grim, and their hands tightened on their weapons.

As the Thungians neared, Totila came forward. His men remained seated upon the ground. This reassured Odoac somewhat. But he was aware of every bit of his advancing age and flagging powers as the huge king of the Tormanna came to him and clasped his hand in a bone-crunching grip.

"Greeting, Odoac, my fellow king! It is too seldom that I see you!" He draped an arm around Odoac's shoulder and turned to wave and nod, giving both armies a good chance to judge how much taller, younger, and finer he was than the Thungian king.

"I greet you, Totila," Odoac answered, carefully omitting the title of king. "Am I right in believing that we are on a similar mission?"

"That is possible. Let us step aside and discuss these matters privily, as two kings should."

Odoac did not want to leave the protection of his housecarls, but he dared not show fear of Totila. "Rest you here, my men," he said, affecting unconcern. "This chieftain and I must take counsel upon weighty matters."

The two men walked a short distance away to a small hillock.

"My wizard tells me," began Totila, "that Alcuina is back after her mysterious disappearance."

"I rejoice to hear it," Odoac said, surprised. "Now I may ask her why she has been so tardy in answering my suit."

"I had similar questions in mind. Perhaps you also wished to discipline your wayward nephew?"

Odoac fumed but strove not to show it. This man had the advice of the cursed Iilma to make up for his lack of royal blood. Why had the Hyperborean not come to a true king like Odoac?

"In truth, the boy has been a trial to me. I brought him up as if he were my own son, for the sake of my dear brother. The wretch had the temerity to plot after my throne." He managed to smile at Totila. "Be glad that you never married, and have no heir."

"That is a situation I intend to rectify soon. After all, it were a shame to leave a royal lady like Alcuina unbedded when all three of our kingdoms are currently without heirs. Now, if you and I were to fall out here upon the road and come to swordstrokes, who would profit? Only the Cambres, for whichever of us prevailed would yet be too weakened to take the field against the Cambres this year."

"An alliance against the Cambres makes sense,"

Odoac said, nodding as if he had not been hoping that this was what Totila would suggest. "There remains the question of our similar aims. This alliance will do us no good if we should fall out over possession of Alcuina and her lands and people."

"These things can be worked out," said Totila persuasively. "And they should be before we proceed further. The lands and people are easy to settle. We simply divide them in twain, north and south, along the Gernach River, which runs nearly through the center of the kingdom. North to me, south to you."

Odoac thought for a moment. "That is agreeable to me. Now, what about Alcuina herself? Each of us is in need of a wife, and I see no way to divide her as we have already divided her land."

"As I see it," said Totila craftily, "you have two goals here: You want Alcuina, but you also want to rid yourself of Leovigild. It would not look good to your men if you were to slay him with your own hand, which you could easily do, I am sure."

"Of course I could slay that puppy," Odoac grumbled. "But you are right, it would be impolitic for me to do so. There would be those who would name me kinslayer even though I but defended myself."

"I, on the other hand, could slay him with impunity." Totila did not mention that he was fairly certain that he had already slain that young man. "Leovigild's life for Alcuina. Do you not think that is a fair trade, since I will after all be getting her with only half her dowry?"

Odoac stroked his beard, pretending to be deep in thought. "I still need an heir, you know."

Abruptly, Totila lost patience. "Use your head, man!

There are plenty of noble ladies with marriageable daughters who would be happy to have a king for son-in-law. Or find some peasant brat and pronounce him the long-lost son of your brother. It is not as if you intended to let him grow to manhood. You could buy fifteen more soft years on the throne with such a move.''

"You speak wisely, my friend," said Odoac, deeply cowed. "Let us agree on this: We shall unite forces against the Cambres. When the fighting is over, if you have slain Leovigild, you shall have Alcuina and the northern half of her kingdom. I shall have the southern half. We shall part friends and march our men home."

Totila thrust forth a hand, and Odoac took it. Neither had the slightest intention of honoring the agreement except at his own convenience. Arms about one another's shoulders, they walked back to their men, smiling.

"Is Odoac such a fool?" said Iilma, incredulous.

King and wizard sat in a small tent of oiled hides half a day's march from Alcuina's garth. Night had fallen, and the men rested against the exertions of the morrow. Iilma had kindled a small, smokeless fire between them, and it cast sinister shadows upon their faces as they conferred.

"Aye, he is a fool, but not so great a fool as that. He is merely a frightened old man with his best days behind him. He wants to hold on to his kingship for his few remaining years, and he knows not who to fear more—Leovigild or me. He does not like this alliance I have forced upon him, but he has no other choice."

"Will you let him march home peacefully after the battle is done?" Iilma asked.

"That depends upon how things look at the time. If

his men have taken many losses and we have taken few, I might well settle with him at that time. If we are seriously weakened, perhaps we must wait another year or two. Undoubtedly we should beat them, but why drain all my power in a second battle if things can be arranged more advantageously? After all, I have great plans, and eliminating my little northern rivals are a small part of them. I do not wish to be weakened for my southern conquests.''

''As my lord says,'' Iilma soothed. ''Might not matters be simplified if Odoac were to be slain in the coming battle?''

Totila thought. ''Perhaps. If he were to be slain by the Cambres. If I slew him, his men would not follow me.''

''Suppose Leovigild was to slay him?''

''Eh?'' Totila was mystified. ''Leovigild? I've already done for the boy. He is dead by now, from the wounds I dealt him.''

''The Thungians do not know that. I can raise a phantom, fashioned in the guise of young Leovigild. The Thungians will see Leovigild strike him down, then you may deal with the phantom, which will die most realistically.''

Totila smiled widely. ''Can you truly do that? Then the Thungians would be bound in honor to follow me, as the avenger of their slain lord.''

''Just so,'' said Iilma, nodding.

Totila slapped his knee in delight. ''Then that is what we shall do! I have never killed the same man twice, but I am willing to do it.''

Odoac and his chief warriors sat around their fire, glumly staring into the flames. They had eagerly anticipated the coming fight with the Cambres. The appearance of the Tormanna had stolen much of the zest from the enterprise. A senior warrior with much gray in his brown beard addressed his king.

"We came hither to get Alcuina's lands, and we'll not do that with Totila here. I say we go home and wait for a better time."

There was a slight grumble of agreement, but another warrior objected. "No! Will we let it be said that the Thungians took the warrior's road only to turn back like whipped dogs without a blow being struck? I'll not live with such shame!" Many roared agreement.

"And so should say all true men!" yelled Odoac, who wanted above all else not to go back and let his men spend the rest of the winter brooding about the fiasco their king had led them into.

"If we get only half her lands this year, what of it? There is always next year. It is just that now the Cambres and the Tormanna are too much for us to take on at one time. By next year, things may be different. We can first take the rest of the land of the Cambres, then turn west to take Totila. But for now we must have this alliance. It binds us to nothing after this fight is won." This time most of the men signified approval. For all its faults, this plan would at least allow them to fight and then return home with honor. None of them cared to contemplate going home to face the women and the old ones should they return with spears unbloodied.

Odoac smiled at his men, hiding his relief. All he asked now was a little land, his reputation as a warchief restored, and the corpse of Leovigild at his feet. All these things he might have upon the morrow.

* * *

"There they are," Conan said.

He stood beside Alcuina upon the walk that backed the palisade. All of the Cambres of fighting age who could elbow a place at the wall were there as well. At intervals along the wall stood bundles of crude, hastily-made javelins and piles of rocks, from fist-sized up to small boulders a foot in diameter. This kind of defensive warfare was alien to the Cambres, but Conan had insisted that it was their only chance in the face of superior numbers. They had learned that his word in these matters was to be trusted.

"There are a great many of them," Alcuina said, trying not to let worry creep into her voice.

The tree line beyond the plain of Giants' Stones was growing black with warriors, the sun casting bronzen gleams from helm and cuirass, the men nearly indistinguishable except for the broad, round shapes of their shields. There were two distinct groups, nearly equal in size but several yards apart.

"They may be allies," said Siggeir with a grin, "but the Thungians and the Tormanna have little love for one another."

A sound of axes cutting trees came to them across the plain.

"They are preparing," Conan said. "Now they make ladders to scale the wall."

"Will they succeed?" asked Alcuina.

"In time they would," said Conan. "This fort stands upon flat ground without motte or moat, no more than a stockade. An experienced army would take this place in little more time than if there were no wall at all. Since those men have probably never assaulted a wall except to steal their neighbors' chickens, they may be stymied for a day or so.''

''Will that be enough?'' she asked.

''If all goes well. You see a great host out there on the plain, but there are only two dangerous men: Iilma and Totila. I must deal with Totila. Rerin says he can settle with Iilma.''

''I pray to Ymir that it be so.'' She drew her fur cloak more closely about her, but not against the cold.

Within an hour the enemy host was moving upon the garth; Conan ordered all except warriors off the wall. Since the enemy had no siege engines, there was little immediate danger to them except from an occasional javelin skimming over the wall. In Conan's opinion, anyone who could not dodge a javelin deserved to be skewered.

''Get ready,'' Conan called. ''Don't begin throwing things until you can't miss them. There is no hurry. They'll make easy targets when they get to the base of the wall.''

All around him were men wearing nervous grins of anticipation. They were eager to fight. In southern armies, half of Conan's work as an officer had been in driving reluctant men to fight. Here he would have to keep a sharp lookout lest they rush to the courtyard, throw open the gate, and run out to fight hand-to-hand, the way they liked best.

The allies came on shouting. Some carried long ladders. Conan could tell from the way the ladders were held that these men had never stormed a wall. They would learn soon enough, however, just as they had learned to deal with horsemen. He scanned the unranked mob of enemies. He saw few of the long pikes

such as he had used against the hunter. He was relieved. With a wall as low as this, such pikes could be
used to force defenders back from the palisade, allow-
ing a few intrepid warriors to make their way up the
ladders and onto the wallwalk. Once the enemy had a
secure foothold on the wall, more could scramble up
the ladders with relative impunity, and the defense of
the wall, and therefore the siege, would be over. Except
for the slaughter of the remaining defenders.

The attackers reached the base of the wall and missiles began to fall on them. They raised their shields
high and shouted at the defenders to come down and
fight like men. The reply was yet more missiles. Clum-
sily, the ladders began to go up. At first they were
easily shoved aside, but the efforts of the attackers
became more determined, and soon the braver men
were essaying an assault on the palisade.

Conan saw a shield lurch over the wall with a bird-
crested helmet behind it. His first blow lowered the
shield and his second clove the helm. In falling, the
man swept the man behind him off the ladder. Conan
reached out to push the ladder aside, but by accident or
design the ladder-bearers had done the correct thing and
positioned the top of the ladder well below the top of
the wall. Thus, in order to shove it aside, the defenders
would have to lean far out over the wall in order to
reach the ladder. A rain of javelins drove Conan back.

Another man reached the top of the ladder without a
shield, but swinging an ax in both hands. He maneu-
vered the bulky weapon with such speed that Conan
was hard-pressed to keep his shield between himself
and the whistling blade. He waited until the ax was
going back for a swing, then stepped in, smashing the
shield's central boss into the man's face and following

the blow with a cut at the man's right side. Ribs
crunched below the edge of the bronze cuirass, and the
man fell screaming. Conan grabbed a spear and wedged
its shaft under the ladder, using the top of the palisade
as a fulcrum to lever the ladder away. His great strength
allowed him to push the ladder back in spite of the three
men clinging to it.

The ladder men along the wall were being similarly
repulsed. Below, men were throwing back the rocks
and javelins, but throwing upward they were severely
handicapped. Some of the defenders derisively caught
the stones in flight and cast them back to good effect.
After a few minutes of that a trumpet sounded.

Conan looked toward the sound and saw three men
standing atop a low mound. One was short, fat, and
gray-bearded. Another wore the skins and antlers of
reindeers. It was the third who drew Conan's attention.
The lowering sun glanced from his magnificent helmet
in multicolored shards. A long, piebald cloak hung
from his broad shoulders. Odoac, Iilma, and Totila.
And now Conan realized that Odoac only appeared to
be short when standing next to the giant king of the
Tormanna. So this was the man he must face.

It was Totila who had sounded the horn, and the men
below began to pull back from the wall, screaming in
their frustration at such unmanly war-making. The defenders atop the wall cheered and shouted taunts at the
withdrawing foe.

"We've beaten them! They run like whipped dogs!"
Siggeir whooped and shouted a traditional victory cry.

"Save your celebrating for tomorrow's nightfall,"
Conan cautioned. "We've stopped them this time. They'll
know the work better next time. By the third assault,

we'll not keep them out, unless some new circumstance comes to our aid.''

''You're cursed gloomy, Cimmerian,'' Siggeir said.

''I am the happiest of men,'' Conan told him, ''after the battle is won.''

''Totila comes!'' called a defender.

The tall king covered the plain with long strides. Odoac stepped along quickly beside him. Iilma was nowhere to be seen. Conan smiled in reluctant admiration. The man might be of base blood as the Cambres maintained, but he was as kingly as any monarch Conan had ever seen reviewing an army, clad in purple cape and plumed helm. Fearlessly, the man walked up to the wall, ignoring the danger from stone and spear. Unwilling to shame himself before his followers, Odoac stood beside him.

''Queen Alcuina!'' Totila called.

''She has no use for the likes of you,'' said Siggeir, spitting upon the ground beyond the wall.

Totila ignored the underling as if he did not exist. ''Queen Alcuina, I wish a few words with you!'' Totila stood planted on the spot as if he were willing to wait for the rest of his life. There was a rustling of skirts and cloak as Alcuina mounted the wall.

''My lady!'' said Siggeir, scandalized. ''Do not demean yourself by parleying with this scum. We've the upper hand now.'' Others agreed loudly.

''Hear what he has to say, Alcuina,'' Conan advised. ''It can have no bearing on relations between you and him, but it may tell us much about how things stand down there.'' He nodded to where the host stood massed. Now that the attack was over, the men were once more divided into two groups.

''Ah, my dear Alcuina,'' Totila called. ''How good

of you to come. This unpleasantness between our peoples pains me sorely, as it does my brother king, Odoac of the Thungians. Yet these matters may be set aright easily. You have not in the past seen fit to answer my suit for your hand. I ask you to reconsider now. After all, when we wed you will still be queen of the Cambres, and of the Tormanna as well.''

"And what does your brother king get from this?'' Alcuina said haughtily.

"Where is my dear nephew Leovigild?'' demanded Odoac. "I have missed him since his hasty and unwarranted flight from my garth. Why is he not up there on the wall with you? Or does he cower in rightful fear of his uncle's anger?''

"What makes you think your nephew is here, you Thungian tub of suet?''

This set Alcuina's men laughing uproariously, and the Tormanna laughed only a little less loudly. Even some of the Thungians were hard-pressed to restrain their grins. The others looked shamefaced, not because their king had been insulted, but because he made such a poor showing in front of these people. Conan missed none of these things.

"Get you gone, both of you!'' Alcuina commanded. "I'll wed neither a swine nor a bandit.''

Totila whirled and stalked away with dignity, each sway of his cloak reminding the viewers of how many champions and chiefs he had slain. Odoac scuttled after him, while the Cambres jeered.

Alcuina stood close to Conan and spoke so only he could hear. "It is a great pity that Totila is such a beast. He would treat my people like thralls. Otherwise, baseborn or not, I'd wed him.''

Conan grinned down at her. "As you've said, a

queen must choose her husband for political reasons. Aye, he's a real man; I'll grant him that much.''

"Now you have seen him close up. Think you still that you can defeat him?"

Conan looked insulted. "I said he was a real man, but I'm a better!"

"What kind of fighting is this?" Odoac groused. "Climbing walls like thralls escaping bondage!" He spat into the fire in disgust. "Why will they not come out and fight us?"

"Because we outnumber them better than two to one," said one of his men reasonably.

"What kind of reason is that for true men?" Odoac snorted. "I am especially disappointed in my nephew. The same blood fills his veins that fills mine. You would think he'd show more spirit. Perhaps some thrall crept into my brother's bed while he was off cattle-raiding, and begot Leovigild. He is a disgrace to the family."

"I spoke with some of Totila's men," said a young warrior hesitantly. "Some of them said that they knew Leovigild by sight, and they had seen him leading one of the horse-ambushes against the Tormanna."

"Indeed?" said Odoac. "Then why did we not see him today? Does he fear to meet his uncle?"

"They told me," said the young warrior, "that he fought Totila, and the king struck him down. They think he is surely slain."

This puzzled Odoac. Had he agreed to a condition that was already met? Was Totila really so clever that he bargained with a game piece he had already taken? It infuriated Odoac to think so, and he did not want his men to think he had been gulled.

"It must have been some other young fool Totila slew. My nephew would never have the courage to face such a man."

Before the fire had burned much lower, Totila himself came to visit his ally. The king strode dramatically into the ruddy glare and stood before the seated Odoac.

"Greeting, Odoac. We had a slow start today, but we began late. Tomorrow we shall have Alcuina's garth in our hands ere the sun sets."

"And Alcuina in yours," grumbled Odoac.

"Such was our bargain," Totila rejoined. "You, of course, shall have—"

"I know what our agreement was," Odoac broke in hastily. "Come, sit by me and have some ale."

The two kings sat, passing the ale-horn back and forth, speaking of inconsequential things. They put on a fine show of solidarity and friendship for the assembled Thungians. The celebration of good fellowship was interrupted when a tall, slender figure stepped from the surrounding shadows into the firelight.

"Greeting, Uncle."

Odoac's breathing became labored, and he grew crimson in the face. "Leovigild! You dare! You—you—"

Odoac struggled to his feet, fumbling at his sword hilt. Totila stood behind him. The Thungians, struck dumb at this unexpected sight, did not move at all.

Smiling gently, the young man before Odoac thrust the spear he was carrying deep into the capacious belly of the king. Odoac looked down in disbelief at the shaft protruding from his stomach. He opened his mouth to scream, but all that emerged was a gush of dark blood. Odoac collapsed sideways, and died.

With a shout, freed from their paralysis, the Thungians

jumped to their feet. Totila was quicker. He whipped his sword out with unbelievable swiftness, and the long, heavy blade was descending through the skull of Odoac's murderer before the warriors were fully on their feet. Those standing nearest were spattered with blood, brains, and teeth. Then they were goggling with wonder at the inert form upon the ground. Totila had made such a ruin of the skull that the features were no longer recognizable.

"The boy must have been mad to try such a thing. Well"—he looked around at the warriors—"it seems that your king and his heir are both dead. We shall burn them both at sunup, with full honors due royalty. Will you see this fight to the end, with me as your leader?" He carefully did not use the word *king* yet.

"We were Odoac's sworn men," said an elder warrior, "not yours."

"And as such you should have avenged him," Totila said blandly. "Yet you did not. I did. Do you owe no service to your king's avenger?"

The Thungians turned shamefaced. Events were happening too fast. It was easiest to let custom decide their immediate actions. "Aye, that is true," said the same elder.

"Then follow me until this matter is settled. Then we may sit and discuss the future of your tribe." With a scrap of coarse cloth, Totila cleaned off the bits of scalp and hair clinging to his sword. He sheathed it, turned, and strode away, his cloak of men's hair swinging behind him.

"Does this mean that the Torman is our king now?" demanded someone.

"We must talk of this," said the elder warrior. He looked down at the two hulks upon the ground. "What possessed the lad to do such a thing? Had he waited, Odoac could not have lived much longer. Then we could have haled him back to be our king. We all loved the boy.''

"Perhaps,'' said a man in elkskin armor, ''he was overcome with shame and rage at this alliance with the Tormanna. It might have robbed him of his wits.''

"We may never know what happened,'' said the elder, ''but now we are faced with a problem: Odoac and Leovigild were the last of the royal house. We have no king now. There are only Totila and Alcuina, and on the morrow Totila will have her.''

They were all silent for a while. The man listening from just outside the firelight had heard enough in any case. Conan, dressed in his black wolfskins and his face blackened with soot, snaked his way backward through the sparse brush of the plain toward the garth. He could do this as silently as any Pict. When he was far enough from the men, he rose and loped to a place at the base of the wall where a rope dangled from the palisade. Swiftly as a squirrel, he pulled himself up the wall and greeted the guards at the top. Many of the men were sleeping at their places on the wallwalk, lest the enemy try a surprise assault in the darkness.

Conan quickly made his way to Rerin's hut and barged in. The old man was performing some spell before his fire, but he looked up as Conan entered. "You were right,'' Conan announced. ''Iilma made his move tonight.''

"I knew it! Early this evening I felt his workings.''

Conan briefly outlined the events he had observed since the fall of night, and the things he had heard spoken among the enemy.

"I wondered how he would do it,'' Rerin said musingly. "It would have been difficult to do in battle, because few men would have seen it. Totila destroyed the false Leovigild's head because it would soon have ceased to resemble him. So now the Thungians have no king."

"No," Conan corrected. "They have one; they just don't know it."

Slowly, both men smiled.

Fifteen

War of Three Nations

When Totila rose and girded himself for battle it was with the deep satisfaction of a man who has planned well and now sees his plans coming to full fruition. He belted on his sword and strode from his tent.

"Are the pyres ready?" he asked one of his men. The man pointed to where two great heaps of wood rose above the plain near the Giants' Stones. "Then let us go and get these carcasses burned," Totila said impatiently. "We've a battle and a royal wedding to accomplish this day."

The Thungians were already gathered around the pyres, which they had toiled all night to build. The Tormanna lounged about, leaning on their spearshafts and showing scant respect for the dead. According to custom, those who had fallen in the battle the day before would be burned when the fighting was over, or carried home for burial if distance and transport permitted.

Iilma joined Totila on the way to the pyres. "Have I not wrought well, my king?"

"Very well, indeed," said Totila. He smiled benignly at his mage. "I was quite close to killing you not long ago, so much had you failed me. But now it looks as if all is working out for the best."

"The best is all I wish for my king," Iilma insisted. He had lost much of his arrogance in recent days, and now he wondered if his craft was under the influence of some baleful star. But how could his latest working fail? He could see no way at all.

Without preamble Totila picked up a torch and thrust it into the larger of the pyres. "Thus I give final rest to the spirit of my brother king, Odoac of the Thungians."

He walked to the lesser pyre and there was grumbling from the Thungians. A funeral oration for a king was supposed to last for hours. This was not proper, but they were about to be shocked still further.

"The Cambres come!" shouted someone.

They all whirled to face the garth. In open-mouthed stupefaction, they saw that the whole host of the Cambres were crossing the plain. In the forefront they could see Alcuina.

"Sacrilege!" said Totila with more wonder than anger in his voice. "Surely even the most desperate of men would not violate a funeral!"

"They bear their spears point-down," said the elder of the Thungians. "And they bring Alcuina with them. Perhaps they wish to pay their final respects."

A broad smile divided Totila's beard. "No. They have come to surrender. Why else would Alcuina come herself? Well, we must prepare to receive her properly." He strode toward the arriving party with Iilma close at his side. "Greeting, Alcuina," he called when they were a few paces apart. "It is good to see that you have come to your senses and decided to end this without further bloodshed."

"What do you mean, Totila?" Alcuina asked. "I have come to attend your double funeral. Royalty should not fail to attend such ceremonies."

"Especially since one of the pyres is mine!" called a voice.

Speechless, Totila watched as the crowd parted, and four thralls emerged, carrying a litter. Upon the litter lay Leovigild, pale, bandaged, but unmistakable. The Thungians goggled in disbelief, then cheered and began to surge toward the youth. He pointed a finger at Iilma.

"That wizard made the phantom that bore my appearance! The phantom slew Odoac, not I!"

Without hesitation, Totila whirled, drawing his sword. Before Iilma could so much as blink, the king's blade sheared through his shoulder and did not stop until it reached his waist. Totila placed a foot against the dying carcass and pushed it free of his sword. He turned back to face Alcuina.

"Thus do I punish such wickedness! I assure you, lady, that I had no knowledge of this thing. I thought that I had avenged the death of Odoac." He gestured at the body of the wizard. "Now I have."

Alcuina's lips curved slightly. "You are truly a man of quick decision, but it will not save you this time. Men will not follow cunning and treachery for long."

As if in confirmation of this, the Thungians were drawing away from the Tormanna and ranging themselves beside the Cambres.

Totila dropped his mask of amiability, and snarled. "They'll follow a real king if there are no others alive!" He advanced upon Alcuina and Leovigild, but now the black-haired champion stood before him with shield and drawn sword.

"It is time that you and I got acquainted," said Conan.

"Aye," said Totila. "For too long has my cloak been destitute of a black scalp. If you can make me tarry with you a while, you may earn a place on my cloak."

He took the famous garment off and tossed it to a retainer. Another man brought his shield. The people backed away to give them room, and there was a collective sigh of anticipation. This would be a rare spectacle.

King and champion circled, crouched well behind their shields. Totila attacked first, springing in to swing a swift horizontal chop at Conan's head. Instead of blocking with his shield, the Cimmerian ducked, cutting at Totila's waist. But the blow was deliberately short and passed in front of Totila's shield. Quick as thought, Conan reversed the blow and cut a backhand blow at Totila's unshielded side. Instead of bringing his shield across his body, Totila reversed his own blow, bringing his blade downward and across to block Conan's sword with his flat, a finger's width from his waist.

A huge cheer went up at the brief exchange, in praise of the men's masterful swordsmanship and the incredible strength of arm and wrist needed to reverse two such heavy swords in midswing. Other men would have sprung apart for the next attack, but these two kept up a dazzling exchange of blows, cutting at leg, flank, shoulder, and head with bewildering rapidity. Time and again, blade rang on cuirass, helm, and shield. So cunning were the fighters that the blows never landed squarely, but always glanced from the armor with little harm done.

It seemed impossible that mortal men could sustain such a pace in their combat, but these two showed no signs of tiring. Their shields were hacked and their armor gouged and dented, but as the sun shone higher in the sky they continued to attack one another with the relentless fury of male beasts fighting over their harems. Neither would abate his attack until the other lay stretched stark upon the ground.

In the end they proved to be mortal after all. Closely matched as they were, they had to tire. Attacks grew less precise, defense lost its swiftness, timing became fractionally less perfect. Sweat poured from both men, and their breathing grew as labored as a smith's bellows. Both bled freely from small wounds on arm and leg.

For the first time, they drew apart. To the watchers it looked as if the two were resting for another prolonged bout. The two combatants knew better. They were equally tired, and the shield arm wears out more quickly than the sword arm. Another blow, perhaps two or even three, and the battle would be decided.

"Thank you for a magnificent fight, Cimmerian," said Totila. "However it falls out, it will be one to remember."

"I salute you, Totila," Conan gasped. "You should have stayed a warrior and not sought to be a king."

"The road of kings is one a man must tread when he knows that greatness is writ upon his brow. Now, let's finish this."

Totila raised his shield once more. Only his eyes showed above its rim. With a shout, he advanced. Silently, Conan did the same. Conan began a charge, but blood trickling from a thigh wound made the sole of his boot slick; he slid on the grass, barely stopping himself from falling. Totila exploited the instant's imbalance, swinging a terrific overhand slash. In doing so, he lowered his shield a few inches, and that was all the advantage Conan needed.

For the first time, Conan used the point. Recovering from the feigned stumble, he darted his arm out to full extension and threw the whole weight of his body behind his blade. The point entered Totila's screaming mouth, crunched through teeth, palate, and skull, and emerged two handsbreadths beyond the splendid helm. Conan wrenched the blade free, and for a moment the huge body stood upon its feet. Then Totila toppled stiffly as a falling tree.

Conan turned to the Tormanna. "Who follows his king into the dark?"

The Tormanna warriors, so confident an hour before, were utterly demoralized. They found themselves without a king, outnumbered in an alien land. Finally the elder who had spoken the night before strode up to Alcuina.

"Lady, our king was of no line and left no heir. If Cambres and Thungians are to unite, then the Tormanna will become your men, too, if we all be treated as equals."

Alcuina glanced at Leovigild, and he nodded slightly. She turned back to the elder. "So be it." The pledging of fealty was a simple matter in the North. She turned to Totila's corpse. "Throw this carrion on the pyre with the false Leovigild. Totila was no real royalty."

"No!" bellowed Conan. "Build him a pyre higher than Odoac's! This was a true king. If I have to, I'll build him one myself, by Crom!"

Alcuina regarded him for a moment, then said, "Do as my champion says. Burn him with sword and helm, and with his cloak."

Dawaz the merchant looked up from the unloading ship to see a familiar figure striding toward his trading post. The long black hair swinging in the breeze was unmistakable, even at a distance.

"Conan!" he shouted, waving.

He dropped his bill of lading and rushed to meet the warrior. As he drew nearer, he saw that Conan no longer wore his bronze armor and carried a long Aquilonian sword. His arms blazed with several gem-set golden bands.

"Greeting, Dawaz," said Cónan. "When does the ship sail south?"

"Tomorrow, as soon as my goods are loaded. How did it go? Did you find the North to your liking?"

Conan did not break stride, and Dawaz turned to follow him. "It was a good winter; not nearly as dull as I had feared. Did the ship bring any good southern wine?"

"The best Turanian. But what of your adventures? You must have wrought prodigies to win so much gold."

At the trading post Conan paused for a moment. "Let's have some wine, and I'll tell you. There is little to tell, though. I have had far more exciting winters." Together the two men went into the post.

A CONAN CHRONOLOGY

by

Robert Jordan

Over the years during which I wrote novels about Conan of Cimmeria, I frequently received letters from fans inquiring about the proper placement in Conan's life of the various novels (both mine and those by other authors), and even of the short stories and novellas. Several of the true Conan aficionados even sent me copies of chronologies they had themselves worked out for all of the then-published works. It was seldom that two of these agreed in every detail with either each other or with the order in which I believe the stories belong. Sometimes they diverged widely.

Now that I am editing the novels, rather than writing them, I receive fewer of these queries and chronologies, but they still come in occasionally. As an aid to those real Conan fans, I present this chronology of all of the Conan stories and novels published to this time.

This chronology is primarily a simple listing of the stories, in the order in which they occur in the life of the Cimmerian, which I originally prepared after I stopped writing Conan novels for distribution to other writers who wanted to take up Robert E. Howard's mantle. In a few cases, where there are questions about the exact placement of a story, a note will give the alternate placement. There are a number of notes at the end of the list, most of which refer to the early publishing history of the original Robert E. Howard stories. Some of the notes give the facts about stories which L. Sprague de Camp (in some cases with assistance from Lin Carter or Bjorn Nyberg) finished, rewrote, and/or edited from outlines or rough drafts prepared by Howard. In instances where a story has appeared under more than one name, I have attempted to list these alternative names as well. It is possible that I have missed a variation somewhere, but I have tried to be as thorough as I could. The note which applies to a particular story will be designated by a number (as #1, #2, etc.) after the name of the author.

I am well aware in undertaking this that there will be disagreements among the readers over whether I have put every story in its proper place. That is all well and good. If you disagree, let me know about it. Perhaps you will even convince me.

TITLE	AUTHOR
"Legions of the Dead"	de Camp/Carter
"The Thing in the Crypt"	de Camp/Carter
"The Tower of the Elephant"	HOWARD #1
CONAN THE RAIDER	Carpenter
CONAN AND THE SORCERER	Offutt #2

CONAN THE BUCCANEER	de Camp/Carter
"Red Nails"	HOWARD #28 (novella)
"Jewels of Gwahlur"	HOWARD #29
"The Ivory Goddess"	de Camp/Carter
"Beyond the Black River"	HOWARD #30
"Moon of Blood"	de Camp/Carter
"The Treasure of Tranicos"	HOWARD/de Camp #31 (novella)
"Wolves Beyond the Border"	HOWARD/de Camp #32 De Camp/Carter
CONAN THE LIBERATOR	
"The Phoenix on the Sword"	HOWARD #33
"The Scarlet Citadel"	HOWARD #34
CONAN THE CONQUEROR	HOWARD #35
THE RETURN OF CONAN	de Camp/Nyberg #36
"The Witch of the Mists"	de Camp/Carter
"Black Sphinx of Nebthu"	de Camp/Carter
"Red Moon of Zembabwei"	de Camp/Carter
"Shadows in the Skull"	de Camp/Carter
CONAN OF THE ISLES	de Camp/Carter

NOTES

#1. "The Tower of the Elephant" was first published in *Weird Tales* for March, 1933. It was reprinted in *SKULL-FACE AND OTHERS* (ROBERT E. HOWARD), Arkham House, 1946; and in *THE COMING OF CONAN* (ROBERT E. HOWARD), Gnome Press, 1953.

#2. *CONAN AND THE SORCERER, CONAN THE MERCENARY,* and *CONAN: THE SWORD OF SKELIOS* (all Andrew J. Offutt) may all three (in the same order) properly come later, after "Rogues in the House." The placement above is based on Conan's stated age of 17, but, as L. Sprague de Camp points out, he behaves in a much more sophisticated fashion than he properly should at that age. It should be noted that the three are linked together in such a fashion as to be able to be read as one novel, though they stand well alone.

#3. *CONAN THE DESTROYER* (Robert Jordan), the novelization of the movie of the same name, may properly be placed later, after "Rogues in the House." L. Sprague de Camp places it *before* the three novels by Andrew J. Offutt.

#4. "The Hall of the Dead" was first published in *The Magazine of Science Fiction and Fantasy* for February 1967. It was written by L. Sprague de Camp to an outline found by Glenn Lord among Robert Howard's papers in 1966.

#5. "The God in the Bowl" was first published in *Space Science Fiction* for September, 1952. It was reprinted in *THE COMING OF CONAN* (ROBERT E. HOWARD), Gnome Press, 1953.

#6. "Rogues in the House" was first published in *Weird Tales* for January, 1934. It was reprinted in *TERROR BY NIGHT* (ed. Christine Campbell Thomson), Selwyn & Blount, Ltd., 1934; in *SKULL-FACE AND OTHERS* (ROBERT E. HOWARD), Arkham House, 1946; in *THE COMING OF CONAN* (ROBERT

E. HOWARD), Gnome Press, 1953; and in *MORE NOT AT NIGHT* (ed. Christine Campbell Thomson), Arrow Books Ltd., 1961.

#7. *CONAN THE CHAMPION* (John Maddox Roberts) may properly be placed later, after "Shadows in the Moonlight" and before "The Road of Eagles."

#8. "The Curse of the Monolith" was originally published in *Worlds of Fantasy*, Vol.1, No. 1, 1968, as "Conan and the Cenotaph."

#9. "The Bloodstained God" was rewritten by L. Sprague de Camp from a Robert Howard story, "The Trail of the Blood-Stained God," set in contemporary (1930s) Afghanistan. It was first published in *TALES OF CONAN* (ROBERT E. HOWARD/L. Sprague de Camp), Gnome Press, 1955.

#10. "The Frost Giant's Daughter" was first published under the title "Gods of the North" in *The Fantasy Fan* for March, 1934, and was reprinted in *Fantastic Universe Science Fiction* for December 1956. In a version that had been revised by Robert Howard, and which was later revised again by L. Sprague de Camp, it was reprinted in *Fantasy Fiction* for August, 1953, and in *THE COMING OF CONAN* (ROBERT E. HOWARD), Gnome Press, 1953, under its present title.

#11. *CONAN: THE ROAD OF KINGS* (Karl Edward Wagner) possibly belongs later, after "Hawks Over Shem" and before "Black Colossus."

#12. "Queen of the Black Coast" was first published in *Weird Tales* for May, 1934. It was reprinted in

AVON FANTASY READER No. 8, 1948, and again in
THE COMING OF CONAN (ROBERT E. HOWARD),
Gnome Press, 1953.

#13. The occurrences of *CONAN THE REBEL* (Poul
Anderson) are generally considered to have taken place
between the events of chapters 1 and 2 of "Queen of
the Black Coast."

#14. "The Vale of Lost Women" was first published
in *Magazine of Horror, No. 15*, Spring, 1967.

#15. "The Snout in the Dark" was rewritten by L.
Sprague de Camp and Lin Carter from an outline and
the first half of a rough draft of the story by Robert
Howard.

#16. "Hawks Over Shem" was rewritten by L. Sprague
de Camp from a Robert Howard story set in 11th
Century Egypt and entitled "Hawks Over Egypt." It
was first published in *Fantastic Universe Science Fiction*
for October 1955. It was reprinted in *TALES OF CONAN*
(ROBERT E. HOWARD/L. Sprague de Camp), Gnome
Press, 1955.

#17. "Black Colossus" was first published in *Weird
Tales* for June, 1933. It was reprinted in *CONAN THE
BARBARIAN*, Gnome Press, 1954. This should not be
confused with the movie novelization of the same name.
See Note #37.

#18. "Shadows in the Moonlight" was first published
in *Weird Tales* for April, 1934. It was reprinted in
CONAN THE BARBARIAN, Gnome Press, 1954. This

should not be confused with the movie novelization of the same name. See Note #37.

#19. ''The Road of the Eagles'' was rewritten by L. Sprague de Camp from a story of the same name, by Robert Howard, set in the 16th century Turkish Empire. Under the title ''Conan, Man of Destiny,'' it was first published in *Fantastic Universe Science Fiction* for December, 1955. It was reprinted in *TALES OF CONAN* (ROBERT E. HOWARD), Gnome Press, 1955, under its present title.

#20. ''A Witch Shall be Born'' was first published in *Weird Tales* for December, 1934. It was reprinted in *AVON FANTASY READER No. 10*, 1949; and in *CONAN THE BARBARIAN*, Gnome Press, 1954. This last should not be confused with the movie novelization of the same name. See Note #37.

#21. ''Shadows in Zamboula'' was first published in *Weird Tales* for November, 1935. It was reprinted in *SKULL-FACE AND OTHERS* (ROBERT E. HOWARD), Arkham House, 1946; and in *CONAN THE BARBARIAN*, Gnome Press, 1954. This last should not be confused with the movie novelization of the same name. See Note #37.

#22. ''The Devil in Iron'' was first published in *Weird Tales* for August, 1935. It was reprinted in *CONAN THE BARBARIAN*, Gnome House, 1954. This should not be confused with the movie novelization of the same name. See Note #37.

#23. ''The Flame Knife'' was first published in *TALES*

OF CONAN (ROBERT E. HOWARD), Gnome Press, 1955.

#24. ''The People of the Black Circle'' was first published, as a serial, in *Weird Tales* for September, October, and November, 1934. It was reprinted in *THE SWORD OF CONAN* (ROBERT E. HOWARD), Gnome Press, 1952.

#25. ''The Slithering Shadow'' was first published in *Weird Tales* for September, 1933. It was reprinted in *THE SWORD OF CONAN* (ROBERT E. HOWARD), Gnome Press, 1952.

#26. ''Drums of Tombalku'' was written/edited by L. Sprague de Camp from an outline and a partial rough draft found among Robert Howard's papers by Glenn Lord in 1965.

#27. ''The Pool of the Black One'' was first published in *Weird Tales* for October, 1933. It was reprinted in *THE SWORD OF CONAN* (ROBERT E. HOWARD), Gnome Press, 1952.

#28. ''Red Nails'' was first published, as a serial, in *Weird Tales* for July, August-September and October 1936. It was reprinted in *TALES OF CONAN* (ROBERT E. HOWARD), Gnome Press, 1952.

#29. ''Jewels of Gwahlur'' was first published in *Weird Tales* for March, 1935. It was reprinted in *KING CONAN* (ROBERT E. HOWARD), Gnome Press, 1953.

#30. ''Beyond the Black River'' was first published in

Weird Tales for May and June, 1935. It was reprinted in *KING CONAN* (ROBERT E. HOWARD), Gnome Press, 1953.

#31. "The Treasures of Tranicos" was first published, in an abridged form as revised by L. Sprague de Camp, as "The Black Stranger" in *Fantasy Magazine* for March 1953. It was first printed under the present title in *KING CONAN* (ROBERT E. HOWARD), Gnome Press, 1953.

#32. "Wolves Beyond the Border" was written/edited by L. Sprague de Camp from an outline and the first half of a story by Robert Howard, which were found by Glenn Lord among Robert Howard's papers in 1965. The events of this story occur simultaneously with *CONAN THE LIBERATOR*. This is the only story in the canon in which Conan does not appear.

#33. "The Phoenix on the Sword" was first published in *Weird Tales* for December, 1932. It was reprinted in *SKULL-FACE AND OTHERS* (ROBERT E. HOWARD), Arkham House, 1946; and in *KING CONAN* (ROBERT E. HOWARD), Gnome Press, 1953.

#34. "The Scarlet Citadel" was first published in *Weird Tales* for January, 1933. It was reprinted in *SKULL-FACE AND OTHERS* (ROBERT E. HOWARD), Arkham House, 1946; and in *KING CONAN* (ROBERT E. HOWARD), Gnome Press, 1953.

#35. *CONAN THE CONQUEROR* (ROBERT E. HOWARD) was originally serialized in *Weird Tales* for December 1935, January, February, March, and April 1936 under the title "The Hour of the Dragon." It is the only full-length novel about Conan written by Howard, though it was never published as a novel during his life.

#36. Chapters 2 through 5 of *THE RETURN OF CONAN* (L. Sprague de Camp/Bjorn Nyberg) were first published as a novella, "Conan the Victorious," in *Fantastic Universe Science Fiction* for September 1957. It was published under the listed title (with 10 chapters, along with a prologue and an epilogue) by Gnome Press, 1957. The novella "Conan the Victorious" should not be confused with the later novel of the same name.

#37. *CONAN THE BARBARIAN* (L. Sprague & Catherine de Camp), the novelization of the movie of the same name, must be considered to lie outside the proper canon and chronology, though L. Sprague de Camp, in "Conan the Indestructible" (included in the Conan novels published by Tor Books) manages to fit it in as a variant early-life story. It is not to be confused with the collection of the same name published by Gnome Press in 1954.

LIST OF CONAN AUTHORS

Robert E. Howard was, of course, the creator of Conan
of Cimmeria and the Hyborian world, but since his
death a number of other writers have continued the tale
of Conan's life. These writers are listed here alphabet-
ically.

ROBERT E. HOWARD
Poul Anderson
Catherine de Camp
L. Sprague de Camp
Leonard Carpenter
Lin Carter
Roland Green (to be published)
Robert Jordan
Bjorn Nyberg
Andrew J. Offutt
Steve Perry
John Maddox Roberts
Karl Edward Wagner

Conan
the
Indestructible

by L. Sprague de Camp

The greatest hero of the magic-rife Hyborian Age was a
northern barbarian, Conan the Cimmerian, about whose
deeds a cycle of legend revolves. While these legends
are largely based on the attested facts of Conan's life,
some tales are inconsistent with others. So we must
reconcile the contradictions in the saga as best we can.

In Conan's veins flowed the blood of the people of
Atlantis, the brilliant city-state swallowed by the sea
8,000 years before his time. He was born into a clan
that claimed a homeland in the northwest corner of
Cimmeria, along the shadowy borders of Vanaheim and
the Pictish wilderness. His grandfather had fled his own
people because of a blood feud and sought refuge with
the people of the North. Conan himself first saw daylight on a battlefield during a raid by the Vanir.

Before he had weathered fifteen snows, the young
Cimmerian's fighting skills were acclaimed around the
council fires. In that year the Cimmerians, usually at
one another's throats, joined forces to repel the warlike

251

Gundermen who, intent on colonizing southern Cimmeria, had pushed across the Aquilonian border and established the frontier post of Venarium. Conan joined the howling, blood-mad horde that swept out of the northern hills, stormed over the stockade walls, and drove the Aquilonians back across their frontier.

At the sack of Venarium, Conan, still short of his full growth, stood six feet tall and weighed 180 pounds. He had the vigilance and stealth of the born woodsman, the iron-hardness of the mountain man, and the Herculean physique of his blacksmith father. After the plunder of the Aquilonian outpost, Conan returned for a time to his tribe.

Restless under the conflicting passions of his adolescence, Conan spent several months with a band of Æsir as they raided the Vanir and the Hyperboreans. He soon learned that some Hyperborean citadels were ruled by a caste of widely-feared magicians, called Witchmen. Undaunted, he took part in a foray against Haloga Castle, when he found that Hyperborean slavers had captured Rann, the daughter of Njal, chief of the Æsir band.

Conan gained entrance to the castle and spirited out Rann Njalsdatter; but on the flight out of Hyperborea, Njal's band was overtaken by an army of living dead. Conan and the other Æsir survivors were led away to slavery ("Legions of the Dead").

Conan did not long remain a captive. Working at night, he ground away at one link of his chain until it was weak enough to break. Then one stormy night, whirling a four-foot length of heavy chain, he fought his way out of the slave pen and vanished into the downpour.

Another account of Conan's early years tells a different tale. This narrative, on a badly broken clay prism from Nippur, states that Conan was enslaved as a boy of ten or twelve by Vanir raiders and set to work turning a grist mill. When he reached his full growth, he was bought by a Hyrkanian pitmaster who traveled with a band of professional fighters staging contests for the amusement of the Vanir and Æsir. At this time Conan received his training with weapons. Later he escaped and made his way south to Zamora (*Conan the Barbarian*).

Of the two versions, the records of Conan's enslavement by the Hyrkanians at sixteen, found in a papyrus in the British Museum, appear much more legible and self-consistent. But this question may never be settled.

Although free, the youth found himself half a hostile kingdom away from home. Instinctively he fled into the mountains at the southern extremity of Hyperborea. Pursued by a pack of wolves, he took refuge in a cave. Here he discovered the seated mummy of a gigantic chieftain of ancient times, with a heavy bronze sword across its knees. When Conan seized the sword, the corpse arose and attacked him ("The Thing in the Crypt").

Continuing southward into Zamora, Conan came to Arenjun, the notorious "City of Thieves." Green to civilization and, save for some rudimentary barbaric ideas of honor and chivalry, wholly lawless by nature, he carved a niche for himself as a professional thief.

Being young and more daring than adroit, Conan's progress in his new profession was slow until he joined forces with Taurus of Nemedia in a quest for the fabulous jewel called the "Heart of the Elephant." The gem lay in the almost impregnable tower of the infamous mage Yara, captor of the extraterrestrial being Yag-Kosha ("The Tower of the Elephant").

Seeking greater opportunities to ply his trade, Conan wandered westward to the capital of Zamora, Shadizar the Wicked. For a time his thievery prospered, although the whores of Shadizar soon relieved him of his gains. During one larceny, he was captured by the men of Queen Taramis of Shadizar, who sent him on a mission to recover a magical horn wherewith to resurrect an ancient, evil god. Taramis's plot led to her own destruction (*Conan the Destroyer*).

The barbarian's next exploit involved a fellow thief, a girl named Tamira. The Lady Jondra, an arrogant aristocrat of Shadizar, owned a pair of priceless rubies. Baskaran Imalla, a religious fanatic raising a cult among the Kezankian hillmen, coveted the jewels to gain control over a fire-breathing dragon he had raised from an egg. Conan and Tamira both yearned for the rubies; Tamira took a post as lady's maid to Jondra for a chance to steal them.

An ardent huntress, Jondra set forth with her maid and her men-at-arms to slay Baskaran's dragon. Baskaran captured the two women and was about to offer them to his pet as a snack when Conan intervened (*Conan the Magnificent*).

Soon Conan was embroiled in another adventure. A stranger hired the youth to steal a casket of gems sent by the King of Zamora to the King of Turan. The stranger, a priest of the serpent-god Set, wanted the jewels for magic against his enemy, the renegade priest Amanar.

Amanar's emissaries, who were hominoid reptiles, had stolen the gems. Although wary of magic, Conan set out to recover the loot. He became involved with a bandette, Karela, called the Red Hawk, who proved the ultimate bitch; when Conan saved her from rape, she tried to kill him. Amanar's party had also carried off to the renegade's stronghold a dancing girl whom Conan had promised to help (*Conan the Invincible*).

Soon rumors of treasure sent Conan to the nearby ruins of ancient Larsha, just ahead of the soldiers dispatched to arrest him. After all but their leader, Captain Nestor, had perished in an accident arranged by Conan, Nestor and Conan joined forces to plunder the treasure; but ill luck deprived them of their gains ("The Hall of the Dead").

Conan's recent adventures had left him with an aversion to warlocks and Eastern sorceries. He fled northwestward through Corinthia into Nemedia, the second most powerful Hyborian kingdom. In Nemedia he resumed his profession successfully enough to bring his larcenies to the notice of Aztrias Pentanius, ne'er-do-well nephew of the governor. Oppressed by gambling debts, this young gentleman hired the outlander to purloin a Zamorian goblet, carved from a single diamond, that stood in the temple-museum of a wealthy collector.

Conan's appearance in the temple-museum coincided with its master's sudden demise and brought the young thief to the unwelcome attention of Demetrio, of the city's Inquisitorial Council. This caper also gave Conan his second experience with the dark magic of the serpent-brood of Set, conjured up by the Stygian sorcerer Thoth-Amon ("The God in the Bowl").

Having made Nemedia too hot to hold him, Conan drifted south into Corinthia, where he continued to occupy himself with the acquisition of other persons' property. By diligent application, the Cimmerian earned the repute of one of the boldest thieves in Corinthia. Poor judgment of women, however, cast him into chains until a turn in local politics brought freedom and a new career. An ambitious nobleman, Murilo, turned him loose to slit the throat of the Red Priest, Nabonidus, the scheming power behind the local throne. This venture gathered a prize collection of rogues in Nabonidus's mansion and ended in a mire of blood and treachery ("Rogues in the House").

Conan wandered back to Arenjun and began to earn a semi-honest living by stealing back for their owners valuable objects that others had filched from them. He undertook to recover a magical gem, the Eye of Erlik, from the wizard Hissar Zul and return it to its owner, the Kahn of Zamboula.

There is some question about the chronology of Conan's life at this point. A recently-translated tablet from Asshurbanipal's library states that Conan was about seventeen at the time. This would place the episode right after that of "The Tower of the Elephant," which indeed is mentioned in the cuneiform. But from internal evidence, this event seems to have taken place several years later. For one thing, Conan appears too clever, mature, and sophisticated; for another, the fragmentary medieval Arabic manuscript *Kitab al-Qunn* implies that Conan was well into his twenties by then.

The first translator of the Asshurbanipal tablet, Prof. Dr. Andreas von Fuss of the Münchner Staatsmuseum, read Conan's age as "17." In Babylonian cuneiform, "17" is expressed by two circles followed by three vertical wedges, with a horizontal wedge above the three for "minus"—hence "twenty minus three." But Academician Leonid Skram of the Moscow Archaeological Institute asserts that the depression over the vertical wedges is merely a dent made by the pick of a careless excavator, and the numeral properly reads "23."

Anyhow, Conan learned of the Eye of Erlik when he heard a discussion between an adventuress, Isparana, and her confederate. He invaded the wizard's mansion, but the wizard caught Conan and deprived him of his soul. Conan's soul was imprisoned in a mirror, there to remain until a crowned ruler broke the glass. Hissar Zul thus compelled Conan to follow Isparana and recover the talisman; but when the Cimmerian returned the Eye to Hissar Zul, the ungrateful mage tried to slay him (*Conan and the Sorcerer*).

Conan, his soul still englassed, accepted legitimate employment as bodyguard to a Khaurani noblewoman, Khashtris. This lady set out for Khauran with Conan, another guard, Shubal, and several retainers. When the other servants plotted to rob and murder their employer, Conan and Shubal saved her and escorted her to Khauran. There Conan found the widowed Queen Ialamis being courted by a young nobleman who was not at all what he seemed (*Conan the Mercenary*).

With his soul restored, Conan learned from an Iranistani, Khassek, that the Khan of Zamboula still wanted the Eye of Erlik. In Zamboula, the Turanian governor, Akter Khan, had hired the wizard Zafra, who ensorcelled swords, so that they would slay on command. En route, Conan encountered Isparana, with whom he developed a lust-hate relationship. Unaware of the magical swords, Conan continued to Zamboula and delivered the amulet. But the nefarious Zafra convinced the Khan that Conan was dangerous and should be killed on general principles (*Conan: The Sword of Skelos*).

Conan had enjoyed his taste of Hyborian-Age intrigue. It became clear that there was no basic difference between the opportunities in the palace and those in the Rats' Den, whereas the pickings were far better in high places. Besides, he wearied of the furtive, squalid life of a thief.

He was not, however, yet committed to a strictly law-abiding life. When unemployed, he took time out for a venture in smuggling. An attempt to poison him sent him to Vendhya, a land of wealth and squalor, philosophy and fanaticism, idealism and treachery (*Conan the Victorious*).

Soon after, Conan turned up in the Turanian seaport of Aghrapur. A new cult had established headquarters there under the warlock Jhandar, who needed victims to be drained of blood and reanimated as servants. Conan refused the offer of a former fellow thief, Emilio, to take part in a raid on Jhandar's stronghold to steal a fabulous ruby necklace. A Turanian sergeant, Akeba, did however persuade Conan to go with him to rescue Akeba's daughter, who had vanished into the cult (*Conan the Unconquered*).

After Jhandar's fall, Akeba urged Conan to take service in the Turanian army. The Cimmerian did not at first find military life congenial, being too self-willed and hot-tempered to easily submit to discipline. Moreover, as he was at this time an indifferent horseman and archer, Conan was relegated to a low-paid irregular unit.

Still, a chance soon arose to show his mettle. King Yildiz launched an expedition against a rebellious satrap. By sorcery, the satrap wiped out the force sent against him. Young Conan alone survived to enter the magic-maddened satrap's city of Yaralet ("The Hand of Nergal").

Returning in triumph to the glittering capital of Aghrapur, Conan gained a place in King Yildiz's guard of honor. At first he endured the gibes of fellow troopers at his clumsy horsemanship and inaccurate archery. But the gibes died away as the other guardsmen discovered Conan's sledge-hammer fists and as his skills improved.

Conan was chosen, along with a Kushite mercenary named Juma, to escort King Yildiz's daughter Zosara to her wedding with Khan Kujula, chief of the Kuigar nomads. In the foothills of the Talakma Mountains, the party was attacked by a strange force of squat, brown, lacquer-armored horsemen. Only Conan, Juma, and the princess survived. They were taken to the subtropical valley of Meru and to the capital, Shamballah, where Conan and Juma were chained to an oar of the Meruvian state galley, about to set forth on a cruise.

On the galley's return to Shamballah, Conan and Juma escaped and made their way into the city. They reached the temple of Yama as the deformed little god-king of Meru was celebrating his marriage to Zosara ("The City of Skulls").

Back at Aghrapur, Conan was promoted to captain. His growing repute as a good man in a tight spot, however, led King Yildiz's generals to pick the barbarian for especially hazardous missions. Once they sent Conan to escort an emissary to the predatory tribesmen of the Khozgari Hills, hoping to dissuade them by bribes and threats from plundering the Turanians of the lowlands. The Khozgarians, respecting only immediate, overwhelming force, attacked the detachment, killing the emissary and all but two of the soldiers, Conan and Jamal.

To assure their safe passage back to civilization, Conan and Jamal captured Shanya, the daughter of the

Khozgari chief. Their route led them to a misty high-land. Jamal and the horses were slain, and Conan had to battle a horde of hairless apes and invade the strong-hold of an ancient, dying race ("The People of the Summit").

Another time, Conan was dispatched thousands of miles eastward, to fabled Khitai, to convey to King Shu of Kusan a letter from King Yildiz proposing a treaty of friendship and trade. The wise old Khitan king sent his visitors back with a letter of acceptance. As a guide, however, the king appointed a foppish little nobleman, Duke Feng, who had entirely different objectives ("The Curse of the Monolith," first published as "Conan and the Cenotaph").

Conan continued in his service in Turan for about two years, traveling widely and learning the elements of organized, civilized warfare. As usual, trouble was his bedfellow. After one of his more unruly adventures, involving the mistress of his superior officer, Conan deserted and headed for Zamora. In Shadizar he heard that the Temple of Zath, the spider god, in the Zamorian city of Yezud, was recruiting soldiers. Hastening to Yezud, Conan found that a Brythunian free company had taken all the available mercenary posts. He became the town's blacksmith because as a boy he had been apprenticed in this trade.

Conan learned from an emissary of King Yildiz, Lord Parvez, that High Priest Feridun was holding Yildiz's favorite wife, Jamilah, in captivity. Parvez hired Conan to abduct Jamilah. Meanwhile Conan had set his heart on the eight huge gems that formed the eyes of an enormous statue of the spider god. As he was loosening the jewels, the approach of priests forced him to flee to a crypt below the naos. The temple dancing girl Rudabeh, with whom Conan was truly in love for the first time in his life, descended into the crypt to warn him of the doom awaiting him there (*Conan and the Spider God*).

Conan next rode off to Shadizar to track down a rumor of treasure. He obtained a map showing the location of a ruby-studded golden idol in the Kezankian Mountains; but thieves stole his map. Conan, pursuing them, had a brush with Kezankian hillmen and had to join forces with the very rogues he was tracking. He found the treasure, only to lose it under strange circumstances ("The Bloodstained God").

Fed up with magic, Conan headed for the Cimmerian hills. After a time in the simple, routine life of his native village, however, he grew restless enough to join his old friends, the Æsir, in a raid into Vanaheim. In a bitter struggle on the snow-covered plain, both forces were wiped out—all but Conan, who wandered off to a strange encounter with the legendary Atali, daughter of the frost giant Ymir ("The Frost Giant's Daughter").

Haunted by Atali's icy beauty, Conan headed back toward the South, where, despite his often-voiced scorn of civilization, the golden spires of teeming cities beckoned. In the Eiglophian Mountains, Conan rescued a young woman from cannibals, but through overconfidence lost her to the dreaded monster that haunted glaciers ("The Lair of the Ice Worm").

Conan then returned to the Hyborian lands, which include Aquilonia, Argos, Brythunia, Corinthia, Koth, Nemedia, Ophir, and Zingara. These countries were named for the Hyborian peoples who, as barbarians, had 3,000 years earlier conquered the empire of Acheron and built civilized realms on its ruins.

In Belverus, the capital of Nemedia, the ambitious

Lord Albanus dabbled in sorcery to usurp the throne of King Garian. To Belverus came Conan, seeking a patron with money to enable him to hire his own free company. Albanus gave a magical sword to a confederate, Lord Melius, who went mad and attacked people in the street until killed. As he picked up the ensorcelled sword, Conan was accosted by Hordo, a one-eyed thief and smuggler whom he had known as Karela's lieutenant.

Conan sold the magical sword, hired his own free company, and taught his men mounted archery. Then he persuaded King Garian to hire him. But Albanus had made a man of clay and by his sorcery given it the exact appearance of the king. Then he imprisoned the king, substituted his golem, and framed Conan for murder (*Conan the Defender*).

Conan next brought his free company to Ianthe, capital of Ophir. There the Lady Synelle, a platinum-blond sorceress, wished to bring to life the demon-god Al'Kirr. Conan bought a statuette of this demon-god and soon found that various parties were trying to steal it from him. He and his company took service under Synelle, not knowing her plans.

Then the bandette Karela reappeared and, as usual, tried to murder Conan. Synelle hired her to steal the statuette, which the witch needed for her sorcery. She also planned to sacrifice Karela (*Conan the Triumphant*).

Conan went on to Argos; but since that kingdom was at peace, there were no jobs for mercenaries. A misunderstanding with the law compelled Conan to leap to the deck of a ship as it left the pier. This was the merchant galley *Argus*, bound for the coasts of Kush.

A major epoch in Conan's life was about to begin. The *Argus* was taken by Bêlit, the Shemite captain of the pirate ship *Tigress*, whose ruthless black corsairs had made her mistress of the Kushite littoral. Conan won both Bêlit and a partnership in her bloody trade ("Queen of the Black Coast," Chapter 1).

Years before, Bêlit, daughter of a Shemite trader, had been abducted with her brother Jehanan by Stygian slavers. Now she asked her lover Conan to try to rescue the youth. The barbarian slipped into Khemi, the Stygian seaport, was captured, but escaped to the eastern end of Stygia, the province of Taia, where a revolt against Stygian oppression was brewing (*Conan the Rebel*).

Conan and Bêlit resumed their piratical careers, preying mainly on Stygian vessels. Then an ill fate took them up the black Zarkheba River to the lost city of an ancient winged race ("Queen of the Black Coast," Chapters 2–5).

As Bêlit's burning funeral ship wafted out to sea, a downhearted Conan turned his back on the sea, which he would not follow again for years. He plunged inland and joined the warlike Bamulas, a black tribe whose power swiftly grew under his leadership.

The chief of a neighboring tribe, the Bakalahs, planned a treacherous attack on another neighbor and invited Conan and his Bamulas to take part in the sack and massacre. Conan accepted but, learning that an Ophirean girl, Livia, was held captive in Bakalah, he out-betrayed the Bakalahs. Livia ran off during the slaughter and wandered into a mysterious valley, where only Conan's timely arrival saved her from being sacrificed to an extraterrestrial being ("The Vale of Lost Women").

Before Conan could build his own black empire, he was thwarted by a succession of natural catastrophes as well as by the intrigues of hostile Bamulas. Forced to flee, he headed north. After a narrow escape from pursuing lions on the veldt, Conan took shelter in a mysterious ruined castle of prehuman origin. He had a brush with Stygian slavers and a malign supernatural entity ("The Castle of Terror").

Continuing on, Conan reached the semicivilized kingdom of Kush. This was the land to which the name "Kush" properly applied; although Conan, like other northerners, tended to use the term loosely to mean any of the black countries south of Stygia. In Meroê, the capital, Conan rescued from a hostile mob the young Queen of Kush, the arrogant, impulsive, fierce, cruel, and voluptuous Tananda.

Conan became embroiled in a labyrinthine intrigue between Tananda and an ambitious nobleman who commanded a piglike demon. The problem was aggravated by the presence of Diana, a Nemedian slave girl to whom Conan, despite the jealous fury of Tananda, took a fancy. Events culminated in a night of insurrection and slaughter ("The Snout in the Dark").

Dissatisfied with his achievements in the black countries, Conan wandered to the meadowlands of Shem and became a soldier of Akkharia, a Shemite city-state. He joined a band of volunteers to liberate a neighboring city-state; but through the treachery of Othbaal, cousin of the mad King Akhîrom of Pelishtia, the volunteers were destroyed—all but Conan, who survived to track the plotter to Asgalun, the Pelishti capital. There Conan became involved in a polygonal power war among the mad Akhîrom, the treacherous Othbaal, a Stygian witch, and a company of black mercenaries. In the final hurly-burly of sorcery, steel, and blood, Conan grabbed Othbaal's red-haired mistress, Rufia, and galloped north ("Hawks Over Shem").

*   *   *

Conan's movements at this time are uncertain. One tale, sometimes assigned to this period, tells of Conan's service as a mercenary in Zingâra. A Ptolemaic papyrus in the British Museum alleges that in Kordava, the capital, a captain in the regular army forced a quarrel on Conan. When Conan killed his assailant, he was condemned to hang. A fellow condemnee, Santiddio, belonged to an underground conspiracy, the White Rose, that hoped to topple King Rimanendo. As other conspirators created a disturbance in the crowd that gathered for the hanging, Conan and Santiddio escaped.

Mordermi, head of an outlaw band allied with the White Rose, enlisted Conan in his movement. The conspiracy was carried on in the Pit, a warren of tunnels beneath the city. When the King sent an army to clean out the Pit, the insurrectionists were saved by Callidos, a Stygian sorcerer. King Rimanendo was slain and Mordermi became king. When he proved as tyrannical as his predecessor, Conan raised another revolt; then, refusing the crown for himself, he departed (*Conan: The Road of Kings*).

This tale involves many questions. If authentic, it may belong in Conan's earlier mercenary period, around the time of *Conan the Defender*. But there is no corroboration in other narratives of the idea that Conan ever visited Zingâra before his late thirties, the time of *Conan the Buccaneer*. Moreover, none of the rulers of Zingâra mentioned in the papyrus appear on the list of kings of Zingâra in the Byzantine manuscript *Hoi Anaktes tês Tzingêras*. Hence some students deem the papyrus either spurious or a case of confusion between Conan and some other hero. Everything else known about Conan indicates that, if he had indeed been offered the Zingaran crown, he would have grabbed it with both hands.

We next hear of Conan after he took service under Amalric of Nemedia, the general of Queen-Regent Yasmela of the little border kingdom of Khoraja. While Yasmela's brother, King Khossus, was a prisoner in Ophir, Yasmela's borders were assailed by the forces of the veiled sorcerer Natohk—actually the 3,000-years-dead Thugra Khotan of the ruined city of Kuthchemes.

Obeying an oracle of Mitra, the supreme Hyborian god, Yasmela made Conan captain-general of Khoraja's army. In this rôle he gave battle to Natohk's hosts and rescued the Queen-Regent from the malignant magic of the undead warlock. Conan won the day—and the Queen ("Black Colossus").

Conan, now in his late twenties, settled down as Khorajan commander-in-chief. But the queen, whose lover he had expected to be, was too preoccupied with affairs of state to have time for frolics. He even proposed marriage, but she explained that such a union would not be sanctioned by Khorajan law and custom. Yet, if Conan could somehow rescue her brother from imprisonment, she might persuade Khossus to change the law.

Conan set forth with Rhazes, an astrologer, and Fronto, a thief who knew a secret passage into the dungeon where Khossus languished. They rescued the King but found themselves trapped by Kothian troops, since Strabonus of Koth had his own reasons for wanting Khossus.

Having surmounted these perils, Conan found that Khossus, a pompous young ass, would not hear of a foreign barbarian's marrying his sister. Instead, he would marry Yasmela off to a nobleman and find a middle-class bride for Conan. Conan said nothing; but in Argos, as their ship cast off, Conan sprang ashore with most of the gold that Khossus had raised and waved the King an ironic farewell ("Shadows in the Dark").

Now nearly thirty, Conan slipped away to revisit his Cimmerian homeland and avenge himself on the Hyperboreans. His blood brothers among the Cimmerians and the Æsir had won wives and sired sons, some as old and almost as big as Conan had been at the sack of Venarium. But his years of blood and battle had stirred his predatory spirit too strongly for him to follow their example. When traders brought word of new wars, Conan galloped off to the Hyborian lands.

A rebel prince of Koth was fighting to overthrow Strabonus, the penurious ruler of that far-stretched nation; and Conan found himself among old companions in the princeling's array, until the rebel made peace with his king. Unemployed again, Conan formed an outlaw band, the Free Companions. This troop gravitated to the steppes west of the Sea of Vilayet, where they joined the ruffianly horde known as the *kozaki*.

Conan soon became the leader of this lawless crew and ravaged the western borders of the Turanian Empire until his old employer, King Yildiz, sent a force under Shah Amurath, who lured the *kozaki* deep into Turan and cut them down.

Slaying Amurath and acquiring the Turanian's captive, Princess Olivia of Ophir, Conan rowed out into the Vilayet Sea in a small boat. He and Olivia took refuge on an island, where they found a ruined greenstone city, in which stood strange iron statues. The shadows cast by the moonlight proved as dangerous as the giant carnivorous ape that ranged the isle, or the pirate crew that landed for rest and recreation ("Shadows in the Moonlight").

Conan seized command of the pirates that ravaged the Sea of Vilayet. As chieftain of this mongrel Red Brotherhood, Conan was more than ever a thorn in King Yildiz's flesh. That mild monarch, instead of strangling his brother Teyaspa in the normal Turanian manner, had cooped him up in a castle in the Colchian Mountains. Yildiz now sent his General Artaban to destroy the pirate stronghold at the mouth of the Zaporoska River; but the general became the harried instead of the harrier. Retreating inland, Artaban stumbled upon Teyaspa's whereabouts; and the final conflict involved Conan's outlaws, Artaban's Turanians, and a brood of vampires ("The Road of the Eagles").

Deserted by his sea rovers, Conan appropriated a stallion and headed back to the steppes. Yezdigerd, now on the throne of Turan, proved a far more astute and energetic ruler than his sire. He embarked on a program of imperial conquest.

Conan went to the small border kingdom of Khauran, where he won command of the royal guard of Queen Taramis. This queen had a twin sister, Salome, born a witch and reared by the yellow sorcerers of Khitai. She allied herself with the adventurer Constantius of Koth and planned by imprisoning the Queen to rule in her stead. Conan, who perceived the deception, was trapped and crucified. Cut down by the chieftain Olgerd Vladislav, the Cimmerian was carried off to a Zuagir camp in the desert. Conan waited for his wounds to heal, then applied his daring and ruthlessness to win his place as Olgerd's lieutenant.

When Salome and Constantius began a reign of terror in Khauran, Conan led his Zuagirs against the Khauranian capital. Soon Constantius hung from the cross to which he had nailed Conan, and Conan rode off smiling, to lead his Zuagirs on raids against the Turanians ("A Witch Shall Be Born").

Conan, about thirty and at the height of his physical powers, spent nearly two years with the desert Shemites, first as Olgerd's lieutenant and then, having ousted Olgerd, as sole chief. The circumstances of his leaving the Zuagirs were recently disclosed by a silken scroll in Old Tibetan, spirited out of Tibet by a refugee. This document is now with the Oriental Institute in Chicago.

The energetic King Yezdigerd sent soldiers to trap Conan and his troop. Because of a Zamorian traitor in Conan's ranks, the ambush nearly succeeded. To avenge the betrayal, Conan led his band in pursuit of the Zamorian. When his men deserted, Conan pressed on alone until, near death, he was rescued by Enosh, a chieftain of the isolated desert town of Akhlat.

Akhlat suffered under the rule of a demon in the form of a woman, who fed on the life force of living things. Conan, Enosh informed him, was their prophesied liberator. After it was over, Conan was invited to settle in Akhlat; but, knowing himself ill-suited to a life of humdrum respectability, he instead headed southwest to Zamboula with the horse and money of Vardanes the Zamorian ("Black Tears").

In one colossal debauch, Conan dissipated the fortune he had brought to Zamboula, a Turanian outpost. There lurked the sinister priest of Hanuman, Totrasmek, who sought a famous jewel, the Star of Khorala, for which the Queen of Ophir was said to have offered a roomful of gold. In the ensuing imbroglio, Conan acquired the Star of Khorala and rode westward ("Shadows of Zamboula").

The medieval monkish manuscript *De sidere choralae*, rescued from the bombed ruins of Monte Cassino, continues the tale. Conan reached the capital of Ophir to find that the effeminate Moranthes II, himself under the thumb of the sinister Count Rigello, kept his queen, Marala, under lock and key. Conan scaled the wall of Moranthes's castle and fetched Marala out. Rigello pursued the fugitives nearly to the Aquilonian border, where the Star of Khorala showed its power in an unexpected way ("The Star of Khorala").

Hearing that the *kozaki* had regained their vigor, Conan returned with horse and sword to the harrying of Turan. Although the now-famous northlander arrived all but empty-handed, contingents of the *kozaki* and the Vilayet pirates soon began operating under his command.

Yezdigerd sent Jehungir Agha to entrap the barbarian on the island of Xapur. Coming early to the ambush, Conan found the island's ancient fortress-palace of Dagon restored by magic, and in it the city's malevolent god, in the form of a giant of living iron ("The Devil in Iron").

After escaping from Xapur, Conan built his *kozaki* and pirate raiders into such a formidable threat that King Yezdigerd devoted all his forces to their destruction. After a devastating defeat, the *kozaki* scattered, and Conan retreated southward to take service in the light cavalry of Kobad Shah, King of Iranistan.

Conan got himself into Kobad Shah's bad graces and had to ride for the hills. He found a conspiracy brewing in Yanaidar, the fortress-city of the Hidden Ones. The Sons of Yezm were trying to revive an ancient cult and unite the surviving devotees of the old gods in order to rule the world. The adventure ended with the rout of the contending forces by the gray ghouls of Yanaidar, and Conan rode eastward ("The Flame Knife").

Conan reappeared in the Himelian Mountains, on the northwest frontier of Vendhya, as a war chief of the savage Afghuli tribesmen. Now in his early thirties, the warlike barbarian was known and feared throughout the world of the Hyborian Age.

No man to be bothered with niceties, Yezdigerd employed the magic of the wizard Khemsa, an adept of the dreaded Black Circle, to remove the Vendhyan king from his path. The dead king's sister, the Devi Yasmina, set out to avenge him but was captured by Conan. Conan and his captive pursued the sorcerous Khemsa, only to see him slain by the magic of the Seers of Yimsha, who also abducted Yasmina ("The People of the Black Circle").

When Conan's plans for welding the hill tribes into a single power failed, Conan, hearing of wars in the West, rode thither. Almuric, a prince of Koth, had rebelled against the hated Strabonus. While Conan joined Almuric's bristling host, Strabonus's fellow kings came to that monarch's aid. Almuric's motley horde was driven south, to be annihilated at last by combined Stygian and Kushite forces.

Escaping into the desert, Conan and the camp follower Natala came to age-old Xuthal, a phantom city of living dead men and their creeping shadow-god, Thog. The Stygian woman Thalis, the effective ruler of Xuthal, double-crossed Conan once too often ("The Slithering Shadow").

Conan beat his way back to the Hyborian lands. Seeking further employment, he joined the mercenary army that a Zingaran, Prince Zapayo da Kova, was raising for Argos. It was planned that Koth should invade Stygia from the north, while the Argosseans approached the realm from the south by sea. Koth, however, made a separate peace with Stygia, leaving Conan's army of mercenaries trapped in the Stygian deserts.

Conan fled with Amalric, a young Aquilonian soldier. Soon Conan was captured by nomads, while Amalric escaped. When Amalric caught up again with Conan, Amalric had with him the girl Lissa, whom he had saved from the cannibal god of her native city. Conan had meanwhile become commander of the cavalry of the city of Tombalku. Two kings ruled Tombalku: the Negro Sakumbe and the mixed-blood Zehbeh. When Zehbeh and his faction were driven out, Sakumbe made Conan his co-king. But then the wizard Askia slew Sakumbe by magic. Conan, having avenged his black friend, escaped with Amalric and Lissa ("Drums of Tombalku").

Conan beat his way to the coast, where he joined the Barachan pirates. He was now about thirty-five. As second mate of the *Hawk*, he landed on the island of the Stygian sorcerer Siptah, said to have a magical jewel of fabulous properties.

Siptah dwelt in a cylindrical tower without doors or windows, attended by a winged demon. Conan smoked the unearthly being out but was carried off in its talons to the top of the tower. Inside the tower Conan found the wizard long dead; but the magical gem proved of unexpected help in coping with the demon ("The Gem in the Tower").

Conan remained about two years with the Barachans, according to a set of clay tablets in pre-Sumerian cuneiform. Used to the tightly organized armies of the Hyborian kingdoms, Conan found the organization of the Barachan bands too loose and anarchic to afford an opportunity to rise to leadership. Slipping out of a tight spot at the pirate rendezvous at Tortage, he found that the only alternative to a cut throat was braving the Western Ocean in a leaky skiff. When the *Wastrel*, the ship of the buccaneer Zaporavo, came in sight, Conan climbed aboard.

The Cimmerian soon won the respect of the crew and the enmity of its captain, whose Kordavan mistress, the sleek Sancha, cast too friendly an eye on the black-maned giant. Zaporavo drove his ship westward to an uncharted island, where Conan forced a duel on the captain and killed him, while Sancha was carried off by strange black beings to a living pool worshipped by these entities ("The Pool of the Black Ones").

Conan persuaded the officals at Kordava to transfer Zaporavo's privateering license to him, whereupon he spent about two years in this authorized piracy. As usual, plots were brewing against the Zingaran monarchy. King Ferdrugo was old and apparently failing, with no successor but his nubile daughter Chabela. Duke Villagro enlisted the Stygian super-sorcerer Thoth-Amon, the High Priest of Set, in a plot to obtain Chabela as his bride. Suspicious, the princess took the royal yacht down the coast to consult her uncle. A privateer in league with Villagro captured the yacht and abducted the girl. Chabela escaped and met Conan, who obtained the magical Cobra Crown, also sought by Thoth-Amon.

A storm drove Conan's ship to the coast of Kush, where Conan was confronted by black warriors headed by his old comrade-in-arms, Juma. While the chief welcomed the privateers, a tribesman stole the Cobra Crown. Conan set off in pursuit, with Princess Chabela following him. Both were captured by slavers and sold to the black Queen of the Amazons. The Queen made Chabela her slave and Conan her fancy man. Then, jealous of Chabela, she flogged the girl, imprisoned Conan, and condemned both to be devoured by a man-eating tree (*Conan the Buccaneer*).

Having rescued the Zingaran princess, Conan shrugged off hints of marriage and returned to privateering. But other Zingarans, jealous, brought him down off the coast of Shem. Escaping inland, Conan joined the Free Companions, a mercenary company. Instead of rich plunder, however, he found himself in dull guard duty on the black frontier of Stygia, where the wine was sour and the pickings poor.

Conan's boredom ended with the appearance of the pirette, Valeria of the Red Brotherhood. When she left the camp, he followed her south. The pair took refuge in a city occupied by the feuding clans of Xotalanc and Tecuhltli. Siding with the latter, the two northerners soon found themselves in trouble with that clan's leader, the ageless witch Tascela ("Red Nails").

Conan's amour with Valeria, however hot at the start, did not last long. Valeria returned to the sea; Conan tried his luck once more in the black kingdoms. Hearing of the "Teeth of Gwahlur," a cache of priceless jewels hidden in Keshan, he sold his services to its irascible king to train the Keshani army.

Thutmekri, the Stygian emissary of the twin kings of Zembabwei, also had designs on the jewels. The Cimmerian, outmatched in intrigue, made tracks for the valley where the ruins of Alkmeenon and its treasure lay hidden. In a wild adventure with the undead goddess Yelaya, the Corinthian girl Muriela, the black priests headed by Gorulga, and the grim gray servants of the long-dead Bît-Yakin, Conan kept his head but lost his loot ("Jewels of Gwahlur").

Heading for Punt with Muriela, Conan embarked on a scheme to relieve the worshipers of an ivory goddess of their abundant gold. Learning that Thutmekri had preceded him and had already poisoned King Lalibeha's mind against him, Conan and his companion took refuge in the temple of the goddess Nebethet.

When the king, Thutmekri, and High Priest Zaramba arrived at the temple, Conan staged a charade wherein Muriela spoke with the voice of the goddess. The results surprised all, including Conan ("The Ivory Goddess").

In Zembabwei, the city of the twin kings, Conan joined a trading caravan which he squired northward along the desert borders, bringing it safely into Shem. Now in his late thirties, the restless adventurer heard that the Aquilonians were spreading westward into the Pictish wilderness. So thither, seeking work for his sword, went Conan. He enrolled as a scout at Fort Tuscelan, where a fierce war raged with the Picts.

In the forests across the river, the wizard Zogar Sag was gathering his swamp demons to aid the Picts. While Conan failed to prevent the destruction of Fort Tuscelan, he managed to warn settlers around Velitrium and to cause the death of Zogar Sag ("Beyond the Black River").

Conan rose rapidly in the Aquilonian service. As captain, his company was once defeated by the machinations of a traitorous superior. Learning that this officer, Viscount Lucian, was about to betray the province to the Picts, Conan exposed the traitor and routed the Picts ("Moon of Blood").

Promoted to general, Conan defeated the Picts in a

great battle at Velitrium and was called back to the capital, Tarantia, to receive the nation's accolades. Then, having roused the suspicions of the depraved and foolish King Numedides, he was drugged and chained in the Iron Tower under sentence of death.

The barbarian, however, had friends as well as foes. Soon he was spirited out of prison and turned loose with horse and sword. He struck out across the dank forests of Pictland toward the distant sea. In the forest, the Cimmerian came upon a cavern in which lay the corpse and the demon-guarded treasure of the pirate Tranicos. From the west, others—a Zingaran count and two bands of pirates—were hunting the same fortune, while the Stygian sorcerer Thoth-Amon took a hand in the game ("The Treasure of Tranicos").

Rescued by an Aquilonian galley, Conan was chosen to lead a revolt against Numedides. While the revolution stormed along, civil war raged on the Pictish frontier. Lord Valerian, a partisan of Numedides, schemed to bring the Picts down on the town of Schohira. A scout, Gault Hagar's sons, undertook to upset this scheme by killing the Pictish wizard ("Wolves Beyond the Border").

Storming the capital city and slaying Numedides on the steps of his throne—which he promptly took for his own—Conan, now in his early forties, found himself ruler of the greatest Hyborian nation (*Conan the Liberator*).

A king's life, however, proved no bed of houris. Within a year, an exiled count had gathered a group of plotters to oust the barbarian from the throne. Conan might have lost crown and head but for the timely intervention of the long-dead sage Epimitreus ("The Phoenix of the Sword").

No sooner had the mutterings of revolt died down than Conan was treacherously captured by the kings of Ophir and Koth. He was imprisoned in the tower of the wizard Tsotha-lanti in the Kothian capital. Conan escaped with the help of a fellow prisoner, who was Tsotha-lanti's wizardly rival Pelias. By Pelias's magic, Conan was whisked to Tarantia in time to slay a pretender and to lead an army against his treacherous fellow kings ("The Scarlet Citadel").

For nearly two years, Aquilonia thrived under Conan's firm but tolerant rule. The lawless, hard-bitten adventurer of former years had, through force of circumstance, matured into an able and responsible statesman. But a plot was brewing in neighboring Nemedia to destroy the King of Aquilonia by sorcery from an elder day.

Conan, about forty-five, showed few signs of age save a network of scars on his mighty frame and a more cautious approach to wine, women, and bloodshed. Although he kept a harem of luscious concubines, he had never taken an official queen; hence he had no legitimate son to inherit the throne, a fact whereof his enemies sought to take advantage.

The plotters resurrected Xaltotun, the greatest sorcerer of the ancient empire of Acheron, which fell before the Hyborian savages 3,000 years earlier. By Xaltotun's magic, the King of Nemedia was slain and replaced by his brother Tarascus. Black sorcery defeated Conan's army; Conan was imprisoned, and the exile Valerius took his throne.

Escaping from a dungeon with the aid of the harem girl Zenobia, Conan returned to Aquilonia to rally his loyal forces against Valerius. From the priests of Asura, he learned that Xaltotun's power could be broken only by means of a strange jewel, the "Heart of Ahriman." The trail of the jewel led to a pyramid in the Stygian desert outside black-walled Khemi. Winning the Heart of Ahriman, Conan returned to face his foes (*Conan the Conqueror*, originally published as *The Hour of the Dragon*).

After regaining his kingdom, Conan made Zenobia his queen. But, at the ball celebrating her elevation, the queen was borne off by a demon sent by the Khitan sorcerer Yah Chieng. Conan's quest for his bride carried him across the known world, meeting old friends and foes. In purple-towered Paikang, with the help of a magical ring, he freed Zenobia and slew the wizard (*Conan the Avenger*, originally published as *The Return of Conan*).

Home again, the way grew smoother. Zenobi gave him heirs: a son named Conan but commonly called Conn, another son called Taurus, and a daughter. When Conn was twelve, his father took him on a hunting trip to Gunderland. Conan was now in his late fifties. His sword arm was a little slower than in his youth, and his black mane and the fierce mustache of his later years were traced with gray; but his strength still surpassed that of two ordinary men.

When Conn was lured away by the Witchmen of Hyperborea, who demanded that Conan come to their stronghold alone, Conan went. He found Louhi, the High Priestess of the Witchmen, in conference with three others of the world's leading sorcerers: Thoth-Amon of Stygia; the god-king of Kambuja; and the black lord of Zembabwei. In the ensuing holocaust, Louhi and the Kambujan perished, while Thoth-Amon and the other sorcerer vanished by magic ("The Witch of the Mists").

Old King Ferdrugo of Zingara had died, and his throne remained vacant as the nobles intrigued over the succession. Duke Pantho of Guarralid invaded Poitain, in southern Aquilonia. Conan, suspecting sorcery, crushed the invaders. Learning that Thoth-Amon was behind Pantho's madness, Conan set out with his army to settle matters with the Stygian. He pursued his foe to Thoth-Amon's stronghold in Stygia ("Black Sphinx of Neb-thu"), to Zembabwei ("Red Moon of Zembabwei"), and to the last realm of the serpent folk in the far south ("Shadows in the Skull").

For several years, Conan's rule was peaceful. But time did that which no combination of foes had been able to do. The Cimmerian's skin became wrinkled and his hair gray; old wounds ached in damp weather. Conan's beloved consort Zenobia died giving birth to their second daughter.

Then catastrophe shattered King Conan's mood of half-resigned discontent. Supernatural entities, the Red Shadows, began seizing and carrying off his subjects. Conan was baffled until in a dream he again visited the sage Epimitreus. He was told to abdicate in favor of Prince Conn and set out across the Western Ocean.

Conan discovered that the Red Shadows had been sent by the priest-wizards of Antillia, a chain of islands in the western part of the ocean, whither the survivors of Atlantis had fled 8,000 years before. These priests offered human sacrifices to their devil-god Xotli on such a scale that their own population faced extermination.

In Antillia, Conan's ship was taken, but he escaped into the city Ptahuacan. After conflicts with giant rats and dragons, he emerged atop the sacrificial pyramid just as his crewmen were about to be sacrificed. Super-natural conflict, revolution, and seismic catastrophe ensued. In the end, Conan sailed off to explore the continents to the west (*Conan of the Isles*).

Whether he died there, or whether there is truth in the tale that he strode out of the West to stand at his son's side in a final battle against Aquilonia's foes, will be revealed only to him who looks, as Kull of Valusia once did, into the mystic mirrors of Tuzun Thune.

L. Sprague de Camp
Villanova, Pennsylvania
May 1984